PUNK-IN

MM ROCKSTAR ROMANCE

AVA OLSEN

NOTE FROM THE AUTHOR

Van is from Montreal and will occasionally use swear words in Quebecois French that you may or may not be familiar with including *tabarnak* (holy fuck) and *câlisse* (also way of saying fuck or shit), and other versions thereof.

PROLOGUE
VAN

FOUR YEARS AGO

> My office. Now.

Nothing like starting off the first day of a new job with a text like that from your boss.

Not that it was entirely unexpected. It had been a crazy-ass week.

Seven days ago, I turned forty.

Forty.

Four decades of my life had passed. Don't ask me how the fuck that happened. One day, I was thirty and looking at forever, then I blinked, and here I was.

Then, five days ago, the woman I'd been casually seeing for the past three weeks dumped me. She said she was sick of my "total lack of commitment." We'd only gone out, like, two or three times; what the hell did she mean by that?

Whatever.

I didn't have the bandwidth to date or to give my social life any thought. The fact that I couldn't remember her last name was a sure sign that the relationship - if you could even call it that - was going nowhere.

Finally, two days ago, my week turned around. In the very best way.

I'd gotten a job offer to work for Bandit Music, the biggest label in the country.

Almost two decades of being on the road, managing bands, and scheduling tours had all led up to this. Now, I was getting the chance to manage not just any band but one that had recently signed with the label.

According to my boss and Bandit CEO, Greg Haddley, Wayward Lane was the next hot thing.

Greg had a proven track record of finding and developing top-selling artists, so I was excited as fuck, to say the least.

And I wasn't going to let anything distract me from this opportunity—not a milestone birthday, and certainly not the loss of a potential relationship that was over before it had even begun.

Picking up my work cell, I texted Greg a quick "I'm heading up now" response and took the elevator to the thirty-fifth floor.

When the doors opened, Greg's assistant motioned me to enter his office.

The space was big and bright, with panoramic views of Nashville.

I was envious. His office was larger than my entire one-bedroom condo.

But it wasn't just Greg in the room waiting for me.

There was a group of guys sitting across from him who looked to be in their early twenties, wearing wide-legged jeans, rumpled t-shirts, and scuffed doc martens. They all had long hair—with one exception—and copious tattoos and piercings among them.

I could smell their cocky attitude even from this distance.

Then I remembered the demo tape and the lead singer in particular. He had a stellar voice and a memorable face.

These were the guys I'd be working with, the band called Wayward Lane. Their blend of punk, rock, and soul had garnered a lot of attention from various labels, and between their sound and their look, it was no wonder.

Greg stood up, buttoned his suit jacket, and motioned for me to come in.

"Ivan, I want you to meet Wayward Lane: Brodie James, lead vocals; Iain Holloway, guitar; Faisel Reed, drums; and Ronin Stadler, bass. Guys, this is Ivan Cross. He's been assigned as your manager and will take good care of you from here on out."

The singer stood up first, the guy with the shaved head, and held out his hand.

Brodie was a few inches shorter than me but long and lean, with a model-perfect profile and tattoos everywhere but his face.

What caught my attention were his intense hazel eyes and a smirk that was difficult to ignore. The guy had a magnetic presence, no question, and he fucking knew it. If he could sing as well as his demo proved, he'd draw in the fans en masse.

He'd also be easy to photograph. The press office would love him.

"How long have you been in this business?" Brodie asked me point blank.

No "nice to meet you" or any polite chit-chat. Let's get right to it.

"Since I graduated from college."

"You mean, like, in the nineties? Can you remember that far back?" he asked with a curl of his lip, and the rest of the guys chuckled.

"Don't knock someone with experience or that decade. Grunge was fucking awesome," I snapped back. "I know my shit. And when things go to shit, which they inevitably do, especially in this business, I'm the one people turn to."

I raised one eyebrow and stared right back at him.

Go ahead, smart-ass. I can play your game.

It was second nature to me now. I was used to dealing with musicians and their gigantic egos.

Brodie's eyes narrowed and I braced myself for a snarky response.

"I personally hired Ivan, so that should tell you everything you need to know," Greg commented. "He's been in this business for as long as you've breathed air. Like he said, he knows his shit, and he's not going to take any of yours. You give your all; we do the same. It means success for everyone."

The guys nodded.

Well, everyone except for Brodie. He just stood there staring at me like I was a puzzle he couldn't quite figure out.

"Now, if you'll excuse me, I have other business matters to attend to," Greg stated and sat back down.

I turned to the band and decided on a friendlier tone.

"How about I take you guys out for lunch, and we can get to know each other?"

"I don't put out on the first date," Brodie sneered.

"I don't date, so no problem," I replied.

The rumble of laughter from the rest of the guys filtered through the room.

"Shit, Dee, it looks like you've met your match."

That comment came from the blond one, Holloway. He was good-looking, too. In fact, they all were. Holloway also had a confident glint in his eyes that I knew meant trouble.

"We'll see about that," Brodie scoffed.

"Yes, we will," I bit out and motioned to the door. "After you."

"Favorite band?" Brodie asked me as we headed out of Greg's office.

"The Smiths."

"What was the last concert you went to?"

"Does it count if it was a band I managed?"

"Yes."

"Maze."

"Cool," Brodie replied as he walked beside me. "You play?"

"Guitar and piano."

"You sing?"

"Sometimes."

"You married?"

"Fuck no."

Brodie's bark of laughter stunned me. It was welcome, though, and the mood between us shifted and became a little less hostile. Not entirely, but I didn't expect to win him over in one conversation.

But I did as promised. I took them to the best barbeque place in the city, and we bonded over our mutual love of smoked meat, beer, and, of course, music.

Brodie and I bantered back and forth, with the rest of the band chiming in here and there.

Later that night, I reviewed their demo again. After meeting them in person, I knew this was the start of something special.

Wayward Lane was going to go all the way, and I would make sure of it.

Their lives would never be the same.

Turns out, neither would mine.

BRODIE

There were very few people I liked on sight.

Lusted after? Sure. Lots and lots of men, that is.

Respected? That was a whole different thing. That took time.

Was curious about? That was rare, too.

Until Ivan Cross. Or Van, as he preferred.

Van ticked every fucking box and then some.

Most people in the music biz I'd met over the past seven years were either conceited assholes, like Greg Haddley, or predatory pricks.

Either way, I was always on guard.

Dealing with people like Greg was a necessary evil if you wanted to make it big. His talent roster spoke for itself, but that didn't mean I trusted him.

But Van? He didn't try to charm me, and I didn't sense any ulterior motives.

I don't know what I'd been expecting in Bandit's head office that day, but it sure as shit wasn't Van.

I'd nearly drooled at the first glimpse of him. The rolling swagger of his walk, the confident air when he returned my sass, the denim blue eyes…

Fuck me, those eyes.

In my mind, I was anticipating some creepy dude with a bad combover who wanted to mold us into the next boy band. Not a hot-as-fuck fortysomething who knew more about rock music than I did. A guy as cool as we were.

We were rockers from up north—wild, know-it-all, snarky, twenty-five-year-olds.

Within an hour of meeting, Van had Holls, Ronin, and Faise at ease, and that was no mean feat.

Me, especially. I didn't warm to anyone I just met.

But something about Van was different.

And my instinct had been spot-on.

In the months after we signed, I discovered Van was unlike any manager I'd ever met. Not only was he honest and hardworking, but he had an ear for picking a great song. He also had no problem going to bat for us when we had creative differences with Greg. Not to mention, Van was one of the few people who called me out on my own shit.

He hadn't just earned my professional respect. My dick liked him too.

My dick liked a fuckton of hot guys. Van was no exception.

Then there was no time for me to worry about my dick at all.

After that first year we went from a band that booked two local gigs a week to a number-one-selling album. We were either in the recording studio or performing or promoting. Our faces and our lives were splashed all over entertainment news.

Once we had our first hit single, things changed.

I was never short of male attention before, but now? I had guys lining up outside my trailer after concerts, in hotels, in bars, everywhere.

All the fucking time.

It was heady, amazing.

My rock n' roll dream come true.

My life was just the way I wanted it. I had my music, my best friends as bandmates, my fans, and plenty of hot, sexy men eager for my bed.

What could be better?

If only I'd known…

CHAPTER 1

VAN

"Explain this."

I tapped on my phone, placed it in front of Brodie, and waited for his answer.

All I got was an eye roll and a huge cloud of pot smoke blown in my face.

"Knock it off and speak," I bit out, waving off the earthy fumes that surrounded me.

Then again, maybe I should take a deep fucking breath because I could use some relaxation right about now.

We'd met at Brodie's house instead of my office, and all the guys in the band were here.

Not that they were paying me any attention. They were too busy smoking, eating leftover pizza, and swallowing shots of tequila.

And it was only ten a.m.

They'd finished recording their second album a month ago, and we'd started the promo launch, including interviews.

But Brodie and I had different opinions on what was

considered appropriate to share with the press. Or how to interact with them.

"You wanted me to do promo. I did it," Brodie smirked, running a hand over his shaved head. His hazel eyes were glassy and bright with amusement.

"I wanted you to answer the reporter's questions about the album and tour. Not fuck around with said reporter right after the interview and then piss him off. He wrote a very unflattering piece on you. Not to mention he's left me and our PR rep several angry voicemails."

"He's just ticked off because I wouldn't go back for seconds. Guy's a fucking clinger."

I grabbed my phone and slammed it on the table. I'd been working sixteen-hour days, and I was at the end of my goddamn patience.

Brodie's ensuing chuckle had all the hair on my body standing on end.

"What the fuck is so funny?" I asked, standing up and pacing.

"You," Brodie sneered, then inhaled another drag. "You're wound tighter than Faise's drums. You need to chill. This guy you're talking about is the closest thing to a tabloid reporter. He tells lies for a living. No one's gonna believe anything he says."

I shook my head. "He already contacted the PR team and told them he's gonna sue. Our lawyers are preparing a ten-thousand-dollar settlement offer as we speak."

"Get the fuck out!" Brodie exclaimed, standing up to face me. "Suing for what?"

"He claims that after your interview, he—" I paused, my stomach doing a weird kind of somersault. "He gave you a blowjob, and you ruined the interior of his vehicle."

"He's suing me for getting cum on his car?"

Brodie burst out laughing, and so did the rest of the guys.

I stepped in closer, getting right up in his face.

Okay, even I could admit that the whole situation was ridiculous. And, yes, I'd probably laugh about it next week. But my boss had reamed me out an hour ago and my ears were still ringing.

So yeah, I wasn't all that amused right now.

"*Tabarnak*, Dee! You just think you can do whatever the fuck you want and, haha, Van is gonna clean up the mess," I snapped.

"Apparently not if my cum's involved," Brodie chuckled again, then gripped my shoulder.

His touch burned through the thin layer of my shirt. I had the strange urge to step closer to him but shook it off. Then he dropped his hand just as quickly.

"Come on, Van. This is hilarious. I stained his car seat, and he's suing me? You can't make this shit up. God, I fucking love this crazy life!"

I should've just chalked the incident up to another rockstar antic, but for some reason, Brodie's flippant manner chafed me. And dealing with the aftermath of his many, many conquests was starting to wear.

And it had only been a year.

My phone rang and I glanced at it.

Incoming call: Dad.

"I've got to take this."

I stepped out onto the patio overlooking the pool. "Hey, Dad, what's up?"

There was silence on the other end of the line.

"Dad?"

"You need to come home," he mumbled, his voice raspy and low.

"Maybe in a few weeks, I—"

"Now. Van. Now. She's gone. My Keira is gone."

I registered his words, but I didn't believe them.

Until I heard my dad's sob, a gut-wrenching cry I would never forget.

I stood frozen in place, unable to breathe or fully wrap my mind around what he was saying.

Mom had been sick for a year, battling stomach cancer. The treatments had been going well, or so I thought. I spoke to her a few days ago, and she'd been upbeat.

"She… she complained yesterday that she was feeling hot, like a f-fever," he stuttered, the words barely above a whisper. "I rushed her to the hospital, but then… it turns out she had an infection. In her blood. It was too late."

"I'm on my way."

I shoved my phone in my pocket, my hands cold and trembling. Then I turned around, but I was unable to move my feet and walk back inside.

"Van? Is everything okay?"

I looked up to find Brodie standing at the door, staring at me like he'd never seen me before.

"No. No, it's not. My mom…my mom is gone. I have to go home."

I didn't notice the tracks of tears on my face until much later.

BRODIE

One moment I was stoned and laughing my ass off, and the next, I was shoving the guys out the door and calling my assistant, Bibi, barking out orders like a goddamn general.

No way was Van driving after just finding out his mother had passed.

Bibi arranged for a driver to pick him up from my place so he could go home, grab a bag, and then head off to the airport. She'd arranged a private flight and pick-up in Montreal.

Before he left my house, I reached up and hugged him, holding him tight. He seemed shocked at first, then slowly slid his arms around my waist and clutched me even tighter.

There were things I wanted to say, but I didn't think "I'm sorry" would ever be enough.

Much as I loved to provoke Van, I liked him. I considered him my friend.

A funny ache in my chest bloomed when I heard his indrawn breath. Then I realized I was probably holding on too long and let go.

A half-hour later, he was gone, and I was left pacing in my house.

I called Bibi again.

"I'm going up there."

"Are you sure?" she asked.

"You didn't see what he looked like, Bibi. He can't be there alone. He has no siblings or any other family outside of his dad."

"Pack a bag, and I'll pick you up."

"You're coming too?"

"See you in an hour. And don't forget your passport."

Five hours later, we arrived in Montreal; weed is legal there, and thank fuck because I was still stoned. Then I realized on the drive from the airport that I didn't even know where his parents lived.

"I've got the info. We're going to the hotel first. Then we'll figure out the rest," Bibi announced, seemingly reading my mind.

When Bibi and I knocked on his parents' door an hour later, Van answered.

The shocked look on his face was followed by tears that had my heart nearly breaking in half.

"What are you doing here?" he asked.

"We thought you could use some friends," I replied.

Van broke down again and nodded, ushering us inside.

"I... normally, I'm the one managing everything, but I can't seem to make a decision. And my father, he... he's still in shock."

Bibi gently placed a hand on Van's. "I'm here to help you organize anything you need. Where's your dad?"

"He's asleep right now."

"Why don't you tell me where the kitchen is, and I'll go make us coffee to start."

"Down the hallway, to the right. And thanks, Bibi."

She nodded and walked off, leaving Van and me standing in his parents' living room. The place was cozy and warm, with a large bay window overlooking the yard.

Suddenly, I was self-conscious like I never was.

What the fuck could I do for Van? What did I know about the kind of loss he was dealing with? I was just a cocky musician with a penchant for mouthing off.

"This was all your idea, wasn't it?" Van asked as he stared at me.

Instead of saying yes, I nodded.

"You never cease to amaze me," Van continued. "Thank you."

"I told you, we're friends. So there's no thanks necessary."

Van stepped closer and pulled me in for a hug.

It surprised me, and when he pulled back, I could see the same look on his face.

Then he wiped his tears and urged me to sit down.

We spent the next hour talking.

Don't ask me what we talked about. I don't remember. I just recall staring into his blue eyes and thinking that I wanted to do something, anything, to help him.

I could tell he was grateful for the distraction. And for the company.

Van was used to being the caretaker. It was nice to give him something in return, even if it was just for a moment.

Yeah, I usually gave him a hard time, but I knew he had my back.

And from that moment on, I had his.

CHAPTER 2
BRODIE

"'m not recording this piece of shit you call a song. It's garbage."

I finished talking and stared at Van and then Greg.

"What?" I snapped. "It sucks, and I won't have my name attached to it."

"You're being unreasonable," Greg replied calmly. "Lawson Raine is one of the most in-demand songwriters in the business."

"I don't care who he is or what his resume says; the song is fucking crap. Van?"

Van's blue eyes settled on mine; then he turned to Greg. "I agree with Brodie. It's subpar songwriting. It's not worthy of the band or their brand."

Greg shook his head. "I know Lawson personally, so I—"

"I don't care if you've fucked him; the answer is still no," I bit out.

Greg glared at me. "Watch your mouth, Brodie. And I know what sells. I didn't get to where I am by making stupid choices. Now—"

"Hold on, Greg," Van interrupted. "Maybe I wasn't clear enough. Brodie and I are in charge of the song selection for the band. You gotta trust his instinct and mine. This song isn't worthy of Wayward Lane. And I know Lawson, too, but this piece is just not cutting it. Come on, you gotta see that."

"Van's right. I've read better lyrics on graffiti walls downtown," I added.

Van's sudden bark of laughter sparked mine.

Then I watched Greg's face turn from pink to purple, the vein in his forehead throbbing.

Not that I gave a shit. I wasn't changing my mind. If Greg wanted to record that crappy song, he could do it himself.

"Fine," Greg mumbled and stood up. "But you better come up with something and fast. Recording for the album starts in three days. If you don't have an eighth song lined up, you're recording this one."

Then he turned around and stomped out of the studio.

"That went well," I chuckled and turned to Van. "And thanks for sticking up for me."

"Of course. And I have a new piece for you to look at. It's not finished, so I didn't want to show it to Greg. But I think it would work for you guys."

Van handed over a set of sheet music, and I carefully read every line. Then I noted the name of the songwriter, Corley Hewitt. I glanced at the edits on the page, and something familiar about it rattled in my brain, but I couldn't quite pinpoint what it was…

"It looks good. Can the writer finish it in time for recording?"

Van nodded. "I'll get it organized."

"By the way, I've got a date for the Bandit party on Friday. I'll send you their details, make sure the guy gets a pass, and anything else he needs for the night."

Van's friendly expression iced over.

"What's the problem?" I asked.

"Nothing," Van paused, running an agitated hand through his hair. "Normally, you don't bring a date to events. Is this someone you're seeing regularly or—"

"Fuck no! I don't date," I scoffed and stared at Van. "It's some friend of Holls from L.A. He's a big fan."

"I bet he is," Van mumbled and tapped on his phone.

"What are you so cranky about?"

"Nothing."

"Why don't you ever bring someone to these things?" I asked.

That was my lame attempt at trying to find out if Van was dating anyone. So far, I hadn't been able to pry any information out of him.

And we talked about everything.

Everything but Van's sex life. And my curiosity needed to be sated.

Despite having my choice of men, I was getting bored. You read that right.

Only one man could hold my attention outside the bedroom, and I was staring right at him.

And lately, the need to have Van inside my bedroom was fucking with my head. Both of them.

All this to say, Van was occupying way too much of my attention lately, and it had to stop. Between that and the tour schedule, my sleep was non-existent. So much that I was now downing sleeping pills like rock candy.

Friday night, things would change. My date would be the perfect distraction.

"I don't have the time or desire to bring a date," Van replied. "Anyway, back to Friday, since this guy is Holloway's friend, for fuck's sake, let him off nicely. I don't have time to deal with the PR team this week."

"Hey, it's not my fault that some guys get the wrong idea. It's not like I tell any of my hookups I want more than a fuck."

"Anything else?" Van asked as he stood up.

"Yeah. Are you going to be there?"

"As usual."

"Good. Save me a dance."

Van laughed as he walked out of the room.

I wasn't kidding, but the joke was still on me.

VAN

I was sitting in my office the day after the party, staring at the PR photos of Brodie.

He looked like his usual self, smiling, or rather smirking, for the camera. But I could tell by his eyes that something was up with him. Even with makeup, he couldn't hide the dark circles and bloodshot eyes.

I knew Brodie was having problems sleeping and had been prescribed pills months ago. Was he abusing them? Mixing them with other drugs?

That anxiety sparked a real concern in me and, next thing I knew, I grabbed my keys and made for the door.

It would be best to drop by and see him in person. If there was a health issue, I wanted to know so we could address it right away.

I sent off a quick text and waited for his reply as I made my way down to the parking garage.

All I got was a "K" in response.

Then I wondered if Brodie's date was going to be around when I got there. That thought had the acid in my stomach churning away.

It was only because I felt protective of him. There were a lot of users out there and men who wanted to take advantage of his fame and money.

And now that we were in each other's lives more than anyone else, our friendship had grown closer.

Lately, though, I was possessive of his time, which was not

like me. I mean, I cared about all the musicians I worked with.

But not like him.

Pushing my strange mood aside, I drove to his house and knocked on the door.

Brodie answered it wearing his usual jeans and nothing else, all his intricate tattoos on display. His hair had grown out a bit, and the black waves were mussed and sticking up on end. But the only thing that held my attention were the violet circles under his eyes. They seemed to be there permanently these days.

"What's so urgent?" he asked as he stepped aside to let me enter.

"Are you having issues with the pills your doctor gave you?"

Brodie shook his head and wandered down the hallway.

"I need them to sleep. I can handle it."

"How many do you take? Are you taking them every single night?"

Brodie's steps faltered, but he remained silent.

"Dee?"

"Two. At least. Maybe three pills. And yeah, every fucking night. Sometimes with a drink or a spliff. A couple of sedatives. It's fine."

"It's not. You shouldn't be taking them every night. And not with sedatives. They're addictive."

"I'm in control, Van! I'm fine. You can see I'm fine. Stop mothering me!" he yelled and stomped into the kitchen.

I followed and watched him as he yanked on the fridge door. He pulled out a bottle of juice and chugged half of it.

"How long?" I asked.

"What?"

"How long have you been on the pills now?"

"Six months or so. Why?"

"You need to go back to your doctor. He's gotta wean you

off them. Don't you get it? The longer you take them, the worse your sleep is gonna get. And the more pills you'll need."

Brodie's eyes blazed. "Get out!"

"What?"

"Get out of my house! I don't need you coming in here and telling me what to do!"

I wasn't going anywhere.

"Dee, this is serious shit when it comes to your health. Not only that, but I have to tell Greg."

Brodie slammed the bottle down on the counter and got right in my face. My heart was pounding furiously in my chest.

I'd already lost someone I loved a year ago. I couldn't lose him, too.

And I knew, I just knew how these things went. I'd seen it many times in my career with many musicians.

He'd start taking more and more, and then he'd need a different pill or drug to wake him up, then there would be a phone call in the middle of the night and…

"Please, Dee, I can't—" My voice cracked, and I reached for him. "I don't want you to get sick or worse. You gotta nip this thing now. Please. Please."

Brodie stared at me, silent. Then something in his gaze flashed, and he nodded, surprising me.

"Okay."

"Okay?"

"Yes. I'll speak to my doctor. And not just about the sleeping pills," he muttered.

"What's wrong?"

He shook his head. "It's nothing. Nothing you can fix."

"Try me."

Brodie shook his head. "Can you come with me? I hate going there by myself. Doctors creep me out."

"Anything you need."

"Thanks, Van. Sorry I yelled at you."

Brodie didn't apologize. Ever. Hearing and seeing him like this was totally unnerving.

"I'm used to it by now," I chuckled, trying to ease the tension.

My heart was still pounding hard, my body was shaking, and my hands were sweaty. Brodie looked so lost that I reached out and pulled him into my arms.

He gripped me tightly, trembling, and I heard a sniffle. He notched his face in my neck, and I rubbed his back in soothing circles.

"I know it's not going to be easy, but it'll be okay. You'll be off the pills in a few months."

Then he began to shake, and I held on even tighter.

"Every step of the way, I'm here. I'm always here."

CHAPTER 3
BRODIE

ONE YEAR AGO

I was waiting for Van to arrive at the national music awards show.

Me and the guys had already settled into the bar at the venue and were tossing back shots. But a half hour passed, and still no sign of Van, and my restlessness took hold.

I texted him, and all I got was the usual "I'll be there soon" reply.

Something was wrong. He'd been quiet for the past month.

Not that I could blame him. His dad passed six weeks ago, and he was still reeling from the grief of that loss. He'd taken two weeks off, and then he was back at work, claiming he was fine.

I didn't buy it for a second.

I couldn't imagine losing both parents in the span of a few years. But even though I suggested he take more time off, he outright refused.

Me and the guys did what we could for him. We knocked

off our antics in favor of laying low and giving Van a break. I called him more often, too, to check in and see if he was okay.

But it wasn't just grief that brought about a change in him.

Something else was going on.

On the one hand, when he was around, his hugs were longer, tighter, and he looked at me with an intensity I'd never seen before. When we did have a disagreement, our fights were even more passionate than usual.

On the other, he was avoiding me. If he didn't need to be on-site, he'd text or call. And I didn't know what to make of his strange behavior.

This shift between us.

My hunger for him hadn't changed. If anything, the desire I felt grew deeper, stronger. And other men weren't doing it for me anymore. I had no interest in anyone else. I finally admitted to myself that this wasn't just about sex. My feelings for Van were...well, I'd never felt this way before about anyone.

I was obsessed.

I just wanted to be near him. All the fucking time.

I was about to text him again, but he was suddenly standing before me.

But he wasn't alone.

A beautiful brunette woman stood beside Van, clutching his arm tightly and staring up at him like *he* was a rock god.

A flare of jealousy ignited, and I held on to my glass so tight it was in danger of breaking.

Who the fuck was this woman?

"Zoe, this is Brodie James, Iain Holloway, Faisel Reed, and Ronin Stadler. Guys, this is Zoe Nord. She's a new member of our PR team and will be accompanying you tonight."

I was instantly relieved. She was here to work and not as Van's date.

But that didn't mean she wasn't interested. Or that Van wasn't.

He never mentioned a special person in his life or that he even had a life outside of work, but it wouldn't stay that way forever.

Zoe whispered something, and Van laughed in reaction, and that right there set me off again.

I was the one who made him laugh. Me. And I fucking wanted him to be mine.

Fuck, that revelation had me waving down the bartender for another shot.

I glanced at Zoe. She still hadn't let go of Van. Until she turned her head and looked at me, then startled.

Van's phone rang, and he slipped away.

"Is something wrong?" she asked me.

"Leave Van alone," I spat out as I glared at her. "He's going through a lot right now."

"He's a work colleague, nothing more. And I resent your implication."

"I don't give a fuck. You leave Van be. We clear?"

Zoe rolled her eyes. "Trust me when I say I have absolutely no interest in Van that way."

"Really?"

"For starters, my girlfriend would be very upset."

Oh.

And just like that, my temper slowed to a simmer.

"Well, good. I'm glad you cleared that up."

"You certainly did." She smirked at me. "Does he know?"

I ignored her, grabbed another shot, and tossed it back.

"I'm looking out for him. Any friend would do the same."

Zoe looked at me with one raised eyebrow, and I knew right then she'd be good at her job. This woman would never fall for any of my bullshit.

Van reappeared at the entrance to the bar and motioned for me to join him. I walked over, and he pulled me aside.

"What's up?" I asked calmly.

Inside, I was a frustrated mess.

"Be nice to Zoe," Van warned. "We want her to stay longer than a month."

"I'm always fucking nice."

Van cocked his head. "I could tell you were arguing with her. You looked pissed, and so did she. What the fuck did you say to her?"

"Nothing that concerns you," I snarled.

My heart was pounding furiously. Then I looked up, and I saw the hurt in his eyes.

He pulled his hand away.

"I clarified a few things, that's all," I mumbled. "You know I hate it when PR people try to put me on a leash."

"I'll remind her that you're not housetrained yet," Van replied, this time with a smile. "Let's round up the others and head in to grab our seats."

"Are you sitting with us?"

"No, I'm with Zoe in the corporate seats."

"Are you coming to the afterparty?" I asked.

"I'll make an appearance."

I ran a hand over my hair. "Can we talk then?"

"Sure, anything urgent?"

"No, it can wait."

But we never got around to having that conversation.

Wayward Lane won two awards that night. Me and the guys were tossed around from journalist to journalist until finally, hoarse and tired from smiling for photo ops, we hit the afterparty.

By the time we'd arrived, Van was gone.

I took it as a sign. It wasn't the right time to face what I was feeling.

VAN

I watched from the highest row in the theater as Brodie and the guys accepted their music awards.

I was so goddamn proud. I took pictures and yelled as loud as every fan in the audience around me.

This wasn't just their achievement. It felt like mine, too. I'd worked with lots of musicians, but working with Wayward Lane, working with Brodie, was something special.

Brodie leaned into the mic. I braced myself for what was about to come out of his mouth.

"We want to thank our amazing fans for their support and also our manager, Ivan Cross. Van is the reason we're standing here today accepting this award, and I'm sharing this with him. And thanks to everyone else at Bandit Music. Well, except for Greg Haddley, he's a fucking prick. Thank you!"

Zoe burst out laughing. "He's a handful."

I ran a hand over my face and sighed.

"You don't know the half of it. Just wait."

"And he's protective of you."

A hot flush crept over my cheeks, and thank god for the low lighting.

"I don't know what you mean," I murmured in response.

Except, I did.

"He nearly took my head off when he saw me touching your arm earlier."

I wasn't blind to how Brodie treated me. Like I belonged to him. But he loved to be the center of attention; that's all it was.

Even still, the thought of Brodie being jealous sent a shockwave of heat through me. It was happening all too often when I thought about him, when I talked to him, or hell, when I just looked at him from afar.

And for someone who thought of themselves as straight, possibly bi-curious, it was a heady realization.

"Brodie's possessive of my time, that's all."

Was I trying to convince Zoe or myself?

"It's none of my business," she replied.

Thankfully, that was the end of that conversation.

When the ceremony was done, Zoe went in search of the guys to manage their interviews.

I headed to the afterparty, but after an hour and several conversations and no sign of Zoe or the band, I decided to leave.

On my way out, I spotted him.

Several VIPs were surrounding Brodie, gazing at him, hanging on his every word.

And it hit me that whatever these feelings were, it didn't matter. It wasn't going anywhere.

He was a rockstar. The Brodie James.

Maybe he flirted with me and was possessive of my time, but it didn't mean anything. It was just his way.

And whatever was going on inside me, I dismissed it. If there was one thing I was good at, it was compartmentalizing.

I shoved my crazy revelation about Brodie aside and locked it away.

I was still raw from my dad's recent passing and that was enough for me to deal with.

For once, I walked out of the venue and I didn't look back.

I knew Brodie would be looking for me.

This one time, he'd have to wait.

CHAPTER 4

BRODIE

"I want to record this song."

My demand was met with total silence.

"Van, are you listening to me?" I grumbled and glanced over at him.

He was ignoring me again. On his phone, typing away.

Story of my fucking life.

The bus was dark, save for the glow of Van's phone. My fellow band members were asleep in their bunks at the back of the bus.

Not me. I could never get to sleep until at least two or three a.m.

That's music life; you get used to late nights and later mornings. And tour schedules that drained your soul if you weren't careful.

I thrived on the chaos of the road. New cities, new people. Not to mention, those people were all vying for my attention, my body, my time. It was a rush.

Or at least, it used to be.

The one person I wanted, well, he was always looking elsewhere.

Or rather, he was always focused on business. The next tour, new songs that needed recording, press junkets, photo shoots… Blah, blah, blah.

Not that those things weren't important, but my dick should be somewhere at the top of that list, right?

Yeah, I was a needy SOB, and I made no apologies for it.

And for a long time now, there was only one dick that my dick was interested in.

Van.

Our intense chemistry was a real thing. To me, at least.

We bickered over a lot of things. And it was never just a one-off. Our arguments were well-known in the band and with our record label. I was confrontational by nature, and I just loved riling Van up.

Most of all, I wanted his attention. And for him to recognize the fire that he'd lit within me.

I didn't know exactly when it happened or why, but over the past twelve months, Van was the only man I wanted.

I know, I know, mixing business with pleasure would be stupid.

I knew it, and Van sure as hell knew it. He probably had something in his contract to that effect—you know, *thou shalt not fuck band members.*

Having sex with my manager would be like handing me a match and a full gallon of gasoline. I'd enjoy the heat, but there would be hell to pay when the smoke cleared.

Still, the dick wants what the dick wants.

"Van," I repeated again.

Finally, reluctantly, he looked up at me.

Deep-set denim blues stared back at me, and I forced myself not to react. Not to say something hot and flirty or downright filthy. It wasn't easy.

Those were the eyes I dreamt about.

The ones I used as inspiration when I was on stage, fucking the mic.

The ones that haunted my every waking hour.

He'd come into my life, the band's life, and I had never been the same.

He was a great manager, a good friend, and a decent guitar player in his own right. But his real talent came in the form of songwriting. He wrote under the pen name Corley Hewitt.

I was the only one in the band who knew about his secret side gig. But I never said anything to Van, though. I pretended not to know. Some people preferred to work in the background, not on center stage, and I could respect that.

Van understood the music business, including temperamental musicians like me and our insane life. He was the kind of guy who took charge of a chaotic situation and turned it into a beautiful symphony.

I'd had a hard-on for him for what felt like forever, and things were only getting worse.

This past year, he'd taken to ignoring me more and more. Barely looked at me when he had to. And always with that professional distance in place.

It made my temper run as hot as my desire.

And can you blame me? Van was not only smart and talented but gorgeous, with a sleek undercut, a sexy dimple in his left cheek, and a chiseled jawline covered in the perfect amount of dark scruff.

I loved a natural man.

Too many times, I imagined how his beard would feel against my thighs, my taint, my hole.

Fuck, that line of thinking was getting me hard again.

He was always the man in charge, and I wanted him to fucking own me.

Van was taller than my five eleven and bigger, broader. I liked that a whole lot too. I had many fantasies about him manhandling me, ordering me around in that gravelly voice of his.

Fuck, I wanted to submit to him, and I didn't submit to anyone.

And Christ, now my dick was painfully hard. But then my brain remembered the problem.

Our work relationship was the first roadblock. I didn't see a way around that one.

I'm pretty sure our age gap—fifteen years—was the next one.

I didn't give a crap about him being older. So I was twenty-nine and he was forty-four. Who the fuck gave a shit? What drew me to someone was their energy, their aura, and his was hot as fuck, forty-four or not.

The third one, the one I didn't like to consider, was that I wasn't sure if he was into men.

Okay, maybe that was the first roadblock—a permanent one.

Or maybe he wasn't out? I didn't know. His personal life was the one topic he never discussed.

At one point, he had a girlfriend. I think. Or was it a boyfriend? Shit, I don't remember. All I knew was it ticked me off that someone was taking his time away from me.

Surprise, I'm an attention whore and a possessive motherfucker.

Could it be that Van wasn't gay, and all the heated looks that passed between us were all in my imagination?

Never, in the four years I'd known him, had he talked about anyone special in his life. And I never witnessed him hooking up on the road either.

Maybe he was he was bi? Pan? Demi?

I hope to fuck this wasn't all me. Falling for a straight guy was goddamn torture. Or so I've heard.

My one-time hookups with strangers were now a thing of the past. And with good reason. Most guys wanted to get fucked by "Brodie James" the musician, not Brodie, me, the person. And I got tired of pumping and dumping. Finding a quick fuck to take the edge off but always leaving dissatisfied.

No tangible connection.

With men I didn't know, I topped. No deviation.

But with Van? Mmm. I wanted to offer up my ass and let him rail me until we were too fucked out to move.

Between my sexual frustration and his ignoring me, I was ready to throw a massive temper tantrum. I had the urge to tell our driver, Sam, to stop the fucking bus right now so me and Van could have it out.

In the middle of the bayou.

Wait, there were alligators and big-ass snakes in this region. Okay, so maybe stopping wasn't a good idea.

But something had to give. And after reading Van's latest song, I was ready to make my filthy intentions very clear.

"Sideline" wasn't like his others. We were hard-edge rock, loud, and brash. And Van (Corley) could write a solid piece for that genre. We'd recorded several of them.

But his latest song was far from that. Rock n' roll angst meets country heartache.

And I swear to whatever deity you wanted to believe in that the song Van had written was about me and him.

I felt it in every lyric.

"Sideline"

I watch you from the sideline
Playing out your heart time
Sideline
Sliding on stage
shameless adulation
Turning my page
Still, I keep on waitin'
Why you, why me?
Not like it was before
And then there are the fans

Reminders of the score
I watch you from the sideline
Playing out your heart time
Sideline
Is your heart for them?
Do you hear mine racing?
Can't go on this way
I got no business chasin'
Every day gets longer
I tell myself more lies
Holding on to what I was
The want I still deny
I'm standing on the sideline
Playing out my heart time
Sideline
I wandered forever
And never felt this way
Until the day you sang to me
Washed my tears away
I'm waiting on the sideline
Wanting you to be mine
Sideline

I swear, I read it two weeks ago, and my mind has been fucked ever since.

That's when I decided, let's do an impromptu concert in New Orleans. We could try out the new song and see what kind of reception it got.

Last time we toured the city, in the spring, I'd been approached by a charity about a fundraising concert.

So, me being me, I called them up, locked it in, and handed the rest to Van.

We'd just wrapped up a long-ass tour in Europe, and everyone in the band was tired, but when I suggested NOLA, the guys were all in. The city was a music and party lovers' dream, and I was looking forward to performing here again.

Or I was.

Until I looked over and saw the stubborn set of Van's chin.

I just knew that getting what I wanted—the song and the man—would be an uphill battle.

"I don't think it's the right song for you or the band. It's a ballad. There's another one here from a new writer," Van looked away again and searched his bag. "It's grittier, raw. It has sex appeal. Letting you read 'Sideline' was a mistake."

"It's anything but!" I snapped back. "I want it. I feel the writer's words, and I know just how it should sound. Me sitting on stage, my favorite Martin acoustic in hand. It's different, but I love it. It's soulful. And if the guys hate it, too fucking bad! I want it, and I'm recording it. The end."

Van stood up and placed his hands on his lean hips.

He wore his usual uniform of dark jeans and a denim button down—a Canadian tuxedo, he jokingly referred to it.

Van was born and raised in Montreal and headed to Nashville when he was eighteen. Apart from being the band champion and a talented writer, he also spoke French.

I told you, he's a sexy motherfucker.

I overheard Van when we did a tour stop in Montreal in the summer, and I nearly came just listening to him say, "Merci bien, mes amies." I had to google it to find out what it meant. "Thanks very much, my friends" wasn't sexy talk, but anything from Van's mouth, especially in French, was the hottest thing ever.

I recently downloaded one of those language apps to learn French. Until Holls found out and teased me mercilessly for the past month.

"Brodie, I think I know by now what sells and what your fans are looking for. And this isn't it," Van replied, interrupting my musings.

"This is the song I want. It's a hit. I know it, you know it."

I got up off the sofa and got in his face. The gentle sway of the bus rocked our bodies back and forth like the magnetic push and pull that was always between us.

One more push and…

I was surrounded by his heady scent of leather and musk. I wanted to lean in and take a long lick of Van's throat.

My eyes caught on the black-beaded necklace he always wore. It was linked with a silver coin that rested in the divot of his neck. I can't tell you how many times I've pictured him naked, except for that necklace.

My cock pulsed, aching, throbbing, inside my tight jeans.

"Maybe it is a hit. But not for you," he muttered, rubbing a hand over his jaw.

"Why?" I pushed him.

"I just can't… I mean, I can't let you make a mistake. And that's what this song would be."

"You're wrong," I bit out. "And I'm tired of you telling me no. I'm the creative drive behind the band; I know what works and when it's time to try something new. I feel this song in my gut, in my chest, in my fucking balls. And when that happens, I know that it's mine."

Van finally made eye contact again. The pulse of electricity between us was tempered with worry.

"Why did you show it to me?" I asked, lowering my voice.

Van's eyes closed, and he shook his head. "A moment of weakness."

"What the fuck does that mean?"

He opened his eyes again, and all I saw was pain.

Longing, heartache.

His gaze was so expressive. It was the only part of him that I could read clearly.

"You really want this?" he replied.

Were we talking about the song or about us?

I nodded. "Never been surer of anything in my life."

CHAPTER 5

VAN

What the hell am I doing?

Why the fuck had I given Brodie that song?

I'd said it out loud: a moment of weakness.

I'd had too many of those lately, and I was going to do something stupid if I didn't get a hold of myself.

We'd finished Wayward Lane's European tour this fall, and I was bone-tired.

Exhausted, lonely, and frustrated.

Confused and unsettled.

It was so unlike me that I'd started to worry, pouring all my uncertainty into my songwriting. There, at least, I could unleash everything.

And what I'd read back had shocked me as much as Brodie's decision to want to sing my song.

I knew that once Brodie latched on to something, once he got that idea in his head, there was no dissuading him.

Arguing was futile, yet it was the one thing I couldn't stop doing.

But I didn't want to hear him whispering my words. It was too intimate.

And I could picture him just as he'd described. He'd be

sitting down, wearing his jeans, his naked chest on display while he cradled his guitar like a lover.

Singing about my longing, my desires.

For him.

My pulse pounded as a shiver ran through my entire body.

The explosive energy between him and me had always been there, right from the start. I'd just been too preoccupied with doing the job to notice what it really meant.

Plus, I'd never had reason to question my sexuality. I'd had hookups with women here and there, but no one had me reacting with anything more than simple lust. And not for years. I'd been too busy getting the band organized: recording, touring, cross-country, worldwide, twenty-four-seven.

My work was my life.

Until this past year.

After I lost my dad, the only living family member I had left, every emotion I'd locked down inside me rushed to the surface.

Dealing with my father's death had me taking a long, hard look in the mirror.

At myself, at my life, or lack thereof. At friendships and relationships. Ones I'd taken for granted before were now front and center. I realized that work couldn't be the only thing that fed my soul.

I needed more. I needed a real connection.

And sometime around the music awards show last year, I felt a shift.

I noticed Brodie, and not in the usual way.

My eyes were now drawn to the way he bit his full lower lip when he played his guitar and the slick of his lip gloss. I wondered if his lips were soft and what they would taste like.

I noticed the way his hazel eyes lit up when we were arguing.

And the way his high, tight ass flexed on stage.

Most of all, I was drawn to the way he fucked that mic. Sometimes, he'd turn and look right at me. As if daring me to make the first move.

I'd never popped a boner at work before, and now it was happening all too frequently. And what could I do about it?

Nothing. Not fuck all.

I worked for him.

Not to mention, I'd never been with a guy before, so what the hell did I know?

And so, our relationship took on a new intensity. It wasn't just arguments about creative differences or the label. And I... I didn't know what the fuck I was doing.

Me, the master organizer, the musician wrangler, the calm in the shitshow that was the entertainment storm, I was fucked up and in over my head.

Over feelings I had for the first time in my life. Over someone I had no business feeling anything for.

I'd never shied away from confrontation, and Brodie never met a sentence he couldn't refute. But lately, I'd done my best to steer clear of him. Not that it was easy. We interacted every day.

More and more, I needed space from him.

To get away from those green-gold eyes of his that seemed to see everything inside me. I swear he was a witch, and I was now cursed.

And I needed to break this hold he had over me. But it wouldn't be easy. There was a pull between us that had me unable to step away.

It had been like that from the start.

Brodie liked to push back against the label's demands. Sometimes, I agreed; other times, we argued until we ended up in a place that worked for everyone. It meant success for him, the band, and the label.

At first, the label hadn't been entirely supportive of

Brodie's outspoken nature or his gender-fluid style. He dressed however he pleased, and he often wore makeup.

In his usual way, he told them bluntly to fuck off as I stood beside him, backing him up.

Brodie was an intuitive musician, and he was the same way with everything in his life. It didn't need to make sense on paper or to other people as long as it made sense to him.

No matter what he said or did or wore (or didn't wear), Brodie was a beautiful person. Creative, talented, special. When he turned his attention to you, you felt like you were the one in the spotlight.

Greg often referred to Brodie as an "entitled brathole." That was his opinion.

The band hadn't shot up to the top of the charts because of me or anyone else at the label. It was mostly Brodie, his unforgettable voice, his presence, his gift. He didn't just sing his songs; he lived them.

I'd enjoyed my tussles with Brodie from the beginning. He was a smart-ass, emphasis on smart. I'd rarely met anyone as quick or as funny.

And I'd ignored his flirting. He did it with everyone, and it didn't bother me.

Until this past year, and I couldn't take it anymore.

Not his teasing, not his flirting with others, and not his hookups with every gorgeous man who paid him attention. And they *all* paid him attention.

Well, not so much lately. Or perhaps he was being discreet —something that was rarely said about rock stars.

And me? I was having a midlife crisis; lusting after a man fifteen years younger and so far out of my league, we might as well be from different planets.

I probably needed a break. If I got away from him for a while, things would go back to normal. These urges for him would fade.

All that reasoning went by the wayside when I was alone

with Brodie, and he was looking at me like he was now, like I was the only thing he wanted.

"I'm leaving," I announced, standing on shaky legs as the bus gently swayed.

Had I really just said that?

"A sabbatical," I continued. "Once this concert is done, I need a month off. Clear my head."

Maybe longer. Maybe for good.

For once, Brodie had nothing to say, his eyes wide.

"Let me memorize this moment. Brodie James has been silenced," I quipped.

His shocked expression morphed into anger, and I braced myself for the inevitable backlash.

He shook his head, his black hair falling into his eyes. I resisted the urge to reach out and touch him, to push those locks back so I could see his face.

When we first met, he'd worn his hair shaved. Now he was growing it out, the thick waves hitting his cheekbones, barely his ears. It was tousled and sexy, and his fans were obsessed with his new look.

Who could blame them? I was obsessed myself.

With or without makeup or sexy hair, he was so goddamn beautiful, and in a way I'd never anticipated. In a way I could no longer deny.

But he was free of the wrinkles I was now sporting. And the occasional gray hair amongst the brown.

"Never gonna happen," he growled.

Before I could stop him, he grabbed my belt loop and yanked, bringing me in so close our hips collided.

I began to shake and thank fuck for being in a moving bus.

Instead of touching him, like my body was screaming at me to do, I reached up and took hold of the overhead bin to stop me from pitching forward.

Brodie shook his head again and leaned into me, his hot breath brushing my ear. "You're not going anywhere. And I work with you, or I work with no one. Try to leave, and you're gonna be in for the fight of your life."

"That's not rational," I responded and looked him in the eye. "And I need time off. So do you. Especially you. Go on vacation. Alone or with the guys, whatever. Maybe some time away from music will be good for you, too. Recording can wait until the new year."

"I'll go on vacation. But only if you come with me."

My heart began to pound so fast I was in danger of fainting dead away.

"What the fuck, Dee? I'm your manager. If you need… company, you can find it anywhere, any day, any city."

"I don't travel with people I don't know or trust."

"Don't you have an old boyfriend you can call up?"

"Don't be stupid, Van. I'm so fucking tired of playing this game!"

He wasn't backing away. Instead, Brodie's hand slid to my lower back, locking my hips in place.

All my attention centered on the heat of his palm, the touch branding me through the layer of denim. Everything in my body buzzed.

Fuck, I hadn't felt this kind of desire in… ever.

One of us moaned. Maybe both?

"Hey, will you two shut it? Some of us are trying to get our fucking sleep!"

I jolted and turned to find Holloway standing at the end of the hallway in nothing but his black briefs, his long blond hair a tangled mess around his tired face.

"Just fuck already and give us some quiet. I swear to God, I love you guys, but I'm going to take my own goddamn bus the next time we do a one-off road trip."

Holloway turned and stomped back to his bunk.

The timing of his appearance was welcome, and it gave me the cold shower I desperately needed.

I stepped away from Brodie, breaking contact, and grabbed my phone.

I felt the loss of his touch more than I'd care to admit.

"This is not over. You and I are gonna settle this thing between us for good," Brodie demanded.

I reluctantly looked over my shoulder.

"There's nothing to settle. After New Orleans, I'm taking a month off. But I have changed my mind. If you want 'Sideline,' it's yours. I'll set up the paperwork. Try it out at the concert. If it resonates, we'll record it in the new year, all right?"

The look in Brodie's eyes told me he was far from okay. Oddly enough, he said nothing in response.

I turned and headed for my bunk, feeling his gaze burning a hole in my back.

Just one more week. I could survive one more week. Right?

I'd survived this past year; what was seven more days?

We'd come close to crossing that line tonight, and tempted as I was, I was also scared.

I was a forty-four-year-old man dealing with a sexual awakening I wasn't prepared for. And I knew that for me, with Brodie, it was about way more than sex. I related to him in a way I never had with anyone before.

There was trust there, and respect, and friendship, too.

But this desire I had for him was just plain foolish.

I never ran from problems, but maybe, just this once, running was safer and smarter than staying put. It wasn't just time for a vacation. It was time for a new path.

One that didn't involve a seductive lead singer from the most popular band in the world.

CHAPTER 6

BRODIE

"The power just cut off again, the fuck?" I yelled and looked around.

Or as much as I could in the dark venue.

I glanced over at Van and then Ace, our tech guy and sound engineer. I could barely see their outlines as they stood in the wings.

"I'll go downstairs again," Ace yelled out.

New Orleans was known for its good times. So far, our rehearsal had been anything but.

Our venue was an old concert hall from the 1920s, with ornate moldings and drafty dressing rooms. The place had character, no doubt. An intimate feel that we rarely enjoyed, and I loved. But the building had electrical wiring from the dark ages. And every hour, for the past four, without fail, the power shut down.

How the fuck could we rehearse like this? And what about the actual concert on Halloween?

"I better be prepared to sing without a mic tomorrow. Everyone got their lighters handy?" I joked.

The lights flickered again but shut down as fast as they'd lit up.

"For once, I agree with Brodie. The hell, Van?" Holloway muttered as he unplugged his guitar. "We can't work like this."

Van finally sauntered out on stage, carrying a flashlight.

It was the closest he'd been to me since last night on the bus. When I was about to finally stake my claim.

I knew in my gut that Van was gonna do a runner, and his words confirmed it.

A month of vacation, my ass.

But I was younger than him, and I had no problem chasing.

"The venue manager promised me that everything would be fixed by tonight. Let's just keep going through the set and do our best," Van replied.

"How?" Faisel stood up and hit his sticks together. "We're a high-powered rock group. We need our amps, we need lights, we need fucking power to rehearse. This is bullshit!"

It was fine for me to go toe to toe with Van, but no one else. No way was I going to let my band brother's comment go unchallenged.

"Chill out, Faise," I snapped back. "It's not his fault. I picked the venue. And we do what we always do. I don't need special effects to sound good. The best musicians do it naturally. Isn't that right, Van?"

He ignored my flirty comment as the lights flickered to life again.

And stayed on this time.

Faise, Holloway, and Ronin gathered around me and faced Van.

"Now that the power's back on, start the set again," Van requested, then turned and walked off.

My eyes lingered on his ass, but I forced myself to look away.

"Can I sing the new one now?" I blurted out.

"What new one?" Ronin asked, looking at me with curious eyes.

All four of us had been making music together since we were eighteen, fresh out of high school in Rhode Island. We'd had eleven years of friendship and road trips. We'd endured a lot together, and I knew this was not the way to mention a new song.

Shit.

Van paused and turned to face us again.

"I found a new piece for you guys. It's different, though. Brodie read it the other night and loved it, so let's test it out," Van replied and headed back to wait in the wings.

In his usual pose, arms crossed, thighs rigid.

I slung my guitar over my shoulder and reached down to my bag. I pulled out the sheet music and passed it around.

"This doesn't sound like us," Faisel commented as he read. "You really want to perform this one?"

I nodded in response. "I know it's not the usual, but that's just it. We need something fresh. Something with a little less rock and a little more roll. Something deep and slow."

As always, my eyes looked around the room and found Van's.

Deep and slow could be really, really good.

"I like it," Holloway replied, interrupting my sexy side-track. "And I agree with Brodie. After that rockfest through Europe, we should try something chill. I'm game."

Faisel and Ronin nodded.

"Let's try it unplugged. I need my baby," I said to Tommy, our instrument guy.

He was busy checking all our backup pieces. He picked up my custom-made Martin and passed it over to me. Then he did the same with Holloway, switching out his electric guitar.

I slid my hands over the smooth surface and held her lovingly.

"Here goes," I murmured as I sat on a stool and began to strum the first chords.

I'd already memorized the song. Hell, I'd read it a hundred times over the past week.

I closed my eyes and sang the first words, letting out the frustration that had built up inside me. My voice was rougher than usual, probably due to the enormous lump in my throat.

It wasn't nerves. I'd sung Van's words before.

But this song? It brought out a strange ache that was stronger than lust.

I can taste his heartache. It mirrored mine.

The intensity of my emotions surprised me.

It knocked the breath right outta my body, and I struggled with the rest of the lyrics. The chorus came out like a husky moan, with Holloway and Ronin backing me up.

When our harmony hit just right, I finally let go.

I unleashed. I fucking flew.

The high I got from performing—even to an empty theater during rehearsal—never got old.

But performing Van's song in front of him and for him? His words were mine. And everything that had led us to this point suddenly made sense to me.

Growing up, my mom often told me I had a young heart but an old soul.

At the time, I didn't fully realize what she meant.

But now I understood. I'd always known my own mind and what I wanted for my life.

And while I may be young in most people's eyes, I'd done and seen a lot of shit. And I'd fucked around more than most.

But now I was ready to move on to bigger, better, more meaningful things.

Just like taking on a new song, I was ready to keep growing.

With my music.

And most of all, with Van.

I just needed to convince him first.

When I finally reached the end of the song, my lungs were near to bursting, and my throat was dry.

The sudden sound of claps and cheers from our crew startled me. I stood up on shaky legs and bowed.

"I told you," I said to Van as he walked back on stage.

His blue eyes met mine. They were guarded and darker than usual.

My pulse kicked up, and my blood raced. The closer he got, the more I sweated. And it had nothing to do with the heat of the stage lights.

Which, thankfully, were still on.

"You did. And I have to say, Brodie, that was even better than I'd imagined."

"I hope the songwriter will be happy," I countered.

I wanted to do Van's song justice. He deserved nothing less.

"I'm sure they'll be ecstatic that *the* Brodie James picked their song."

"They better be. I'm very selective. I know what I want."

Van stared at me and swallowed hard. I watched as he licked his lips, my eyes locked on his tongue.

I had to taste him; I needed to…

Bam. The lights went out again.

"Maybe this place is haunted," Holloway joked. "Isn't NOLA full of ghosts?"

"No such thing as ghosts. Right?"

A cold draft blew over my shoulders, and I startled, taking a step forward, bumping into Van. Our bodies collided, and I gripped his arm tightly.

"Brodie," Van growled my name in that gravelly voice of his, and goosebumps popped up all over my skin.

The lights flickered on again.

"Van, we have a problem."

Fuck, not now.

Van pulled away, and I was about to protest, but not in the face of Regan, our lead security.

"What's up?" Van asked.

Regan crossed her arms. "There's a growing crowd of fans camped outside the building. And someone from the press has arrived."

Van sighed. "Since I'm the PR rep on this trip, I'll go out and talk to the reporter. Let's hope that appeases them until the day of the concert."

"I'll go with you; let's see what's going on outside," Regan replied, flanking Van as they walked away.

"You guys keep rehearsing. I'll be back in a few," Van yelled out.

I stared at his back as he walked away, Regan close by his side.

She said something to Van, and he tipped his head back and laughed.

Was she flirting with him? I was about to follow them when I received a smack upside my head.

"Stop mooning over him and get back to work," Holloway teased. I whacked his shoulder in response, and he whined. "Careful, dude. Don't mess with my arms, or I won't be able to perform."

"I never have problems performing," I replied with a cheeky grin.

Everyone groaned.

"What? It's true," I scoffed.

"Enough fucking around, let's rehearse," Faise grumbled.

Faise was extra grouchy this trip, and I wondered what the fuck was going on with him. He was the quietest of all of us and usually the most good-natured. Except when he was in the grips of his cocaine addiction and couldn't get a hit. But he'd been clean for three years.

Unless…

Before I had a chance to say something, Holloway leaned into me.

"I feel for you, brother, but I don't think Van's willing to cross that line," Holls warned. "I see the way he looks at you lately, but are you sure you want to take that chance? We talked about this before. No fucking around with each other or our crew. Nothing that can mess with our dynamic or our contract."

I was about to reply sarcastically until I noticed his dark brown eyes were serious for a change.

"I'm done with the fucking around, Iain."

It was rare that I used his first name. He raised one blond eyebrow.

"I mean it. I just want him."

His eyes widened, and his arms went slack, his guitar almost falling out of his hands.

"Careful, don't jinx us by wrecking your favorite instrument two days before a show."

"Are you serious, or are you punking me?" he asked.

"No punkin' involved; at least, not until Halloween."

"Haha. I mean it, are you serious?" he asked again and stared at me.

I met his gaze and nodded.

"Never thought I'd see the day." He whistled and backed up. "But I guess it was only a matter of time. You two would be hot together. Volatile as fuck, but still."

"Volatile, my ass, it's called chemistry. And it only took you eleven years to finally admit you think I'm hot," I teased right back.

I was ready for a relationship, but I'd never be ready to shut my smart mouth.

"You know you're not my type. I like 'em big and brawny." Holloway chuckled, then turned to the rest of the band.

"Are you assholes gonna gossip all evening, or are we gonna rehearse?" Faisel yelled out.

"We're ready," Holloway replied with a wink.

I sure as fuck was.

CHAPTER 7

VAN

Regan and I stood in the foyer of the venue, looking out through the stained glass windows that flanked the front entrance.

Her team on the outside radioed to say that the crowd around the theater was at least a hundred people and growing.

It wasn't unusual for word to get out about rehearsals and for superfans to line up in hopes of catching a glimpse of the band as they entered or exited the venue. And the guys loved that sort of thing, taking impromptu selfies with fans and signing autographs.

But for our security team, it was a fucking nightmare.

Our location, near Bourbon Street, was in a busy section of downtown. Between cars and pedestrians, it was chaotic, especially as more and more people gathered.

My concerns about someone trying to push through our security people began to mount. I'd seen people rush the band before and nearly topple them over.

It was scary as fuck.

"Call the local police. We need them to work crowd control. This is more than the usual."

"Already on it," Regan replied as she pulled out her phone. "I've got a contact from the last time we were in town. He's sending over several squad cars."

Then she tapped her earpiece and spoke to her staff, giving clear, concise instructions.

Regan worked in the military and private protection for over a decade before joining the security company this year. She knew her shit. The band members liked and respected her, even when she had to lay down the law.

Some of my nerves settled, but not all of them.

Of course, most of it had to do with Brodie. About protecting him. Protecting all the guys in the band, but Brodie most of all.

He'd been the target of crazed fans before, and sometimes the attention on him was overwhelming. The rest of the guys were popular in their own way, but they didn't trigger the kind of frenzy that Brodie did.

Between his intense performance style and his knack for spouting off whatever crazy shit was on his mind, he was a fan favorite.

My favorite.

Then I heard someone call out his name.

The crowd was loud and getting louder. Voices roared, and then suddenly, there was the boom of music. With Halloween festivities starting early and all the bars open, we were in the thick of party central.

As usual, we had four security members at each exit, front and back, and two inside with the band. That was only ten in total. Would it be enough?

We headed outside to get a better view of what was going on.

And fuck, it was a street festival. There were loads of people with cups and bottles in hand, dancing and singing. The band's most popular song, "Filthy Pain," was blasting—from someone's cell or a nearby bar, I couldn't tell.

More people walked out of the bars and restaurants lining the street and joined in.

Then I spotted the news van parked nearby.

A reporter and his cameraman pushed through the crowd, getting in front of the four security guys we had around us.

With short brown hair and dark glasses, the reporter shoved his mic in my face as his colleague stood behind him.

"Are you the band's rep? Can we get a statement? How long are Wayward Lane here in town?"

I looked at Regan and nodded. Then I turned to the reporter. "No cameras for this part. Just you."

Regan stepped forward and waved the reporter through, telling his cameraman to stay where he was. Neither guy seemed happy given the circumstances but tough shit.

Out of the corner of my eye, I spotted blue and red flashing lights flickering in the distance.

Regan stayed with her team, and I ushered the reporter into the foyer so I could hear above the din.

I loved a good party as much as the next person, but down here, things got wild. The last time we did a concert here, the afterparty alone had gone on for two days.

I held out my hand. "Ivan Cross, I'm—"

"The band's manager, I know," the reporter replied and shook my hand, a cocky grin on his face. "You're always in pictures with Brodie and his security team. You work very closely with him, right?"

I ignored that question. I was his manager, so my work with Brodie was self-explanatory.

And if it wasn't, it was none of this guy's business.

I cleared my throat. "The concert Wayward Lane's hosting on Halloween was an unscheduled event based on the band's interest. The guys loves this city and the fans here. All the proceeds from the concert will be donated to a local charity that focuses on helping low-income families throughout the year, especially at Thanksgiving. If you'd like to conduct an interview with the band after the concert, please contact me to book it in advance."

I pulled a business card out of my back pocket and handed it over.

The reporter did the same.

"Sorry, I forgot my intro. I'm Beau St. Germain, the entertainment reporter for Channel 10 News. A pleasure."

I nodded. "You too, Beau. If you want a formal interview with the band, fire off an email and I'll add you to the schedule."

"I'll do that, Ivan. And I'll look forward to meeting you again on the thirty-first." He smiled. "Thanks."

"My pleasure." I motioned to the door again.

Beau glanced back at the lobby. No way in hell was I going to let him in to see the guys now.

I pushed open the front door for him. Beau shifted his gaze to look at me again and nodded.

Thick humidity and the barrage of noise hit me full force. Regan greeted us, and the reporter made his way back through the crowd.

"We okay?" I asked Regan.

"Police have arrived, so I'm coordinating with them. It's probably best if the band leaves by the back entrance tonight. I know they like to see the fans but let's leave it until the concert. I don't feel good about letting them out in this. There are too many people who are drunk as fuck already. I've also called up some of my staff who were on leave today, just in case."

"Sounds good. I'm heading back in. They've got a private party at ten tonight; we all set for that?"

Regan nodded. "I've been in touch with the organizer."

I left Regan to deal with the nightmare outside while I ventured back to deal with the one inside.

Not that watching the band rehearse was a nightmare, far from it.

The power going off, however, was definitely a pain in my ass.

Not only that, I didn't trust myself with Brodie. My professional mask was getting harder and harder to wear.

I couldn't wait until this week was over and I was off. Distance would be a good thing.

I stepped into the lobby and glanced up at the gold art deco ceiling, soaking in the history of the place, wondering about all the musicians and artists who had come and gone through these doors. The place held a lot of memories.

As I wandered through, I thought about all the interesting places I'd had the privilege to witness in my life. And where I was going next.

Not just professionally but personally.

I hadn't considered, until recently, that I might be bi or pan. Was it the gender or the person I was attracted to? I thought back to previous women I'd hooked up with. There was physical attraction there, but that was it. Once the sex was over, I was ready to bolt. And sometimes, the sex wasn't all that great. I wanted to feel something beyond basic lust, but I never did.

If I were being totally honest with myself, there had been men that I'd noticed in recent years. At parties, press junkets, on tour. But as I got older and years passed, it felt like I'd missed my opportunity. Like I was too old to explore my sexuality, or maybe I just didn't have the courage. I don't know.

Everything in my life, especially over the past four years, was focused on my career. As friends coupled up and had families of their own, I found myself an outsider.

Alone.

Then I lost my parents.

First, my mom died from cancer, and then my dad from heart disease. I still hadn't closed their home in Montreal yet, the memories too fresh and painful.

And after my dad's death, I questioned everything.

What was going to tether me as time wore on? What was going to fuel me outside of work? I hadn't really thought about those things until I lost my folks, but now it was always on my mind.

I found solace in my songwriting. It wasn't difficult to understand why. It was familiar, cathartic, and comforting.

And I also took comfort in my friends, most of whom I worked with.

But especially Brodie.

I'd never had a more stimulating partnership than working with him. We were years apart, but when it came to music, there was an understanding between us, an unspoken synergy. I'd even been tempted to tell him I was the songwriter he admired, but I didn't.

Maybe someday.

And yeah, all this to say, I was spending way too much time reflecting.

More so this year when I was making my way through grief. But as the pain evolved, my body's needs resurfaced. But I didn't want a hookup. I wanted more.

And all those questions about my love life, or lack thereof, came rushing back.

I always recognized Brodie's attraction. But now? Now, I couldn't think about anything else.

Brodie had already ruined my concentration. Fuck, even my songwriting had changed. Everything became more intense. Like "Sideline," my words conveyed all the stuff I was feeling inside but could never voice in real life.

Less hard-edged and more heartache.

Not that my heart was involved; that would be crazy…

I opened the door to the theater and slid inside as quietly as I could.

There was Brodie, standing under the spotlights in those

painted-on jeans and a loose tank top, his tattooed arms bare. Turning his head over his shoulder, our eyes met.

Despite the distance between us, my breath caught.

Like the first time, like every time since. I didn't recognize what it meant four years ago, but I sure as fuck noticed now.

The beautiful Brodie James.

Why would he want me when he could have anyone?

Would I risk my career to have one night with him rather than nothing at all?

My body knew what it wanted.

My head told me to get the fuck gone.

CHAPTER 8

BRODIE

After a long-ass rehearsal and more technical glitches, it was time to call it a night.

Van had already scampered off, saying something about setting up interviews for concert night. I'm sure he wasn't lying about it, but if I knew him—and I fucking did—it was an excuse to avoid me again.

To avoid a conversation that needed to be had.

Van could express so many emotions in his songs, but not so much when it came to real life.

I remember after his mom passed, then his dad, how silent he was—always holding stuff in. I could see how much he was suffering, the grief that weighed heavy on him. His eyes so bloodshot and weary, his face an icy mask of pain.

I offered what I could, even when he tried to shut me out.

I'd try to change his mood in my usual way. I'd make a joke—about myself or the band or something, anything, to distract him—and at least he'd laugh.

Any reaction was better than nothing at all.

That experience taught me that, more than anything, I wanted to be the person Van could talk to. That shoulder he could lean on.

All of us leaned on him all the time. Me most of all. But except for close family and friends, I've always been kind of a selfish brat. Taking more than I give.

But I didn't want to be that with Van.

I was so far beyond lust for him at this point that I didn't recognize myself.

Bad enough that Van was in my every waking thought; he'd ruined my libido for anyone else. The guys would laugh their asses off if they knew I hadn't had sex with anyone for the past eleven months and thirteen days.

But who's counting?

My attempts at flirting with Van had failed so far, so what was I going to do now?

I still didn't have an answer.

Meanwhile, the guys were hyper as hell and itching to hit the town hard. I couldn't blame them. New Orleans had a party scene that rivaled L.A.'s. Better, even, because it wasn't fake or staged here.

This town was a music lover's dream, and every corner we passed had me wanting to tell our driver to stop and let me out so I could sit in one of the dimly lit clubs and soak up the sultry atmosphere. I'd need some kind of disguise, though, or I'd be mobbed and chaos would erupt. Been there, done that, had the bruises to prove it.

Then I remembered the private party.

Ugh.

When I got back to my suite at the hotel, I showered and ordered a shitload of room service.

Surprise, I'm not such a prima donna that I can't order my own food. When my assistant, Bibi, wasn't on hand, that is.

Like most of our staff, she was on vacation after a long, grueling tour. And I didn't mind at all. I had privacy on this trip and more time to think about how the fuck I was gonna talk to Van.

A half-hour later, and with no further answers, I sat down

in my hotel bathrobe and scarfed down a turkey club with cajun fries and iced tea, extra sweet.

After stuffing my face, I responded to a group text from my family.

I was the youngest of four, so my phone was never silent.

My three siblings were all married now with kids. Family get-togethers were loud and chaotic, and I wouldn't trade them for anything.

Jack was my oldest brother at thirty-six. He's with an orchestra in Denmark, and I kid you not, his ego's as big as his cello. Chamber musicians are rock stars in Europe and party like ones, too. Yeah, Jack got along with my band brothers just fine.

My sister Vi taught piano back in Rhode Island, not far from my folks. She's crazy talented, and I had a mind to invite her to our next event so she could play with us.

Then there's Harriet. We're fourteen months apart. But unlike the rest of our musical clan, Harriet's a psychologist. She, her husband, and my six-year old nephew had recently moved to Georgia, about a three-hour drive from my home in Nashville.

I gotta admit, it's nice to have family nearby. Not that a plane ride was long, but still.

Mom: When are you coming home?

Thanksgiving

Vi: Not before?

We're in NOLA until the beginning of November, then back to TN for a few weeks.

Jack: I thought you were done touring for the year?

The concert was last minute, my decision. All the proceeds will go toward helping a local charity. I wanted to do it.

Harriet: Why doesn't the press ever report about stuff like that? Instead, it's you mooning the crowd or shouting raunchy comments.

That's showbiz. How's Dad?

Mom: He's working on finishing the kitchen remodel. Knowing him, I doubt it'll be ready for Thanksgiving. We may have to order takeout.

I've eaten worse on holidays.

Harriet: I gotta go. Marlon just jumped in our pool, and he took our neighbor's cat with him.

He's definitely my nephew.

Harriet: No question. You can look after him over Thanksgiving weekend and give me and Raj a break.

Happy to, love you guys

I placed my phone aside and headed to the closet to decide what to wear.

I'd prefer to slip into jeans. Hell, I'd prefer to wear grey sweatpants and a t-shirt. I could put on a wig and have my security team sneak me into a local bar instead.

Maybe after I made an appearance at this shindig.

Remembering Van's warning, I picked a black leather

corset vest and a mesh top to go over it. Then, one of my trademark kilts, in purple this time. At the last minute, I slipped on a lace and silk thong. I preferred being commando, but sometimes I loved the feel of lingerie.

I'd often wear it on stage. But it wasn't just a performance look. It was me. I didn't abide by gender conformity. I wore what I liked and in a way that felt natural to me. It caused some backlash when I was younger, but I held firm.

I never understood why people would hate on someone for being themselves. What did my wearing makeup or lace underwear, or not being hung up on gender stereotypes have to do with anyone else?

After lacing up my black knee-high boots, I threw on several silver and gold rings and earrings. Some charcoal eyeliner, lip gloss, and a bit of styling crème to tame the unruly waves of my hair, and I was good to go. I sent a group text to see if my bandmates were ready.

> Hey, assholes, can we leave now?

Van: Driver's pulling up in ten. Regan and Dawson are on their way to your suite.

> You're not going with?

Van: I am, but in another vehicle

Holloway: Yo fuckers, I'm getting my dick sucked. I'll be ready in ten.

Ronin: He's busy getting his hair done. He wishes the stylist would suck him off.

Holloway: Fuck off, I score more than you

Faisel: Meet at Brodie's room and go down together

I'm riding with Van

Faisel: Can't we all ride in the same vehicle? There's only five of us.

Van: Let's meet at Brodie's suite. Play nice at the party for an hour or two; then we'll head to Crimson Bones for the rest of the night. I booked a VIP room. I'll be ready on-site with NDAs.

Normally our PR person came along when we went out and handled all of that shit.

Suddenly, guilt ate away at me. Van had been working non-stop the last week leading to our trip here and now during.

Tours were hell to organize. Last-minute gigs like this one, even more so. And now he was dealing with the press and NDAs.

I'd have to find a way to thank him personally. I know what I'd like to give him, but in the interim, something non-sexual would have to do.

My phone buzzed. My bodyguards were here.

I opened the door and was greeted by Regan and Dawson. "The boys are meeting us here. Can we all fit in one car?" I asked as the nearby ping of an elevator sounded.

"Not with our additional security staff," Regan replied and began talking into her earpiece.

Dawson glanced at me and gave me a thumbs up.

I liked the guy and had worked with him for as long as I'd been around Van.

Dawson was intimidating to look at, a massive wall of

muscle and six feet four, but he had a laid-back personality that fit in well with the band.

I stepped into the hallway to join them and noticed my bandmates walking toward us with their bodyguards flanking.

"Are we set?" Regan asked.

"No, we're waiting for Van," I replied. "Nice look, Holls."

"Right?" He grinned and ran a hand over his hair.

The stylist had parted Holloway's blond, shoulder-length hair in the middle and feathered it. With low-rise, wide-legged pants and a tight collared shirt that was open to his navel, he was rocking the 70s look.

Until he did a turn and started twerking, causing all of us to groan out loud.

"None of us want to see your lame attempt at dancing," I quipped.

Holloway chuckled. "You're just jealous of my smoking hot ass."

Ronin kicked Holloway in said ass, and they tussled, nearly toppling over. They hit the wall with a loud thud, and the sound reverberated down the hallway.

Dawson crossed his arms and pinned them with a dark look that had both Holls and Ronin standing at attention.

Dawson and Holloway were always at odds. Holloway tried to escape his security on more than one occasion, and it had caused a rift between them. That's why Dawson was my primary now and not his.

"What do you think of my fit?" Holloway asked my bodyguard.

Dawson responded by shaking his head.

I heard the ping of the elevator, and I knew it was Van.

I began to shift my balance from one foot to the other, rocking back and forth. If I had room in the hallway to pace, I would've done so, like I did before a performance when my nerves hit.

Then I saw Van step into view, and my belly fluttered like the first time I'd ever graced the stage.

Instead of his usual denim outfit, Van wore a slim-cut navy-blue suit.

It fit him to perfection: simple, classic, timeless.

Instead of a button-down, he'd worn it with a white tank top underneath and his necklace, of course. I nearly swallowed my tongue as he drew near. My heart raced so fast that my ears buzzed, and my vision narrowed.

I watched his powerful stride, sure and confident. Fuck, he was gorgeous.

But then I noticed his eyes; they were bloodshot, with dark circles underneath. That nagging guilt crept up on me again, but I pushed it aside for the moment.

"Looking hot, Van," Holloway yelled out and nudged my shoulder.

I smacked my bandmate upside the head, messing his hair.

"Not the hair, man, that's sacred," he quipped.

He went to smack me in return, but Dawson caught his wrist and stopped him.

"Careful now, they're insured," Holloway joked, and Dawson dropped his arm like he'd been burned.

"Grow the fuck up," I heard Dawson whisper.

"Excuse me?" Holloway replied and got up in Dawson's face.

Okay, not his face. He only came up to Dawson's chest.

"You heard me," Dawson snapped back, his face as red as his hair.

"Look, you have no—"

"That's enough," Regan interrupted, and everyone shut up. "We need to get a move on."

She nodded at Dawson and the other security personnel, then motioned for us to follow her.

Van drew close, moving in step beside me like always.

"You look amazing," he whispered in my ear, so low I almost didn't catch it.

I glanced over and noticed his eyes locked on my mouth.

Straight men didn't look at me that way. That I knew for damn sure.

But Van was wrong. He was the amazing one.

His smell alone, God, it was heady. Leather, musk, and amber. It was delicious.

I wanted to grab him by the lapels of his suit, shove him against the nearest wall, and show him just how talented my mouth really was.

Singing was the least of it, and PR obligations be damned.

Ignoring my body's instinct, I took a deep breath and tried to calm down.

"Thanks," I replied, my voice suddenly hoarse. "You look handsome yourself. Even though I prefer you in denim."

Or nothing at all. Yes, I would definitely prefer that.

"Gotta change the look sometimes, especially if I'm going to be photographed with the most seductive man on the planet."

I tripped, tumbling into Regan.

Thankfully Dawson was walking behind and caught me before I, or Regan, face planted on the carpeted floor.

I shook my head and mumbled my apology. "Sorry, I stumbled over something."

Yeah, my tongue.

Did Van have any idea what he'd just said to me?

He'd called me popular, provocative, and hot in the past, but it was always in the context of selling my image to the fans. But Van calling me seductive stoked the fire inside me that was always simmering.

For the first time in my life, I prayed *not* to get a boner as I walked beside the man I wanted more than my next breath.

My cheeks heated and, fuck, I was blushing now? I think the last time that happened, I was seventeen.

By the time we got to the elevator, I was all but jumping out of my skin.

Hot, bothered, restless, shook.

Thank fuck the rest of the guys took the first elevator down.

Dawson and I waited patiently with Van and Regan. I tried to distract myself and not stare at Van, but it was a losing battle.

Van being Van, he pulled out his phone and began to swipe. "The party tonight is hosted by Juliana Green. She's a longstanding patron of the arts in this city and is, I'm told, a big fan of yours."

"Got it." I nodded. "Operation kiss ass is now in play."

He chuckled and shook his head. "You've got such a way with words."

"Not like you," I replied.

"What do you mean by that?" Van stopped me, gripping my arm.

Shit, I almost gave away my knowledge of Van's songwriting.

"Come on, you're the manager, the negotiator. You've got a much better way with words than me."

Ping. The elevator doors opened, and we were ushered inside.

Saved by the proverbial bell.

CHAPTER 9

VAN

his elevator ride is taking too fucking long.

After booking up interviews for concert day and taking care of last-minute details for tonight, I managed to snag a half-hour nap, and then it was time to shower and change for the evening.

I hated suits, but given that I was the band's rep for, well, everything on this trip, I made the effort. But I refused to wear a dress shirt and tie.

We were in the music biz, after all, and no one expected conventionality.

I was texting back and forth with the organizer of tonight's party as I rode the elevator up to Brodie's suite.

But all my thoughts about work short-circuited as soon as I walked down that hallway and spotted Brodie with his back to me, standing with the band.

I'd never seen him wear that vest before, but it was sexy as hell. It cinched his waist and was held together by black laces that crisscrossed down his back, the edge of the vest hitting the upper curves of his ass.

I smiled as I caught sight of his kilt. Not for the first time did I wonder what, if anything, he was wearing under it.

He wore them on stage all the time; sometimes, it was the only thing he wore.

As we made our way to the elevator, my eyes wandered back up to Brodie's face, his eyes rimmed in dark liner, his mouth slick with gloss.

I didn't know which was sexier, him all-natural or made up. Either way, in my eyes, he was a gorgeous human being.

And even if you stripped away his physicality, he would be the same to me.

His talent, his drive, his connection to his fans - it had everything to do with who he was as a person, not what he looked like.

He turned his head toward me, and a slow grin graced his lips.

There was power in that secretive smile of his, and it had me shaking, my hands so sweaty I nearly dropped my phone.

"Remind me again about the woman hosting this party," Brodie murmured as he leaned closer to me, his shoulder brushing mine, his hot breath hitting my ear.

I shivered and shook my head, trying to get my brain and mouth to work together again.

Some people assumed Brodie's smart-ass attitude meant he didn't give a shit about anything. But he took his job seriously. No matter what, he showed up when called and gave the fans and supporters what they wanted. It was the reason why the label allowed him leverage, room to say whatever he pleased.

If the fans were happy, everything was good.

"Um... Juliana... Green," I managed to reply, my voice hoarse.

I cleared my throat and took a deep breath.

"She's a socialite and donates a lot of her time and money to causes in the city. She and her husband own a trucking company and several other businesses. They heard about the concert and the fact that we're donating the proceeds to one of their favorite charities, so they were only too happy to host a meet and greet. There will be limited on-site press for photos only since this is a private event. If anyone tries to get a statement from you, let me know."

"You better stick close to me. You know how aggressive the media can get."

I met Brodie's intense gaze and swallowed hard.

"You're a seasoned pro by now. I think you can handle it."

Brodie was about to argue with me, but we finally hit the parking garage and the doors opened.

Regan went first, then Dawson flanked Brodie, and I walked behind.

We headed for the two black SUVs, parked side by side.

Brodie got in the back seat of the first vehicle, and I followed. The rest of the band headed for the second car.

Once everyone was ready, we ventured out into the busy New Orleans night.

Every street we passed had colorful architecture and people outside talking, singing, and dancing. I loved the flow of the language down here, including the smattering of French that I recognized and felt at home with.

Maybe the day after the concert I'd take some time and explore a bit. Visit a few local clubs and soak up the atmosphere. And have a sumptuous meal or two.

I noticed Brodie's leg tapping out a nervous rhythm and, without thinking, reached out to touch his thigh.

"You all right?" I asked, then quickly pulled my hand back.

"Yeah, you know me. These private events aren't really my thing. I'm good with faces, but names, not so much. And I hate making small talk with the who's who of whatever city we're in. High rollers are usually so full of themselves."

"Yeah, not like rockstars," I quipped.

Brodie gave me his favorite finger.

Some things never change.

"What about after? The club? Do I have to go?"

I paused, completely surprised at his question.

Brodie loved to party and hang out with his band brothers. And he was never short of male attention when they went out. Plus, he had a day off tomorrow to recuperate from whatever shenanigans he got up to tonight.

I had the electronic NDAs loaded in my phone and ready to go.

Even though the thought of having to deal with whoever caught Brodie's eye tonight made me ridiculously pissed off. So much so that the grip on my phone was near painful.

I usually avoided the party circuit, leaving that to their PR person. I was a shit dancer, and club music was not my jam to start with. And I tried to avoid any place where Brodie would hook up.

But now that I thought about it, he seemed to be doing that less and less…

"You don't have to, but it's the perfect time to blow off some steam since you have all day tomorrow to rest."

"I don't care about clubbing anymore. Or that whole scene."

Was Brodie seeing someone? Was that why he didn't want to go out and get laid like the rest of the guys?

"Have you… are you…"

Fuck, I was tongue-tied.

"What?" he asked, staring at me.

"Are you seeing someone? Is that why you don't wanna go out?"

My question was met by silence and a glare I knew all too well.

"Are you kidding me?" he snapped.

I shrugged. "No. You're acting out of character. I just assumed—"

"Don't assume," he bit out. "Have you heard me talk

about anyone? Have I brought anyone around to meet the guys?"

"No but—"

"If I were seeing someone, you'd damn well know!" he snarled.

"Okay, all right. I'm sorry I mentioned it."

I wasn't. I was unreasonably happy about Brodie's proclamation.

"Since you did, there is someone I want." Brodie leaned into me so close I could see the specks of dark green in his gold eyes.

The fire was still there, but it wasn't anger.

I began to sweat in earnest despite the air conditioning.

"Unfortunately, I don't know how he feels about me. He probably thinks I'm just trying to get into his pants, and given my reputation, that's fair. Still, I don't want anyone else. Haven't for a long time. But I can't seem to get through to him. And not getting what I want is making me edgy," he paused and bit his lip. "Don't make presumptions, all right? And you can take that NDA and shove it up your—"

"We're here," Regan called out, interrupting Brodie's snark.

"Brodie—" I started, but Dawson was already out of the car and waving at us to follow.

"We're not done," Brodie shook his head and gripped my arm. "Tomorrow. As you said, we don't have anything on the schedule. I want you to spend the day with me."

I wanted to, fuck, did I want to. But I had work and... yeah, work.

If the head of the record label had any inkling about my newfound feelings for their number one artist, I'd be out on my ass in a heartbeat.

"I—"

"Please, Van."

The quiet way Brodie asked, the seriousness of his tone,

caught me completely off guard. He sounded pained. It was so unlike him that it made my pulse kick up again and my stomach drop.

"I don't know if that's a good idea."

It was the best idea. My heart wanted me to go, but my head kept telling me to stop.

Brodie's entire demeanor shifted, and his face iced over.

"You know what? I changed my mind. I'd love to go out later. Maybe a quick fuck with a hot guy—or two—is just what I need to get over these annoying as fuck feelings that have pained me long enough," he snapped and stepped out of the vehicle, slamming the door.

I rushed out after him, but he was already headed inside with his detail.

I barely had time to register the venue, a stone mansion with intricate carvings and green ivy climbing the brick walls. Huge trees lined the property and gave it a feeling of privacy.

I was too unsettled by Brodie's sudden anger to appreciate it like it deserved.

One thing I did notice, however, was that the house was crawling with security personnel.

Regan was already talking to someone stationed at the front door. I nodded as I passed and entered the house. The rest of the band were already inside, waiting in the foyer. A huge crystal chandelier hung over us, illuminating a space filled with antiques and art.

I walked up to Brodie, but the angry look on his face had me pausing.

"Not now, Van," he cautioned.

Then he turned his back on me, sauntering to the far corner to talk to Holloway.

Regan and Dawson stepped up beside me. I felt Regan's stare.

"Everything okay?" she asked.

"I think so."

I didn't know what the fuck I was doing.

"Are you sure?"

"Not at all." I shook my head.

"I'm not stupid, you know."

"Excuse me?"

"I see the way he looks at you. If you're having a lovers' spat—"

I choked on nothing but air and my own spit and started to cough.

Everyone turned to look at me, but I waved them off. I cleared my throat.

"It's not… we're not, I mean, I'm not sure—"

She held her hand up. "I don't need to know unless it compromises his security."

"Can we just forget this entire convo?"

Regan nodded and crossed her arms. "With pleasure."

This night was going to be a long one.

I pulled out my phone and checked my messages, texting the organizer to let her know we had arrived. I was supposed to do that when we left the hotel, but I'd forgotten completely. Not surprising, given the source of my distraction.

I glanced up and noticed a brunette woman in a black velvet dress walking down the stairs. Then I remembered the email with the party details. This was our host for the evening.

"Welcome to my home, Green Estates. I'm Juliana. I'm honored to meet y'all, and thank you for coming this evening," she announced.

When she got to the bottom of the stairs, I headed over and did the intros.

A half-hour later, I was standing in a packed ballroom filled with loud chatter, louder music, and the best damn food and liquor I'd had all year.

Brodie, of course, continued to ignore me as he did the rounds.

He charmed everyone, young and old alike. Eventually, they convinced him and the band to sing an impromptu song, which he graciously agreed to. No mic, no instruments save for a piano.

He was spectacular.

Brodie showed the audience his innate talent, and they lapped it up.

The applause went on and on until Brodie finally jumped up on the piano stool and whistled, silencing the room.

"Thank you all so much. Promise me you're gonna bring that passion to our concert on Halloween night! And if you think tonight's performance was good, you ain't seen nothing yet. We've got a new song, and New Orleans gets to hear it first."

More cheers and catcalls rang out as Brodie hopped down and grabbed his drink, toasting with the guys.

He finally looked over at me and raised his glass, then downed the drink in one go. I watched him flag down a waiter for another round, giving him a broad smile. The server was obviously enamored, given the way he was blushing and leaning into Brodie real close.

He wasn't the only one.

For the past two hours, Brodie had been swarmed by good-looking men all vying for his attention. And he hadn't exactly been ignoring them.

He didn't want anyone else, my fucking ass.

I, in turn, stayed glued to my phone to distract myself.

One bourbon became two, then three, and then I had to cut myself off or risk doing something stupid like getting shitfaced and causing a scene in front of two hundred people.

I placed my last drink aside, determined to restore my concentration, but my eyes, like a magnet, were drawn to him.

Another guest, a man worthy of his own billboard, sidled

up to Brodie, offering a million-dollar smile, a long once over, and then, a business card.

I watched, holding my breath, as Brodie glanced at the man and then the offered card.

And when Brodie took that card in hand…

Let's just say my reputation for patience – and my professionalism - had finally reached the end.

CHAPTER 10

BRODIE

After two hours of smiling and putting on a good face (and singing), I was done.

Don't get me wrong, the adulation was always welcome, but I'd had all the peopling I could handle.

All I wanted was to be left alone.

After what happened on the ride over, I was uneasy and vulnerable like I rarely was.

And it was all because of Van.

Even though I'd been approached by several hot men tonight, I felt nothing. Not a spark, not a lick of desire.

But when the last guy handed me his card with an open invitation to get together later tonight, I took it.

Not because I was going to call him, no.

But because Van stared at the guy like he was ready to rip his head off. And I, of course, could not resist poking the bear.

I wasn't above playing dirty to get through to him.

Was it my most mature moment? Hell no. But all's fair in love, right?

Then I realized that doing such a thing only played into Van's idea that I was only interested in getting in his pants.

One and done, and on to the next guy. And that was far from the truth.

I handed the card back.

Lookit me, acting all mature and shit.

Suddenly, Van was by my side and introducing himself to… Leon… Liev… I couldn't remember. The guy looked like a Norwegian model—all white teeth and icy blond hair.

"I'm Ivan Cross, Wayward Lane's manager. I'm afraid that Brodie isn't doing interviews until the night of the concert," Van snapped and passed over his card. "If you want to set it up, you contact me."

"Oh, I'm not with the press," Blondie replied, giving me a flirty grin. "Not at all."

Van's expression grew darker, and his cheeks flushed.

"We gotta hit the road, but it was nice to meet you," I held my hand out.

Blondie gripped it for much longer than a normal handshake.

Van's scowl was downright lethal.

"Same. Are you sure you don't want to get together later?"

"I have to rest up the voice, and I have an early morning, but thanks."

"No worries, then. I'll see you at the concert."

Blondie winked at me, nodded at Van, and sauntered off through the crowd.

"Sorry, I thought he was media," Van muttered and made to turn away.

I reached for his arm and held on, pulling him in close to me.

"I gave the card back. I'm not interested."

"It's none of my business." He shook his head and glanced up at me.

Was that relief I saw in Van's blues?

"Van—"

"Not now," he echoed my earlier reply.

"Later?"

"Tomorrow."

My stomach flipped over. He hadn't walked away or said no. That was a win in my book.

"Can we get out of here? I want to head back to the hotel."

Between the show of Van's jealousy (whether he recognized it or not, that's what it was) and the anticipation of spending time alone with him tomorrow, my sex drive was worked up. I had some serious jacking off to do.

"No club?"

I shook my head. "I was just running my mouth earlier, letting my temper get the best of me."

"Hey, asshole," Holls called out as he sidled up beside me. "Ready for the next party?"

"I'm heading back to the hotel."

"Don't be a bummer. Come on, man, live a little. You've been acting like a fucking monk lately, when was the last time you got your dick—"

"Shut it, Holls," I bit out.

"He's got a point," Van interrupted. "There might be talk if the rest of the guys are out having a good time and you're nowhere to be seen. The label won't want the media or the fans thinking there's been a falling out."

I rolled my eyes. "We can't fucking win. You want to limit our access to the press, but then we have to cater to them?"

"You know how it is. Let's go for an hour, make an appearance, and then you can leave."

"Fine, let's get it over with," I grumbled and chugged the rest of my drink.

"Don't sound so put out. It's a club, not serving time." Van chuckled. "Also, I invited Killmine, the opening band. They're a local act but up and coming. They're looking forward to meeting everyone."

"Why didn't you say so earlier?" I replied. "For that reason alone, I'll go."

"Before we leave, let's say our goodbyes to the host."

A half-hour later, we were back in the SUV on our way downtown.

Van showed me the stats on the band he'd invited, or as much as he could between replying to the texts he kept receiving and the calls he answered.

"Turn off the notifications for the night and relax."

He finally looked up at me. "There's no such thing. And I'm getting the final press schedule done for the thirty-first so I can free up my schedule tomorrow."

Oh. In that case...

"I didn't fully think this trip through," I stated, staring into his eyes.

"What do you mean?"

"I mean, you're shouldering a shitload of stuff because it wasn't in the plan, and I feel... guilty."

He smiled at me, and my pulse began to throb.

"You're sweet to be concerned, but it's nothing I haven't handled before."

"Sweet? No one has ever used that word to describe me. How many drinks have you had?" I teased him.

"More than I should've," he admitted and cocked his head, a lock of his hair falling over his left eye. "And take the compliment. You're not a selfish asshole like some people I've worked with. Snark hides your sensitivity. And your bark is way worse than your bite."

"You might enjoy my bite."

Van coughed but didn't reply.

Suddenly, our SUV came to an abrupt stop. Regan and Dawson got out first, as usual.

"Christ, there's press here already. Someone must've blabbed," Van sighed as he looked out his window. "No autographs before we head in. Just wave and keep moving."

The back door opened and Van stepped out. I followed him, but we waited until the second SUV pulled up beside us and the rest of the guys piled out.

There were camera flashes and callouts, so we turned and waved. I gave the practiced smile and the shot that the press wanted.

Not really.

They wanted dirt—on who I was fucking, how much I was drinking, if I was fighting with my bandmates. I didn't have anything to give them, which was hilarious if you think about it. Sure, I liked to drink, and yeah, I'd had my issues with pills in the past, and yes, I was a randy fuckboy, but not recently.

My salacious rock star persona was not living up to the hype. I couldn't give a shit, but still, if the fans only knew…

There was a massive lineup of people waiting to get into the club, and once the flashes started going off, the fans spotted us. Screams erupted, and phones came out.

This part never got old. It was still a rush to be recognized.

"Keep moving," Regan urged as we made our way up the stairs and into the club.

Crimson Bones lived up to its name, with red walls and gothic touches, including massive black chandeliers and artwork inspired by Mardi Gras celebrations. It was cool and funky, something I couldn't say about many clubs I'd visited.

One thing was the same. The heavy beat of house music blasted through my body as we made our way up the stairs.

Van walked ahead, talking to the host. And then we were whisked down a long hallway that opened to a massive room, a balcony VIP that overlooked the main club below. We had our own bar up here and waitstaff to cater to us.

Then, I noticed the crowd already seated at the bar. A group of guys younger than us and all dressed similar to Holloway in 70s style.

These were the guys from Killmine.

Van, as usual, took charge and made the intros.

"Nate Filier, Xander Delaire, Heath Lang, and Otis Wayne."

Nate was the lead singer, a tall, lanky guy with a brown shag and a deep voice that rumbled like a foghorn. Xander played bass, Heath drums, and Otis lead guitar.

"Nice to meet y'all," Nate smiled and greeted us. "And thanks for the invite, Van. This club is the coolest place in the city, *fantastique*."

"*De rien*," Van replied.

Nate's face lit up. "You speak French?"

Van nodded. "I don't use it much day to day, but I love the language. I was raised in Montreal. Being down here feels like home."

"Well, *bienvenue à la maison*."

I had no idea what Nate said, but it sounded cool.

"Pleasure to meet you guys," I held out my hand. "Van has said nothing but great things. Drinks are on us."

Soon we were all shooting the music shit, downing shots, and chilling out. Van even joined us, taking a few shots while we hung out.

I was relieved to see him relax for a change.

Me and my band brothers could always handle a fuckton of liquor, but the boys from down south beat us, no contest. I don't know how they managed to drink so much and still walk a straight line.

I tried to focus on the conversation going on around me, but inevitably, my focus was on Van.

An hour later, Holls and Ronin announced they were hitting the dance floor. Faise didn't want to go, but Ronin hauled him over his shoulder, and that was that.

Our security team followed, along with the boys from Killmine.

I stayed behind with Van and Dawson.

"Looks like it's just the two of us," Van yelled out over the boom of the music as he ordered a bottle of sparkling water.

We sat on one of the leather couches overlooking the party below.

"Three," I pointed over my shoulder to Dawson, who was standing guard behind us.

"Go on and dance with them. I'm fine up here," Van held up his phone. "I've got work to keep me busy."

I shook my head and moved closer, draping my arm across the back of the couch.

"I'll go if you go."

"No fucking way." Van laughed and pointed to his shoes. "I've got two left feet. Swear to God."

I'd never seen Van dance. Not when he was watching us perform, not at events. Never. He claimed he had no rhythm, but I didn't believe him.

"I think you're lying." I stood up and held my hand out. "Get up."

Tequila flooded veins had me ready to gamble.

"No," Van waved me off, his cheeks flushing.

"No one can see us but Dawson, and he won't tell." I looked over at my security. "Will you?"

Dawson shook his head and turned to face the audience down below.

"Come on, dance with me."

"Brodie—"

"Get your tight ass up off that couch."

Van vaulted off the cushion and faced me. "*Câlisse!* You just can't let up, can you?"

"No, I can't. You should know this about me by now."

My heartbeat was louder and faster than the pounding pulse of the music around us.

But I didn't get closer. I stayed where I was.

I don't know if it was the alcohol or my brain finally

clicking into gear, but I had a sudden realization. I would be clear in my intentions toward Van, but it was up to him.

I wasn't gonna take something he wasn't willing to give.

Even though I knew desire when I saw it, he was still holding back.

He wasn't out? Or maybe he wasn't comfortable with his sexuality? Then there was the fact that we worked together.

All of those reasons were sound.

And Van and I might be a fucking disaster waiting to happen.

Yet, here I was. My body sweating, hands trembling, waiting, fucking dying for Van to come close and touch me.

I never hungered for anyone like I did for him.

It was humbling and so fucking frustrating that I wanted to scream.

But I held back.

Until he took a step toward me.

Then all bets were off.

CHAPTER 11

VAN

eave.

Leave now, and don't look back.

I ignored the common sense loop in my head and closed the gap between Brodie and me.

With the way he'd ordered me to get off the couch, I thought for sure he'd make the first move. But he just stood there, frozen in place. His hands tightly fisted, his chest moving in and out at a rapid pace, his eyes glittering in the darkness.

I stepped into his space and slid one arm around his waist.

He groaned, and I answered.

One simple touch triggered an intense desire that threatened to consume me. My dick liked what we were doing a hell of a lot more than I'd anticipated. My dick got so hard, so fast, that I was lightheaded, aching, throbbing.

From one touch.

I pulled him closer until our hips collided, and we started swaying to the pulsing music.

I wasn't lying when I said I was a shit dancer, but then again, that wasn't what we were doing. We were barely moving in time to the beat.

I splayed my palm against Brodie's back and traced the gap in his corset vest. Slipping my fingers underneath the laces, I gave an experimental tug.

His breath caught, and mine followed.

I was surrounded by his scent. Deep and spicy, warm, as heady as the man himself. It had me dying to taste his skin.

Then I ran the tips of my fingers under the laces and reveled in the feel of his smooth, bare skin against mine.

I brushed my lips against his ear. "You've never worn this before."

"Do you like it?" Brodie asked, his body trembling.

"I more than like it."

I pulled back to look at his face, his cheeks flushed and his eyes glassy.

"Brodie? Are you okay?"

He blinked and nodded. "I'm more than okay. I just...it's been so..."

He paused and licked his lips.

Brodie lost for words was an anomaly I wasn't prepared for.

My eyes were transfixed on his slick mouth.

Not for the first time, I wondered how soft his lips were and how he would taste.

It dawned on me just how closely I'd been watching him all along.

The expressiveness when he sang. The way he bit his lip when he was frustrated. The curl of his sneer when he was angry. The way his lips stretched wide when he laughed out loud.

I wanted to taste it all.

"Guys, we have a problem."

Dawson's booming voice startled Brodie and me.

I turned without thinking, realizing, too late, that my rock-hard dick was tenting my trousers.

Thankfully Dawson's gaze didn't waver from mine.

"Regan and the secondaries are having issues with a drunk on the dance floor. They're headed out with the guys. We need to leave. Now."

A possible security threat had my dick deflating just like that.

But instead of stepping away from Brodie, I took his hand as Dawson guided us out of the VIP room and down the stairs.

Brodie made no effort to let go.

And fuck me, holding his hand felt as natural as everything else between us.

When we got outside, I noticed Regan and her team with the rest of the guys, including Nate and his bandmates.

As we drew closer, my eyes hovered on Holloway, who was holding his hand to his cheek.

"What happened?" I asked.

"Some asshole wouldn't take no for an answer, so I told him to fuck off. Then he punched me. Or he tried to," Holloway replied and rolled his eyes.

Dawson gently pulled Holloway's hand aside and inspected his face.

"I'm fine. He just grazed me; he was too drunk to do any real harm," Holloway insisted and drew his head back.

"Do you need to go to the hospital?" I asked and looked around. "Did anyone else get hurt?"

"It was just Holls," Faisel replied. "He defended himself, and then Regan was there to get us away before it could escalate."

"He's gonna have a bruise for sure, but it didn't break the skin. Are you dizzy or nauseous?" Dawson asked.

Holloway shook his head. "I told you, he barely hit me. I'll ice it. I'll be fine. For fuck's sake, I've had worse injuries on stage."

Dawson crossed his arms and continued to stare at Holloway. "Did you defend yourself like I taught you?"

"Fucking right, he did," Nate commented. "It was like a scene from a goddamn movie! You gotta teach us those sick martial arts moves, Holls."

"No one is teaching anyone anything right now," Regan interrupted. "Let's get in the vehicles before we draw a crowd."

Nate stepped up to me and offered his hand. *"Merci encore* for inviting us tonight, Van. We really appreciate it. Can we talk after the concert?"

Then I remembered I was still holding onto Brodie's hand. I dropped it and stepped away from temptation, reaching for Nate.

"Yeah, of course," I nodded and shook Nate's hand. "Looking forward to Halloween."

"It's going to be a night to remember," Nate replied as he and his band brothers gave hugs to the Wayward Lane boys and waved goodnight to the rest of us.

Killmine headed back into the club while we headed for the SUVs.

Brodie walked and talked with Holloway, making sure his friend was okay. I was following behind them when Brodie turned around and gave me a glare over his shoulder.

I wasn't happy about our disruption either, but now was not the time.

Reality was seeping in, along with doubts and concerns that began to float to the surface of my mind.

I'd almost kissed Brodie in that club.

A step I'd never taken before with any man. Never mind someone I worked with. For.

What the fuck was I doing?

My legs were weak, and my hands were shaking, my phone almost slipping out of my fingers.

The heated pull between me and Brodie was undeniable, so fucking real.

I didn't know whether to be ecstatic or laugh out loud at the predicament I was in.

I'd never crossed the professional line. It was just asking for trouble, and yet... I wanted to be reckless with him.

Brodie made me feel things I'd all but given up on ever feeling.

I found myself alone in the SUV with Dawson and Lennie, a secondary bodyguard, while Brodie went with Holls, Ronin, and Faise.

My phone buzzed, and I glanced at the notifications.

Holloway's incident at the club was already making the rounds of social media.

There were many concerned comments asking if he was okay. Like the pro he was, Holloway posted a photo of him and Brodie in the car, smiles on both their faces. That would calm the fan frenzy for now.

Without thinking, I zoomed in on Brodie and saved the picture as a screenshot.

Then my phone rang.

It was my boss.

Greg was a smart businessman but a total control freak. You don't make it to the top of the music world by being anything less.

We'd had our share of arguments over stuff like press access and creative control, but overall, I respected Greg. Brodie, of course, had his fair share of fights with him. Brodie was never shy about speaking up—for himself or for others. He was determined to walk his own path, even if it put him at odds with the label.

Greg knew talent and he rewarded it. He respected his musicians and they returned it. For the most part.

Not that I was being all that respectful myself.

Only a half hour ago, I was eager to shove my tongue down the throat of Greg's biggest star. I could just imagine the anger that would unleash if Greg found out about that.

Esti de câlisse de tabarnak... Translation: fuckity fuck fuck.

"Everything's under control," I answered in my calmest voice.

The band, yes. Me? Fuck no.

"Are you sure about that?" Greg's voice boomed out on the other end of the line. "What happened?"

"Some drunk got aggressive, and Holloway defended himself. The team got them out of there before it could escalate. Everything's fine."

"Yeah, I saw the picture Iain posted, but I want to hear it from you. Please tell me he doesn't have a concussion."

"He said the guy barely grazed him. There was no blood or anything, just a red welt. Apparently, Dawson taught him self-defense moves."

"Interesting. Maybe the rest of the band should receive the same training." Greg paused. "How're things shaping up for the concert?"

"Great. We met up with Killmine, and they're gonna be an awesome opener. Rehearsal took longer than normal, but the venue's historic, so the tech and the power are temperamental."

"Is that going to be a problem? The last thing we need is three thousand pissed-off fans if we have to cancel."

"There will be no canceling. Brodie and the rest of the guys can improvise if they need to. They're professionals."

Unlike me.

"And interviews? What kind of coverage have we got?"

I leaned my head back and sighed. It was past one in the morning, and I'd been up since six. I was tired and frustrated, but I swallowed it back and answered my boss.

"So far, twenty-four interviews the night of. Mainly local stuff, five national. And two entertainment shows from L.A."

"Good, and since we're not making any money on this one, make sure to play up the charity angle. At least we'll buy good press with the fans."

"It's not an angle," I snapped. "Brodie didn't push for this event just so the band could look good. Despite his sharp tongue, he actually cares about people."

There was silence on the other end of the line.

Shit.

Biting off the head of my boss was not going to benefit anyone.

"I realize that, Van, but this is still business. Everything we do has a reason and purpose. I'm sure the band feels the same. Especially Brodie. He's not just a musician; he's a brand, and he knows it."

Yeah, he did. But he wasn't always happy about it. So many people wanted a piece of him, and there were certain parts he wasn't willing to give. I tried as much as I could to protect him, but I didn't always succeed.

"He's a person too. And you can rest easy; everything will happen as it should. This concert will be a win for everyone."

I knew Brodie. He would've paid out of his own pocket if the label had said no to this gig. Once his mind was made up, nothing stopped him. I admired his tenacity, his fire. It was the first thing that drew me to him.

"I'm sure it will." Greg paused. "One more thing. Brodie hasn't been seen with anyone lately. I want you to confirm a date for him for concert night. A local celebrity, a guy who'll get people talking. He can be seen with Brodie at the after-party. That'll drive speculation and fan engagement."

Arranging "dates" for high-profile musicians was nothing new, but Brodie never needed help in that department. And now, just the thought of having to set him up with some gorgeous model made my blood boil.

"I've got a few ideas," Greg continued. "My assistant will send along a list with contact details. Set it up."

"And if Brodie refuses?"

I barely managed to choke out the question.

"Convince him otherwise. That's what I pay you for."

CHAPTER 12

BRODIE

"N o."

"Dee—"

"I said no, Van. That's it. End of discussion."

"This came directly from Greg. I don't have a choice in the matter and neither do you."

Today was off to a shitastic start.

Last night wasn't any better. It could've been.

If Van and I hadn't been interrupted…

Fuck, when Van grabbed hold of me in that club and teased the skin on my lower back, I nearly came in my lace underwear.

He was about to kiss me, and I was more than ready for it.

Fucking hell, I just about had a heart attack, and we'd done nothing but brush our hips together.

Then we were whisked out of the club by Dawson, and my attention pivoted to Holls.

Despite my friend's assurances that he was okay after his scuffle, I could see that the incident had shaken him up. I stayed with him on the ride back, but he insisted he was fine.

Holls hugged me after we exited and assured me that all he needed was aspirin and a good night's sleep.

Van was on his phone per usual as he exited the SUV at the hotel. He looked irritated and stressed.

It was late and we all needed rest, so, like a mature rock star, off I went to my own room. Alone.

Frustration didn't begin to cover it.

All I really wanted to do was to knock on Van's hotel room door, shove him onto that king-sized bed, and show him that these lips were made for his. They were gonna rock his fucking world, pun intended.

I was going to give him all the pleasure. I was going to ruin him for anyone else.

Admittedly, I had a rockstar ego.

But I came by it honestly.

The same couldn't be said about Greg Haddley.

Since when did I need to hire a fucking date for an event? And making Van organize this? It pissed me off on so many levels. And more so because Van acted like it was no big deal and I should just acquiesce. (I'm not just a pretty face; I know big words.)

"I'll agree to it, but only if you can be my date," I replied, smiling at Van.

We were huddled around the coffee table in my suite, the remnants of breakfast and coffee mugs littering the space.

I hadn't slept enough. I'd hardly slept at all.

As soon as I entered my suite last night, I yanked down my underwear and wanked off to the thought of finally slipping my tongue deep inside Van's mouth. I pictured him lying on his back as I made my way down his body. The visual was so clear, so sexy, that I worked my dick furiously, using pre-cum and spit as lube.

Van would devour me with those denim blues of his and groan out my name.

With only a couple of tugs on my throbbing dick, I was there. I came all over my hand, my kilt, the rug.

Then I passed out on my bed and woke up at nine.

To a knock on my door and a weary looking Van on the other side of it.

Hungover, cranky, and hungry as hell, I let Van in. But all my irritation vanished as I took in the concerned expression on his face.

I ordered room service and took a quick shower while Van worked on his phone.

Okay, maybe the shower wasn't so quick. I did manage to jerk off again under the heated spray of the water.

Hey, the man I was lusting over for what seemed like forever was in my hotel room, looking sleep-rumpled and sexy. Can you blame me?

An hour later, with full bellies and caffeinated veins, Van sprung the news on me.

And I, to say the least, was not taking it well.

Fucking Greg.

"You know I can't do that, Brodie, come on. I've got a shit-load of stuff on my plate for this event," Van snapped and passed over his phone. "Here's the list of possible dates Greg sent. Review their pictures and profiles and let me know which one you… want."

Van looked as happy about this as I did, a dark scowl on his face.

"None of them," I answered without looking at his offered phone. "I want none of them."

"It's just for show. And when the head of the label tells you to do something, you do it."

"What's he going to do if I say no? You think he's gonna threaten me? Or the rest of the guys? I don't fucking think so. Fans are already clamoring for our next album, our next tour. How many tens of millions did we make for him this year alone? We're the ones paying his fucking mortgages, not to mention the alimony for his four ex-wives. He should be kissing my ass, not threatening it."

Van burst out laughing, and the deep, husky sound filled me with a happiness I couldn't explain.

It was just the best sound in the world.

The crinkles at the corners of his eyes deepened, and that dimple in his cheek made an appearance.

I drank in the sight of him like an addict needing my fix.

God, did he know how fucking beautiful he was? I wanted to see him laugh every goddamn day.

"How about you do it for me, then? Since I don't want to get fired," Van replied as he rubbed a hand over his jaw.

He hadn't bothered shaving this morning, and I was a fucking fan. I wanted that scruff on my face, my nipples, my thighs… and shit, so much for the morning wank session.

"I'll agree to it on one condition."

"You don't need to barter to get me to spend the day with you. I'm here, aren't I?"

I leaned forward on my elbows. "I thought this was a business breakfast."

"It is, but it's also you and me. I wouldn't be here if I didn't want to be. I could've just called or texted."

Van raised one eyebrow, and I nodded in return.

"So, what are we doing sitting in this hotel room? We've got a city to explore."

If I wanted to convince Van that taking a chance on me, on us, was worth the risk it entailed, I needed to show him that I was all in.

And not just in a horizontal way.

Not that I didn't think about that every moment of the day, but there was more to him and me than sexual chemistry.

Much, much more.

I got up and held out my hand, hoping, please, God, just fucking take my hand.

I watched the expressions flitting over his face—the

nervous way he licked his lips, the movement of his throat when he swallowed hard, the slight trembling in his hand when he placed his phone in his pocket.

Finally, he reached out, placing his palm against mine.

All my senses electrified. Like that first moment when I walked on stage—the buzz, the anticipation, the fever—it was the best feeling ever.

"First up, more coffee and beignets," I declared as Van stood. "Then, a tour of the French Quarter and lunch at a hidden place that only locals know about. An afternoon at a jazz club on Bourbon Street. Oh, and an authentic Creole dinner, somewhere intimate."

"That sounds amazing," Van replied as he pulled me in close, our hips and thighs touching.

No more caffeine was necessary. I was wide awake now.

"But we'll have Dawson with us. And you'll need to wear a disguise or something."

I nodded. "Don't you have a baseball cap I could borrow? The one you wear when we're on tour. It's got a red and blue logo. I like it."

"My Expos cap? Yeah, I have it with me. It... it belonged to my dad. He was a baseball fanatic, especially when Montreal had a major league team. I take that cap with me everywhere."

Van's eyes welled up, but he quickly blinked away his tears.

"He's always with you."

"He is."

I gripped his waist, the heated muscles quivering under my palm. I slid my hand around to rest on his lower back and pulled him in even tighter. God, being this close to him was already making this the best day ever.

"This okay?" I asked.

"More than," he admitted, his deep blues filled with a longing I recognized.

He reached up and cupped my face.

"I've never… I mean… with a man." He shook his head. "I think I'm bisexual or pansexual. I'm not sure. But I've never been with a man. Never kissed one, nothing. I thought maybe I'm too old, but here we are."

"You're never too old. It's just like singing," I murmured as we shared the same breath. "You don't always know what you're gonna sound like or if you're gonna hit those notes, but you gotta try."

"I'm nervous as fuck."

His hands were trembling. I turned my head and brushed my lips against his palm.

"I know. We take this at your pace; there's no rush."

"Why me? You could have anyone. Like one of those models Greg wants you to be seen with."

Van practically growled, his blue eyes darkening. It gave me enormous satisfaction.

"Stop right there. I'm here with you," I squeezed his waist and moved in closer. "Why do you think I haven't been with anyone else in ages? Even the guys have noticed my lack of a sex life. Hell, Greg, too, and that's why he suggested the 'date,' right?"

Van's face flushed, and the color suited him. "No one? For how long?"

"Eleven months and thirteen, no, fourteen long fucking days."

"What?"

Van practically shouted, his eyes widening.

"Hush, that's between you and me and this hotel room. I don't want to ruin my rock star reputation."

"Are you serious?"

I cocked my head. "Would I joke about something like not having sex in almost a year?"

"No wonder you were extra cranky on tour."

I glared at him, but it had no effect.

He just smiled at me like he knew a secret. Well, he did now.

"The one and done is… done. I need more. I need a sexy man who challenges me in and out of the bedroom. AKA you," I insisted.

"We haven't even kissed yet; how do you know it's gonna be good between us?"

I rolled my eyes and licked my lips. "Please, I know you. You're thorough about everything. Intense, talented, passionate."

Van's cheeks were bright red.

In all the years we'd worked together, I'd never seen him blush, not with anyone. I loved that only I could make him flush like that.

"Come on. It's a beautiful fall day. The sun is shining and we've got a moment to ourselves. Let's go have fun," I encouraged, trying for a lighter tone.

I was all in to take things slow, but we needed to get the hell out of this hotel room and away from the temptation of that nearby bed before I taught Van a lesson he was not yet ready to learn.

Van nodded. "Let me text Dawson."

He stepped out of the circle of my arms and I reluctantly let him go.

It was gonna be difficult to stop myself from touching Van now that I knew I wasn't the only one in over my head. His admission was just what I needed to hear.

He wanted me.

And sooner or later, when we finally took that first step together, it wasn't just his world that was gonna blow up. It was mine.

In that, I had no doubt.

CHAPTER 13

VAN

I was riding a high that I hadn't felt in forever.

Between last night's almost kiss and this morning's revelations, I was jacked up with so much adrenaline I could've power-walked the whole way around the city.

Brodie wore his disguise; my baseball cap, a grey scarf, mirrored aviators, and a distressed leather jacket. My heart twinged with a strange ache as I looked at him in my dad's hat.

All the childhood memories I had of Dad and me involved hot summer days at the stadium and yelling so loud for our team that we lost our voices.

Happy times, the feeling of home…

Brodie touched the brim and nodded at me, giving me that gorgeous smile of his that kickstarted my heart again.

Fuck, were we really doing this?

I set aside my analytical brain for the time being, letting my worries take a backseat as we headed out into the heart of the city to play tourist for the day.

Regan wasn't keen on letting Brodie out with just one security personnel, so I suggested Dawson and Lennie. The four of us made an interesting group.

We found a local café, suggested by the hotel staff, and stuffed our faces full of delicious fried beignets and huge bowls of café au lait.

After the jolt of caffeine and sugar, we walked around the French Quarter, stopping at street vendors and listening to buskers who were as talented as musicians you saw on stage. And I got to practice my *Français* when we entered a store that sold locally made soaps and cologne.

Thankfully, no one recognized Brodie with his shades on, his hair tucked up under the cap, and his jacket and scarf covering his tattoos.

I almost reached for his hand a time—or three—but caught myself.

He walked closer to me than usual, our bodies occasionally brushing against each other. I liked it. I liked it a lot.

And it would have to do for now.

For lunch, Brodie had us walking uptown to a place called the Oyster Shack. And it was, literally, a bright blue shack at the end of the block. But the smells, fuck, the smells were so good. Deep-fried goodness and spices.

Lennie lined up to place our order, along with two dozen people, most of them locals.

It was well worth the half-hour wait.

We ordered po' boys and muffuletta sandwiches and split them amongst us, washing it all down with the sweetest tea I'd ever tasted.

Then, we made our way down to a place off Bourbon Street, which was particularly crowded for a Monday afternoon. Then again, it was the day before Halloween, so the party was getting started early.

"That's the place Armand was talking about," Brodie pointed across the street to a red neon sign that read "Stoney's Jazz."

"Who?"

"The concierge at the hotel. I called down before we left to get recs on the best music joints."

"And this place is good?"

Brodie nodded. "So he said. Let's find out."

We stepped inside a dimly lit room filled with an eclectic range of colorful antique furniture and a mahogany bar that was already packed with patrons.

"There's a table in the corner."

He turned and grinned at me.

"Great minds, I was thinking the same thing."

A hostess greeted us and steered us toward that very table.

I sat at the back beside Brodie, with Dawson and Lennie on either side of us. We ordered a round of IPAs and sat back to enjoy the crisp brew.

A jazz trio—stand-up bass, drums, and singer—took to the tiny wooden stage in the opposite corner.

With our hands hidden under the table, Brodie slid his left over my right, and we interlocked our fingers tightly.

I wished he could take off his sunglasses so I could see his eyes, but he had to leave them on.

So far, he'd gone under the radar, and we wanted to keep it that way. Then it occurred to me that wearing sunglasses indoors might attract questions, too, but no one paid us any mind.

That was the great thing about New Orleans. Eccentric was normal.

"Is there anything better than live music?" I asked him, my eyes lingering on his mouth.

"I can think of one thing, but it's a close call." He smiled. "This is just what I needed. This singer is amazing."

I nodded in agreement and sat back, the soulful strains of the music settling into me. The singer's voice was smooth, sultry, and with just a hint of a gravelly undertone. I let it carry me away to another time and place as she switched between English and French.

The song spoke of longing and love and put to mind silky sheets, glistening bodies, and heated kisses.

Brodie rubbed his thumb against mine, and it was all I could do to sit still and not lean over and take what I wanted.

I never knew I could have an insatiable hunger for a kiss. But there it was.

It shocked me.

Almost as much as Brodie's confession this morning.

He hadn't had sex in almost a year. A year… That's, like, ten years for a rockstar.

And there was the fact that he was letting me set the pace.

In all the years I'd known him, Brodie was always determined when it came to what and who he wanted. Never shy with an opinion or a move.

And usually, he made the first move.

His understanding of my needs touched something deep inside of me. It was wholly unexpected but in the best possible way. This sensitive side of Brodie was as attractive as all the other facets of his personality. And I was longing to learn more.

But I was still wrapping my head around the fact that he not only wanted me, but only me.

I was going to have a hell of a hard time setting him up on that "date," even though I knew it would all be for show.

My fear was that his date would be a much better bet than me. Someone who didn't have my inexperience, someone who didn't have the added complication of working for him.

Brodie's life would be a lot easier if he'd find someone like that to hook up with. If he just ignored this chemistry between us and we went back to our usual roles—manager, singer, colleagues, friends.

Easier for me, too.

Then again, I knew his stubborn mindset. And I knew mine.

He may be letting me drive this relationship for now, but he wasn't going anywhere. He was gonna stick with me until we reached our destination.

All I could feel was my want for this man. And his for me. It was as real as the hand I was holding.

Did I know what the fuck I was doing? No. But I wanted to keep going.

The singer ended the song by hitting the longest, lowest note, and I felt a surge of emotion that brought tears to my eyes.

Reluctantly, I let go of Brodie's hand so we could clap along with the rest of the audience. The singer took a bow and turned to her bandmates, who nodded at the patrons.

Dawson and Lennie waved the server down and we ordered another round of beer. They got into a conversation, and Brodie turned to me.

"I miss places like this. Just blending in, feeling normal," he admitted.

"You said goodbye to normal years ago."

"I know. And I'm grateful." He nodded. "I know I'm lucky. A lot of artists struggle their entire careers. I don't regret anything. It's just that lately, I need more than recording, touring, and partying. I need a life outside of that. And someone to share it with. A family of my own."

My mouth dropped open.

Brodie wanted a family? That was one surprise I was not prepared for.

"Where has deep, introspective Brodie been all these years?" I teased.

"I'm only this way with you. Everyone else gets the sarcastic version."

I mulled over his comment but hesitated to ask what I was dying to ask.

"You look like you want to say something, Van. Go ahead. You can ask me anything."

I leaned in closer and brushed my lips against his ear. "You said you want a family of your own. Do you mean kids and everything?"

"Kids and everything," he confessed.

A dark flush stained his cheeks. He'd probably deny it, but I noticed.

Brodie James as a dad?

I tried to picture it, and I was surprised at how easy it was. He'd be the fun one, the rulebreaker. And his kids would probably be hellions like him.

"I come from a big family, yeah? Four of us siblings, plus my parents, nieces and nephews, cousins. I love it. When I'm with them, it grounds me. They still treat me like the annoying but obviously best-looking James in the family. They have my back, no matter what happens with my life. And I have theirs."

"I know what you mean. When my parents were alive and I'd travel back home, it felt like I could finally breathe again. All the pressure and stress from work took a vacation. I didn't appreciate or realize just how much I was going to miss them. I miss coming home. I certainly wouldn't call my Nashville condo that. It's just a place where I sleep and do laundry. There are no memories or feelings attached to it. God knows, I never do any writing there; that should tell me something."

"Writing?" Brodie asked.

I guess now was as good a time as any.

"You're not the only one with secrets." I sighed and took his hand again under the table. "I'm Corley Hewitt. I've been songwriting for nearly twenty years. It helped pay the bills while I was a road manager and before I started at Bandit. And I still love it."

I paused and looked at Brodie.

"I can't see your eyes, but your body language tells me that you're not surprised about this."

Brodie took a sip of his beer and nodded.

"I've known for a few years. One night, when we were rehearsing, you dropped off a new song for us to look at. But it wasn't the final version; there were notes and edits, and I recognized your handwriting."

"The guys know?"

"Nope. Only me. I don't think they pay attention to things like your handwriting."

No, they wouldn't.

"But you did."

"I did, and I do. I notice every single thing about you, Van."

A shiver wracked my body.

"Why didn't you say anything?" I asked.

"It was none of my business. If you wanted to tell me, you would. And now you have."

"So—"

"So?"

"What do you think of my songs?"

Brodie burst out laughing.

Okay, that was not the reaction I was expecting.

I tried to pull my hand back, but he gripped it tighter.

"We've recorded what, seven of them over the past four years? What do you think? I love them. Especially your new stuff, like 'Sideline.' It's more emotional."

"Well, my muse is very inspiring," I whispered and squeezed his hand.

Brodie's cheeks flushed.

"You're a gifted writer, Van. And now that you know that I know, it's the perfect time to say we should collaborate. Write together."

"Really?"

"Oh yeah."

"I've never had a writing partner before."

"There's a first time for everything," Brodie responded with a teasing grin.

Songwriting was the least of it.

CHAPTER 14

BRODIE

Did I feel bad about ignoring my band brothers's texts to spend the day with Van?

Nope. Not one fucking bit.

I texted them back after we left the jazz club and sent them pics of me and Van as we made our way about town. Holls was taking it easy after last night, Faise didn't respond at all, and Ronin was busy hooking up with some guy he'd met the last time we were in town.

Given their replies (or lack of), I felt no guilt.

And spending the day with Van was not an opportunity I was going to waste.

After the jazz club, we strolled along Bourbon Street. Then we found a Creole restaurant a few blocks over and stuffed our faces full of crawfish étouffée and spicy grilled sausage. We capped it off with chocolate bourbon pecan pie and a couple of espressos.

I offered Van the last bite of pie, but he waved me off. I stuffed the mouthful in and moaned like the needy food slut I was. I'd traveled all over the world, but the food scene in this city was something else.

Van shifted in his seat and gave me a dark look.

"*Tabarnak*, could you be any louder?" he asked as he sipped his coffee.

I recognized the Quebeçois swear word. Van used it when things got fucked up on tour.

"Yes, I could."

I was about to wink at him, and then I remembered my sunglasses. Going incognito had its downside. Still, the day had been one I wouldn't trade for anything.

Instead of winking, I took the last bite and moaned again.

Van leaned forward.

"Stop it," he demanded and glanced at Dawson and Lennie.

They were busy finishing up their dessert and conversation, not paying us any mind.

Both guys had been great all day. They were friendly, but they let me and Van do our thing. I'm sure they caught the handholding at the club, but if they did, they showed no reaction.

They'd seen all kinds of antics that me and the boys got up to on the road and at home.

Holding hands with Van was the least of it.

"Why? I'm just giving an honest reaction. It's not my problem if you don't like it."

"I like it too damn much, and you know it. You sound like you do on stage when you sing 'Filthy Pain.'"

One of our biggest hits. It was a fierce song and full of appropriately filthy lyrics.

I always enjoyed performing that one, especially when I knew Van was watching.

One of his hands dropped below the table, hidden from view.

I smirked and leaned forward until our noses almost touched. I licked my lips and heard his sharp inhale.

"Now that I know you want me, I sure as fuck don't know how I'm gonna hold back. If I could, I'd climb across this table and give you the best goddamn kiss of your life. Or maybe I'd slide underneath and suck your big cock down to the back of my throat."

Van nearly dropped his espresso cup, the dark liquid spilling over the edge.

I grabbed a napkin and wiped his hand. "Careful there; I have a need for that hand in the near future."

His neck and face flushed a gorgeous shade of pink as he shook his head. "Can we please just stop talking about kissing, sucking, or cocks? Please?"

"I love it when you beg."

"Brodie—"

Fuck, Van growling at me like that sparked my lust like nothing else.

I smiled at him. "I want you to join me on stage tomorrow."

"What?" he startled again.

"I'm changing the topic like you asked. I want to perform a duet with you."

He shook his head. "I'm not a professional performer."

"You can sing. I've heard you."

"Not like you."

"Duh."

Van threw the napkin back at me as he tried not to smile.

My laughter let loose. I was doing a lot of that today—a sign of good things to come... in more ways than one.

"I know you're a talented guitarist. Come on, it'll be fun," I urged.

"I'll have to run it by Greg—"

"Fuck what he thinks! It's our show."

"He's still your boss."

"Not at this event," I replied. "Come on, Van."

Van finally nodded.

"Okay. One song. But you need to carry most of the vocals. And I need a guitar. I didn't bring mine with me."

"You can borrow one of my babies, but handle with care."

"Of course. But I'm warning you: I haven't played in a long while. When I'm songwriting, sure, but not in front of others. Not since, well, before my mom passed."

That was three years ago.

"She was into music, right? Wasn't she a teacher?"

A smile graced his lips. "She was. High school. She loved teaching. I learned to play the piano before I could ride a bike. There was always music in our house, whether it was the radio, or my mom on the piano, or my dad playing the guitar. She also sang in her church choir; she was a great alto vocalist."

"But you never caught the performing bug?"

Van shook his head.

"I picked up a lot of instruments with ease, but I was good, not great. I just didn't have that drive to be on stage. You know what I mean, you have to want it more than anything. But I still loved music, and I wanted to work in the industry. So I did a double major in college—music and business. And I started writing. But I couldn't live off that in the beginning. Still, songwriting feels natural to me and probably where my real talent lies. And, of course, managing unruly rock stars and their crazy lives."

I had a mind to ask him why he didn't write full time now, but then his phone buzzed and jolted on the tabletop, interrupting our conversation.

He picked it up and began to tap and swipe, his frown growing deeper the longer he scrolled.

"Greg's office has taken the liberty of choosing your date for the night since you haven't responded," Van bit out.

I held out my hand, and he passed over his phone.

My "date" for Halloween was a stunning man with copper hair, pale blue eyes, sculpted cheekbones, and a pout that, a year ago, I would've had no hesitation exploring. Greg certainly knew how to pick a hot man.

I passed the phone back and watched Van's face.

"The guy's name is Colm McDade. He's a twenty-five-year-old model and actor, currently starring in a reality TV show here in New Orleans. He's also just landed his first major movie role," Van read out. "He'll show up before the concert for a meet and greet, stay for the show, and then on to the afterparty."

"This is stupid," I replied. "I don't need a date, and I sure as fuck don't want one. Not if he's not you."

"This is what Greg wants. It's one night."

"Can I ditch this guy at the afterparty?"

"There'll be media on hand for part of it."

"I'm going to call Greg and tell him to shove this stupid idea up his controlling ass."

"Maybe you'll change your mind," Van stared at the screen. "I'm sure, given this model's age, you'll have much more in common with him than with me."

Van wouldn't look at me.

"Don't. Don't do that after everything that's happened, especially not after today."

Van took a sip of his coffee.

"I'm sorry. I just… this, you and me, now, feels surreal. In the very best way. But still. I feel like I'm gonna wake up tomorrow, and it will all be a dream. *Un rêve fantastique*."

"It's a fucking dream, all right, but it's very real. It's one that I've thought about and wanted for longer than you can imagine."

I rubbed my knee against his under the table, and he let out a pained sigh.

"See? That's what I'm talking about. You say things like that, and, well, no wonder you have guys lining up outside your bedroom door," he mumbled.

"Hookups were different. I didn't think about or talk to them this way."

Van shook his head. "This heartfelt side of you is fucking with my head."

"Which one?" I teased. "And you bring it out in me. When we first met, I thought this was a simple case of lust," I pointed between us. "But then, as we got to know each other and worked together, the wanting never waned—just the opposite. We have a connection on so many levels and in a way that's hard to put into words. I've never felt like this about any man. Just you."

"Brodie—" Van leaned forward and reached for me but stopped short.

I didn't have the same inclination. Fuck it.

I took his hand and held on tight. Then I slid my fingers along his wrist and found his pulse beating fast and strong.

The conversation beside us ceased.

A shiver washed over me, goosebumps popping up along my skin.

"Love it when you say my name."

Van bit his lip, and his head fell back like he was trying to hold on to his control. I knew mine was short-circuiting.

He withdrew his hand from mine and sat back, crossing his arms.

"Let's leave this conversation for later. We should get back to the hotel."

"Finally, something we agree on," I replied, giving him a filthy grin.

Van chuckled.

"To get ready for tomorrow. You need to rest your voice, and I need to get back to work on the set schedule. I'm still worried about the tech issues. If we lose power, we're screwed."

"We'll be fine, no matter what happens. But I guess you're right. I need to get my beauty sleep. I want to be in tip-top shape for my 'date' tomorrow night."

Van's jaw clenched as he flagged down our server and paid the bill.

"Fake date," he responded.

"That's right. Remember that. Maybe I can pawn him off on Holls or Ronin."

"Unfortunately, not."

"We'll see."

My mind began to spin with ideas about what to do. I was tempted to call Greg like I'd threatened, but I didn't want there to be any backlash on Van. And that's where it landed. I was a hothead sometimes (okay, a lot of times), but now I had someone else to consider.

Whoa. That was a mindfuck. Considering someone else?

For now, I'd go along with the date request. It was, after all, for show. And showbiz was my biz. But I was determined that this was not gonna cause a setback for me and Van.

Today wasn't an anomaly, and I wasn't taking a step back.

There was only up from here.

CHAPTER 15

VAN

My phone started ringing and pinging at six a.m. and didn't let up.

I was used to the concert day chaos, but I was normally better rested.

And therefore, in a better mood.

But it had taken me forever to fall asleep last night.

No surprise why.

Brodie had blown my mind, teased my cock, and jump-started my heart.

Fuck, my heart was racing like a marathon runner ever since he touched me in that club, and it had yet to slow down.

When we got back to the hotel last night, I had a mind to invite him up to my room because I didn't want our day to end. I wanted more touching, more teasing, more talking.

We were still us, but that crackling chemistry was flowing stronger than ever, snapping and sparking with every look and every laugh.

I was ready for that first kiss, but I wanted time to savor it.

So, when his phone began to chime with text messages

from the band, and I had work to catch up on, we said a quiet goodnight in the hallway and went our separate ways.

It had never been so hard for me to walk away from anyone or anything.

All those previously suppressed thoughts and curiosities when it came to my sexuality were unleashing at an alarming rate now.

My imagination was running as wild and hot as my pulse.

I lay in my big, empty bed hours later, under the cool cotton sheets, and pictured Brodie on top of me, under me, beside me.

I'd trace every inch of his striking tattoos with my tongue. Then I'd pin his arms to the bed and make him mine, his legs wrapped around my hips, his tongue deep in my mouth.

Brodie was headstrong and defiant, but with me, he was also soft and sweet.

In my fantasies, I was the one in control, and he submitted to me. Only me.

In bed. In the shower.

In front of the window, on the couch, on the tour bus…

I took my throbbing cock in hand and jacked off. I was leaking so much pre-cum, that the sheets were already a mess.

I reached across to the nightstand, desperately seeking my bottle of body lotion. I squirted a good amount in my hand to create a smoother glide.

One slick rub later, I groaned out loud as pleasure consumed me. It was so fucking good.

Not as good as Brodie's callused fingertips would feel against the sensitive skin of my dick. And my balls.

Oui. Yes. More.

Feet flat on the mattress, I pumped my hips as my strokes got faster, my moans louder.

How would it feel to slide my dick in the heat of Brodie's ass, between those taut, smooth cheeks? Yeah, I'd seen his bare ass a time or two (more) on tour. It was high and round and fucking perfect. I wanted to pound that ass until he screamed my name.

My previously slumbering sex drive was revved up and ready to fuck.

One, two more tugs, and I was coming in a rush all over my stomach, my hand, the sheets. Pleasure suffused my entire body as I cried out Brodie's name, fucking my fist frantically.

What a mess, but goddamn, I hadn't come that hard in, well, a very long time.

Calmer, satiated, I finally drifted off and woke up five hours later. My hand was stuck to the dried cum on my stomach.

I rolled out of bed and hopped in the shower. Where I wanked off again. This time to the image of Brodie on his knees, sucking my dick deep in his throat.

Finally wrung out, I finished washing up and got dressed.

Oddly enough, I was still hyper as hell. I ordered room service and got to work.

Work, remember? That's why you're here.

I confirmed the final press details, the after-party schedule, and texted Ace to get his feedback on any other potential tech issues at the venue.

I sent a good morning text to Brodie at ten a.m. since I knew he always went to bed late and slept in.

Well, I sent the text at ten.

But it took me an hour to write it while I paced the room like a teenager with a first crush.

> Morning gorgeous. You ready for today?

No shit, that took me sixty minutes to compose. I'm a songwriter, didn't you know?

Then I waited. And waited. He was probably still asleep.

An hour later, he replied.

> Brodie: You're the gorgeous one. Sorry for the delay. I just got up. I couldn't fall asleep last night, and it's all your fault. Tell me I'm not the only one.

> You're not. What the hell have you done to me?

> Brodie: Oh honey, we're just getting started.

Honey? A hot thrill zipped through my body at that endearment.

My phone rang, but I didn't recognize the number.

"Ivan Cross speaking."

"Morning, Mr. Cross; it's Colm McDade from Helix Talent. Bandit Music emailed my agent about the Wayward Lane concert and afterparty. I'm the one who's been chosen to accompany Brodie James."

The voice on the other end of the line was like a bucket of ice water.

My raging libido cooled at the thought that this Colm guy might be a better match for Brodie than I ever could be.

"Oh, yes. Sorry I haven't been in touch yet. You were on my list of calls this morning."

My very last one.

"No worries. I should've texted or emailed first, but given the time, I thought it best to call and get everything organized," he responded.

"Of course, and thanks. Can you arrive at the venue around seven? Text me upon arrival, and I'll head out to meet you and provide your pass. The concert starts at nine, but the guys always do a meet and greet for VIPs. You can also have a meal with them in the break room before showtime. Then, after the concert, you come backstage, and you and Brodie can leave for the afterparty."

"Sounds awesome! I'm a huge fan, so this is a total honor for me."

He sounded like a genuinely nice guy—good manners, enthusiastic.

I hated him already.

"Good, great. But no statements to the press, okay? You pose for pictures and give your name, and that's it. If they ask how you know Brodie or where you met, ignore them. Any of that line of questioning you leave to me. Understood?"

"Of course. I'm good with my role. I've done these types of events before."

"Perfect, then you know the drill. I'll send along the NDA for you to e-sign and return to me. And that's it. Do you have any questions?"

"What should I wear? Some celebrities are very particular that their date is coordinated. Especially on Halloween."

"The band is dressing up in Day of the Dead makeup and costumes. If you could do something similar, that would work. But don't fuss. We realize this is last minute."

"Cool. And I'm really looking forward to meeting Brodie tonight. All the guys in the band, of course, but yeah, this will definitely be in my top five memorable dates."

Me too, but not for the same reason.

"See you tonight, Colm."

"Cheers."

With that out of the way, I fired off the NDA and took care of the rest of my emails.

Some of the press at the concert were invited to take pictures for the first hour of the afterparty. I got their credentials verified, and then I texted Brodie to remind him to be on his best behavior.

Right.

Just got off the phone with your date. Seems like a nice guy. Give the press the shots they like. But no comments. Keep it about the event and the charity we're supporting.

Brodie: You mean, no pics of him grabbing my ass? Wait. I forgot. Only you're allowed to touch my ass from now on.

My dick perked up at that idea.

Funny. Hand holding, arm around the waist, or side by side for the photo ops.

Brodie: I'll stand side by side, but I ain't holding his hand.

Maybe we should forego the duet. I'm not sure about the optics.

I was nervous that I was going to fuck up on stage. And more importantly, I was concerned that everyone in the audience, my boss included (via video), would know something was up between Brodie and me.

I wasn't ready to answer those questions, not when we barely knew the answers ourselves.

We'd done a shit job of hiding our bourgeoning flirtation in front of our security staff yesterday, but singing? Together?

That was special to me. Intimate.

I didn't perform for audiences on a regular basis. When I did, I tended to wear my heart on my sleeve.

I hoped to fuck he didn't want to sing "Sideline" together.

Watching him sing it the other day was just the way I'd imagined. He gave it his all and put so much emotion behind the words it took my breath away.

I wasn't sure I could watch it again, never mind sing it. With him. To him.

Brodie: The duet stays. You, me, and "Sideline." And I don't give a fuck about optics.

Fuuuuck.

And if the media starts asking questions?

Brodie: I know how to say no comment. You just worry about you.

What do you mean?

Brodie: Try not to eye-fuck me too much.

But I'll be singing with THE Brodie James. I don't think I can help it.

I waited for his response, watching the three dots appear and then disappear.

Brodie: Good

CHAPTER 16
BRODIE

"Where's my guitar strap?" I asked, looking around the stage. "And the mic isn't working again. What's going on?"

All afternoon, it had been like this.

A few items we'd stored in the drafty dressing rooms went missing. The lights flickered on and off. Strange echoes filtered into the theater.

And, of course, the tech was twitchy at best.

I had to wonder if it was the state of the old building or one of our road crew playing Halloween tricks on us.

Or both.

But so far, everyone I'd asked was as mystified as I was about what was going on.

"Maybe it's the ghost," Holls yelled out.

"What the fuck are you talking about?" I asked.

Holls walked over to me and lowered his voice. "So, Tommy was talking to the maintenance guy, and apparently, there's a ghost who lives in this building. In 1975, the most popular local band in New Orleans played here on

Halloween night. The band started the concert by announcing their breakup, and at the end of the show, the singer collapsed and died. Can you believe it? The guy was so distraught over the breakup of the band, his heart gave out. And now his lonely spirit roams the building."

I rolled my eyes at Holls's dramatic tale. "Maybe you should consider an acting career since you obviously enjoy make-believe."

Holls gave me two middle fingers in response.

Ace came running out of the wings, handed me my strap, and then checked the mic.

"Sorry, guys. I went over the setup early this morning with Tommy. It was fine. Everything was in its place and working as it should be. I don't understand what's going on."

"It's okay, Ace. Maybe the theater staff moved stuff around. It'll all work out in the end," I replied, giving him a reassuring nod while he checked the mic.

I didn't know if it would, but it was always good to be confident.

Ace was the best at what he did, and he'd never let us down.

This was a one-off situation.

But the next time I did something like this, I'd hand over the venue selection to someone who knew about these things.

Apparently, this know-it-all didn't, in fact, know it all.

At least I'd done the smart thing this morning and rested my voice. Tea with honey and no talking. To anyone.

Until now, of course.

I hadn't sung since rehearsal (except one song at that private party), and I wanted to be prepared in case the mics did go out, and I had to sing with nothing to accompany me but the acoustics in the venue. It rarely happened, but I'd done it before.

Projecting your voice for that kind of performance was no easy feat.

I'd plan for the worst and hope for the best.

Speaking of best… I looked around the theater, but my favorite person was MIA.

I knew Van was working. I saw him downstairs, heading into one of the dressing rooms while talking on the phone.

At my request, Ace had placed one of my guitars in there for Van to use. Knowing him as I did, Van was probably already practicing for our duet.

Just thinking about being on stage with him had all the nerves in my belly lighting up like fireflies on a summer night.

I just knew that singing with, and to, my Van, was gonna be the most memorable performance of my life. Would the fans love it? I had no way of knowing. Would it be the most meaningful to me? Fuck, yeah.

We'd have to try the song together at least once before we hit the stage. But first, me and the guys tested out a few songs just to be sure the glitches were gone.

Ace stepped away, and I tried the mic again.

"Thank fuck!" I blurted out, and the clear sound echoed in the theater. "Let's do 'Filthy Pain.'"

Ronin opened the number with his distinctive bass line.

When the rest of us joined in, the sound was awesome.

Despite the mishaps, this place was made for music lovers, and I couldn't deny I loved how the sound carried.

Twenty minutes later, guitar still in hand, I went in search of Van.

I found him downstairs in my dressing room, strumming away and singing in that low, husky voice of his that had goosebumps popping up all over my skin.

I wanted to stand and stare at him and soak in the moment, but too soon, he spotted me.

Then he smiled. Not his professional one but a genuine grin, dimple and all. My pulse kicked up, and my heart beat a wild rhythm.

I was so far gone for this man it was out of control.

"You ready to practice?" I asked as I shut the door behind me.

The door clanged with a resounding thud.

I grabbed a nearby stool and sat down across from him.

"I'll sing; you rest your voice," Van replied as he began to strum the song's opening notes.

Instead of replying, I nodded and joined in on my guitar.

Professional me flew out the window when I flubbed up a few times, my hands shaking. I was too entranced with the man across from me to concentrate.

It was a heady realization for someone who'd spent the past four years sliding out on stage in front of tens of thousands of people like it was as normal as breathing.

I didn't know how the fuck I was gonna perform this duet tonight in front of an audience. Watching Van play my baby and sing lyrics that meant so much to him was wreaking havoc with my already tenuous control.

He hit the third verse, but we were interrupted by a knock on the door.

"It's Ace. Your makeup and hair people have arrived."

Van paused his playing. "Come on in!"

The doorknob rattled but the door stayed shut.

"Did you lock the door?" Ace yelled out.

"No," Van replied and got up, turning the handle. The door didn't budge.

He tried again, pulling hard.

Finally, on the third try, it opened.

The loud groan of the hinges was like something out of a horror movie soundtrack.

"Sorry about that." Van stepped aside and motioned for them to come in. "I guess we need lubricant."

"Never leave home without it," I piped up.

"Smart man."

The comment came from a sharp-dressed man in his forties, accompanied by an equally stunning woman of around the same age. They entered the dressing room, suitcases in tow.

"I'm Foster Jones, and this is my colleague, Sasha Decour. Hair and makeup to the rescue."

"Nice to meet you," Van greeted them. "Thanks for accommodating our last-minute booking. I'll get the rest of the guys down here, but you can start with Brodie. Not that he needs any improvement since he's stunning as is."

Foster clutched his chest, and Sasha sighed.

My face heated as I let Van's comment sink in. Who knew I was such a praise slut?

Van quickly stepped out of the room, and I set my guitar aside.

"Just let me change into my outfit first."

"Of course, it'll take us a few minutes to organize our tools," Foster replied with a smile.

I headed into the adjoining room to search the clothes rack.

A movement in the corner of the room caught my eye, but when I turned, there was nothing there. A cold draft surrounded me, but I shrugged off the strange feeling.

Holls and that ridiculous story about the ghost circled in my head, but I dismissed it.

I selected my black leather kilt and corset vest since it would complement the Day of the Dead makeup look perfectly. I paired the outfit with my favorite combat boots and headed out to find the rest of the band sitting down, getting their makeup prepped.

Foster and Sasha spent the next hour creating intricate designs on our faces. And glancing at my reflection, it was worth it.

Everyone thought so, except for Faise, who was acting even more cranky than usual.

"I don't like the smell of this stuff. And how much longer is it gonna take?"

"Sorry, Foster. Despite years on stage, Faise is still a makeup virgin. Just ignore him."

I got a middle finger from our drummer in return.

I had to talk to him. Maybe he was just burnt out from the tour, and this gig pushed him over the edge.

I hoped to fuck he wasn't using again. Whatever the issue was, his attitude the past few days hadn't improved.

Not that I was one to talk, but when it was just us four, there were always jokes and laughter. And I didn't like feeling this tension from him. It threw our dynamic off, and we couldn't work like that.

"Could you excuse us for a moment?" I asked Foster and Sasha.

They nodded and left us alone in the dressing room.

"Seriously, Faise. What's up your ass lately? You've been in a shitty mood since we left Nashville. Speak."

He shook his head.

"Silence isn't going to work anymore. I'm only going to ask once because I need to save my voice. Tell us what's going on. Are you okay? Are you... using again?"

"Fuck no," he snapped back. "The hardest thing I'm ingesting lately is tequila and pot."

Faise sighed and ran a hand through his black hair. Then he leaned forward and hung his head.

"It's my brother. Rae lost his job six months ago, and then Hannah left him. Ever since, he's been on a drug and alcohol binge. I didn't realize how bad it got until we came home from Europe two weeks ago. Mom called me in a panic. She went by his place to see him and found Rae unconscious. Turns out he's addicted to heroin. He's gone through his savings; the mortgage on his condo is in arrears. I managed to get him into an addiction treatment center in California just before we headed down here."

Judging by their expressions—or what I could see beyond the makeup—Holls and Ronin were as shocked as I was.

"Why didn't you say anything sooner?" I asked. "You know we always have your back. Rae is your family; he's like our family, too."

Faise stood up and paced. "I think I'm still in shock myself, you know? He was the perfect one. Graduated top of his class from business school, married the right woman, and had a high-profile job. Always the son my parents wanted me to emulate. Part of me still can't believe what's happened. He's got a long road ahead of him. I know how hard it is."

"I'm so fucking sorry. I was worried it was you."

We'd all had our share of drugs in the beginning when fame was new, and the pressure to perform hit us hard.

Faise most of all when it came to coke. His severe mood swings were the first thing we noticed.

My addiction to sleeping pills and sedatives was well known. The vicious cycle of crazy tour schedules, running at two hundred percent all the time, and always being on catches up to you. It took me a long time and a lot of therapy and support to finally wean myself off the pills.

I walked over to Faise and pulled him in for a hug. Holls and Ronin joined us.

"What can we do?" Ronin asked as he pulled back. "Anything you need, Rae needs, tell us."

Faise stepped away and shook his head. "I'm good. But after this gig, I need to head home to see to Rae's condo and his finances. I need time off before we head to the studio again to record. A month at least."

"Of course, whatever you need," I replied. "Do you want one of us to go with you?"

"I'll go," Ronin offered.

"We can all go," Holls added.

Faise shook his head. "Thanks, but I think it's better if I go alone. Or maybe just one of you. Dee, you know I love you, but if the media finds out—"

I nodded. "I get it."

In the past few years, I'd been subjected to greater press scrutiny than the rest of the guys. I didn't court it, but it was what it was.

The impact that had on my relationships, any kind of relationship, was starting to be seen and felt. How that would play out with Van had yet to be seen.

Faise turned to Ronin. "Could you come with me? You're heading to Cali anyway to see your sister."

"Of course," Ronin replied and pulled Faise in for another hug.

"Okay, that's enough emo bullshit." Faise pulled back and wiped his eyes. "Fuck, I probably ruined my makeup."

"It's Halloween, no one will notice."

"Thank fuck for that."

CHAPTER 17
VAN

It was two hours until showtime, and nerves were running high.

The power shut down several times. Usually, only for a minute or two, and then we were good to go again.

I got on the phone with building management to rail them out about the issue, but there was not much they could do at this point.

We'd roll the dice and see what happened.

Some of our equipment was missing or misplaced, which had Ace in a state of near meltdown.

And I was inundated with more press requests. Many of whom were about to arrive shortly.

The band was dressed up, made up, and scarfing down dinner before greeting the VIPs.

But Brodie's "date" had yet to arrive.

Part of me wished the guy would be a no-show, even though I knew that was ridiculous. It would anger Greg, and the last thing I needed was that stress on top of everything else. I was having a hard enough time concentrating as it was.

My phone buzzed, and I mentally prepared myself to put out another fire.

> Colm: I'm here.

Shit.

> I'm heading out.

I made my way through the maze of narrow hallways at the back of the building until I reached the entrance. I nodded at our security folk at the door and glanced outside.

There was Colm, dressed up in a tattered black tuxedo, his face painted with an elaborate skull design, not that different from Brodie and the rest of the band. The only thing I recognized from his headshots was his copper hair. He had a bowler hat in one hand and a walking stick in the other, like a Halloween version of Fred Astaire.

I stepped outside and waved him over.

"Colm, come on in."

"Hey, Ivan! Sorry, I'm late. I had to drive from Lockport, and the traffic was crazy."

Now that he was standing near me, and despite the makeup, I noticed Colm's perfect smile, big blue eyes, and chiseled profile.

He rushed over and shook my hand. "Is my costume okay?"

"You look great. And call me Van," I replied as we headed back inside. "You hungry? The guys are having a bite."

"I don't know about food; I'm suddenly really nervous. I need some liquid courage for sure."

"Just be yourself, and you'll be fine. Trust me, the guys are down to earth. You're gonna have a great time."

"Good to hear."

The rest of our walk was made in silence. Well, except for my phone constantly buzzing.

We'd set up the space behind the stage as the VIP room with catering and security. I motioned for Colm to enter.

Brodie and the rest of the guys were done eating and were now downing shots. The real party was finally getting started.

"Guys, this is Colm McDade. He's Brodie's date for the evening," I announced.

I felt weird as fuck saying that.

Jeers and whistles rang out.

And I didn't enjoy the appreciative looks sent Colm's way.

Not that Brodie seemed to be giving the model the slow once over like Holls or Ronin, but still, a hot guy was a hot guy. Anyone would notice Colm, makeup, costume, or not.

"I'll let you guys get acquainted. If you need me, I'll be in the dressing room downstairs."

Far away from Brodie and his "date."

Maybe that was me being stupid because I knew this was all for show, but I was vulnerable now that I'd finally admitted how I was feeling about him. Exposed in a way I rarely was.

I needed my protective layer of work around me.

"You need to stay here, Van. Eat, have a drink with us," Brodie insisted after he greeted Colm with a handshake.

I shook my head. "I've got guests and then reporters to corral."

Brodie gently gripped my arm and pulled me in close to him.

Touching me right now was not a good idea. I needed all my brain cells focused on the job.

"Van—"

"Dee, do your thing and get to know Colm. Sell the date to the press."

The rest of the guys were chatting up Colm and not paying us any attention, so I placed my hand over Brodie's.

"I'll see you on stage in two hours. If I don't get stage fright," I quipped.

"I can't fucking wait," Brodie replied and squeezed my fingers.

Someone in the room laughed, and I looked over. Holloway's gaze locked on me and Brodie, his eyes comically wide.

Shit.

I pulled my hand back and headed for the exit.

Regan was standing just outside the door, tapping away on her phone.

"The VIPs are starting to arrive. Once they pass the security check, do you want me to hold them there, or can we let them in the room?"

"Send them on back."

I waited in the hallway as guests started to file in. I greeted each one and had a quick look inside the room again to make sure the guys did the same. Soon, the room swelled to just over fifty people. It was small compared to our stadium tours when we had VIP groups of five hundred.

One of the last VIPs to arrive was the man I recognized from the party last night—the one who'd offered his card to Brodie.

I had a mind to kick him out of the building for no reason other than I was jealous as hell.

Instead, I shoved my caveman ideas away and put on my practiced smile. I greeted him as warmly as everyone else. Once he was inside, I took some satisfaction in watching the man's face fall as Brodie introduced him to Colm.

Maybe this fake date thing wasn't so bad after all.

I prepped my notes for the post-concert interviews, and then I wandered over to the stage to make sure everything was set as it should be.

Earlier mishaps were now under control.

I headed back to the VIP room and noticed the guys from Killmine had arrived. They were dressed up as characters from the Wizard of Oz, with Nate as Dorothy, right down to the pigtails and the ruby slippers. And judging by how they were joking and laughing with Brodie and the rest of the group, as well as the VIPs, they were having a great time.

Some bands hated the promo stuff, but it was part of the biz. If you wanted to go big, you had to do it.

Bandit was always on the lookout for the next hot thing, and Greg wanted my opinion on the group. Based on what I saw of their previous performances, they had the makings of a band that could go far in this business. Greg was going to offer them a contract and the opportunity to open for Wayward Lane's next world tour. It was a good deal and one I hoped they would take.

"Van!" Nate yelled out and worked his way through the crowd to greet me.

"Hey Nate, cool costume."

He laughed. "Thanks, but I didn't think through the shoes. These heels are fucking killing me already."

"The price of beauty and fame. You ready?"

"Ready to puke my guts out. Never been so nervous to perform in my life," he replied and took another gulp of his drink. "You got a moment to talk?"

"Yeah, of course."

Nate motioned to the corner of the room. I glanced around, my eyes inevitably snagging on Brodie as he charmed the VIP crowd.

Forcing my gaze away, I followed Nate.

"What's up?" I asked.

"Greg Haddley reached out to me today. He's offered us a contract."

I smiled and reached out my hand. "I knew it was coming; congrats!"

Nate grinned in return and shook my hand. "*Merci*, we're over the fucking moon excited. It doesn't seem real yet. But I wanted to pick your brain about something. Do we have to keep our manager in this case, or will Bandit assign a new one? I haven't seen the contract yet, but in confidence, we've had a lot of disagreements with our current rep. Greg reached out to him twice, and he didn't return the calls. Thankfully, after that, Greg called me directly. I nearly had a heart attack. I mean, this is our dream, right? You don't get offered a recording contract every day. And you don't ignore phone calls from the head of the biggest label."

"Did your manager give you an explanation?"

"Nope. He's not replying to my texts. There's another band he represents that I feel he's favoring. When the offer came in for tonight's show, he didn't want us to do it. Said it would suit someone else. That's a major red flag. Who wouldn't want to open for Wayward Lane? Especially in our hometown. I had to push back and tell him to take it."

"I know it's not easy to change managers, but sometimes it's for the best. It sounds like this person doesn't have your best interests in mind. Bandit has a roster, and they can assign one to you. Or I can refer you to a few independents who are reliable."

Nate bit his lip. "That's good to know. I just wanted to get your insight on it. You've been with Wayward since the beginning, and everyone in the band has nothing but mad respect for you. We want a rep who believes in us and will be our champion."

"We'll find you someone who does just that."

"Awesome."

I glanced at my phone and noticed the time.

"You're on in twenty."

"Thanks, Van."

"Anytime. You guys have something special. I knew it, and so did Greg. You're gonna do great."

Nate nodded and downed the rest of his drink in one go.

"Am I interrupting?"

I turned to find Brodie behind me, his eyes full of fire.

"Not at all."

"I wanted Van's business input. Thanks again."

Nate nodded and headed back over to his bandmates.

"You two seem awfully chummy," Brodie muttered.

"It's purely professional."

"It better be. I'm not above staking my claim on you here and now, and fuck the record label, the press, and my so-called date."

I shook my head in disbelief. "You can't seriously be jealous."

"Oh, no?"

"How's Colm?" I asked as I raised one eyebrow.

Brodie bit his lip. "He seems like a great guy. Ronin's about ready to make his move."

I looked over, and sure enough, the bass player was standing extra close to the model.

Great.

"Tell Ronin to back off until the party is over tonight. Then he can do whatever the fuck he wants. As long as he's discreet."

"Don't worry about it. Everyone'll just assume we're having a threesome. We're rock stars, after all."

I all but dragged Brodie to the farthest corner of the room.

"Have you… wait, that's none of my business."

What the hell was going on with me? I'd never been the possessive type before, and I was about to make an ass of myself.

I stepped around Brodie, but he held firm.

"Have I what? Slept with Ronin? Or anyone in the band? No. We made a promise to each other years ago, and we've stuck to it."

The relief I felt was immediate.

"That's not to say we haven't enjoyed watching each other from time to time."

That statement had me curious and curiously aroused.

"I'm gonna need a drink," I bit out, and Brodie finally let go.

His laughter followed me out of the room.

CHAPTER 18

BRODIE

SHOWTIME

stood in the wings, watching Nate and his band amping up the hometown crowd and filling the theater with a shitload of energy.

He'd confided in me about the contract from Bandit, and I couldn't be happier for him and the rest of the band.

For them and for us.

Having Killmine on tour next year would be an exciting ride and, hopefully, a successful one. These guys loved to party, for sure, but they also knew their shit.

I listened to Nate's impressive vocal range as he and Otis played off each other, sharing the mic for a while. When Nate finished up the song, he and the rest of the band took a well-deserved bow—several of them.

Greg Haddley was a pain in the ass, but he knew talent and drive when he saw it. Signing this band was a very smart move.

And so was this concert.

So far, everything tonight had gone off without a problem.

The power was working, the sound was amazing, the fans were screaming, and the energy was unleashing.

I paced back and forth in the wings, walking off my pre-concert nerves.

And they were high.

But mostly, I was filled with heady anticipation. Performing was in my blood, and there was nothing that could equal it.

Well, maybe a few things. Sex was right up there.

Speaking of sex, I turned to find the object of my desire standing behind me, watching me.

Before, Van was always guarded.

But now he gave me a once over like he fucking owned me, and it made my adrenaline spike even higher.

"Thank you, guys!" I heard Nate yell out to the crowd. "Fuck, what a warm welcome. But I expected no less from my hometown. *Les bon temps roulez ce soir!*"

I motioned for Van to come closer.

"What did Nate just say?"

"The good times are rolling tonight," Van replied as he stared into my eyes.

If I could get Van alone, they certainly would.

The crowd erupted in more cheers and whistles.

Van and I stood behind the curtains in our own little world, locked in some kind of trance with each other, unable to tear our gazes away.

Instead of giving me a pat on the shoulder like he usually did before I went out, he slid one hand around my waist and pulled me in close.

If our crew noticed, no one said anything. I sure as fuck wasn't going to complain. I'd been waiting for this kind of moment with Van for what felt like an eternity.

He leaned down, and when his breath hit my ear, I full-on shivered.

"Every time I see you get ready to take the stage, it's like the first time. Never seen anything like it. You blew my mind back then and every day since, and you sure as fuck do the same now. Only, it's not just my mind that's fucked. It's everything."

"Jesus Christ, Van, are you trying to give me a hard-on before I go out there in front of three thousand people?" I growled.

His low, husky laugh made my heart clench.

"I'm gonna go grab my guitar, well, your guitar. I'll see you on stage in an hour."

Van gave my waist one last squeeze before he walked away.

Good thing, too, and thank fuck for the distraction of Nate on stage, or I'd give the audience a very different kind of show.

"Now that we've got you amped up and ready to fuck… I mean, ready to fucking rock," Nate chuckled, "I am proud as hell to introduce your headliners for the night. They just wrapped up their sold-out European tour two weeks ago and decided on one last show to close out their year. And on Halloween, no less. Lucky, lucky us, *oui*?"

I peered my head around the curtain. Another round of applause had Nate nodding.

I turned back and saw Holls, Ronin, and Faise headed towards me.

"That's right, folks, you should be excited. Not only will they be performing their hits tonight, but all the funds from this show are going to Harvest King, a local food-focused charity that helps families in need. So, let's give a warm New Orleans Halloween welcome to the band that merges punk with rock and soul, the one… the only…Wayward Lane!"

The roar in the packed theater was muffled by my earpiece, but I felt the vibration through my entire body. I rolled my shoulders, looked at my band mates, and nodded.

No matter how many times I performed, I was still in awe.

I stepped out onto the stage and waved to the crowd as the heat of the lights hit me. I walked over to thank Nate, giving him and the rest of the guys a hug.

Then, I grabbed hold of the mic and did what I did best.

"*Bon soir!*" I yelled out in my limited French, wishing everyone a good night. "Thank you, Nate, and holy shit, what a fucking set by Killmine! Give them another round of applause, folks!"

The crowd erupted again, and I smiled as the band waved one last time and left the stage. As my guys got their instruments ready, I continued with the intros.

"I speak for everyone in the band when I say we are beyond happy to be back in New Orleans and to celebrate Halloween with you guys. What do you think of our costumes?"

Screams and shouts echoed around me.

"Personally, I think Ronin looks way better with a face full of Halloween makeup; what do you think?" I chuckled as he gave me the middle finger.

"I love you, Ronin!" someone in the audience screamed.

"I love you too!" he yelled back.

I looked around and saw that everyone was ready to go.

"All right then, folks, are you ready?" I asked.

The replying screams bounced off the walls and reverberated through my bones.

"I didn't hear you!" I yelled into the mic. "I said, are you fucking ready?"

The next wave of cheers and screams erupted like a soundwave tsunami, and I swore the entire stage moved.

"That's more like it! Let's start with 'Ragged Edge.'"

Holls strummed the opening guitar chord, Ronin joined in on his bass, and Faise rounded it out with a slamming drumbeat.

Then, there was no more time for nerves.

I belted out the opening chorus, embracing the energy of

the crowd, feeding off it, feeling the ebb and flow that surged in my veins.

I glanced to my left and spotted Van in the wings, holding my baby, barely visible in the shadows. But I felt him like he was right there beside me.

It hit me just then that I took for granted he'd always be there. My rock, my inspiration. Seeing and feeling his presence always gave me that extra oomph on stage, but tonight?

I made love to that mic.

And someday soon, I'd be doing the same to Van.

After we'd performed the songs from our first two albums, including "Filthy Pain" and "Nine Gone Wrong," we took a short break.

When we returned, I grabbed my acoustic guitar and sat on one of the stools Ace had set up for us.

I ran a hand through my sweat-drenched curls and took a deep, cleansing breath before I spoke into the mic.

"We've got a new song for you tonight. And when I mean new, I mean no one, except for you, has heard this before. It's a heartfelt piece I hope you love as much as we do."

Whoops and hollers rang out.

"But first, I want to introduce you to the person who wrote this song. He's the man who made tonight's event possible. This is someone very special—" my throat nearly closed over, but I swallowed past the lump. "He's very special to me and the guys. For me personally, he's my muse and the most incredible man I've ever met. Please give a warm welcome to Ivan Cross."

The rumble of applause rolled through the venue as Van walked onstage with my guitar in hand.

In his usual denim outfit and cowboy boots, no Halloween

costume in sight, he was the best damn thing I'd ever seen. He smiled at me and then waved to the audience.

I was so excited to perform with him I nearly slipped off the damn stool and fell on my ass.

Van took the seat beside me, and our knees brushed against each other.

One touch, and I was vibrating. It was all I could do not to reach over.

The lights dimmed, the orange glow setting off the dark stage.

"Someone better be recording this," I commented into the mic.

There was laughter from the crowd, whistles, and claps, many of them already holding up their phones.

I looked over to see Ace with his phone in one hand, giving me a thumbs-up with the other.

"This song is different from our other stuff, but when you hear it, you'll know why I had to make it mine." I looked at Van and all but fell into his indigo eyes. "This is called 'Sideline.'"

Three, two, one.

We strummed our guitars, playing out the first notes.

I sang the chorus, and then we played off each other.

Back and forth, and then harmonizing together.

And the way Van looked at me as he sang, I swear our souls connected on a level I'd never felt with anyone.

Like he was right there inside me, and I was living his song.

Together, we merged and unleashed something greater than ourselves—a moment in time that would live on after us.

The song was us.

I'd performed with lots of musicians over my career—some of the most popular in the world.

None of them could compare to him.

Was this the best performance of my life? From the audience's point of view, maybe yes, maybe no.

But I poured every bit of myself into it. And the emotions behind the music?

Everything but me and Van faded away.

No fucking joke; my eyes welled up as I sang the last chorus.

My makeup was probably a ruined mess by the time the song was done, but I didn't give a fuck.

I gave it my all. And all I had was his.

If Van didn't know by now that I was all in with him, that I was, in fact, in love with him, he'd never know.

The audience sure as fuck did.

CHAPTER 19
VAN

Seeing my song performed by an artist always gave me a high.

And watching Brodie sing several of my works over the years was an even bigger thrill.

But having a chance to perform this song, with Brodie, to his fans?

I'd never experienced anything like it. Never.

No, my voice was not nearly as smooth as his, and I couldn't hit some of those high notes, but none of that mattered.

Everything between us on this stage made perfectly imperfect sense.

We were just Brodie and Van out here.

Two people making beautiful music together, taking our connection to a higher level. A place beyond age, and jobs, and tours, and schedules.

All the frustration I'd poured into the song about feelings that were new to me, feelings I was unsure about, released.

Maybe life wasn't linear, and the answers I was searching for were hidden in plain sight.

As I sang, I stared at Brodie and watched him watching me.

He'd been there all along. But until this trip, I'd never let myself hope he could want anything more than friendship. And more than our shared passion for music.

Then I saw the tears in his eyes, and I felt the heartache in his voice.

I felt his desire for me with every husky note that poured out of him, a honeyed growl that rumbled from deep inside.

How was it possible that I'd reached forty-four years of age and only now knew this feeling?

Was I in total denial most of my life, running on automatic?

All I knew was that the man across from me was the most extraordinary gift of my life. Working with him, creating with him, and now, falling for him.

Holy fuck, I was falling in love with Brodie…

As we reached the end of the song, my body caught up to my emotions. My hands trembled, my voice shook, and everything in my vision blurred.

The onslaught of cheers, claps, and hollers around us was nothing but white noise.

The only sound I recognized was the beat of my heart, fast and out of control.

I blinked, and Brodie came in to focus again. He stood up, wiped his eyes, and acknowledged the crowd, then urged me to get on my feet and join him.

Finally, I stood on wobbly legs as he placed his arm around my waist, steadying me, supporting me.

Never thought I'd ever lean on someone else for a change and Brodie, least of all. But as I turned my head and stared into his eyes, I saw the truth.

I knew exactly how he felt about me.

I'm pretty sure everyone in that theater knew it, too.

Suddenly, the rest of the guys rushed out to surround us

while black and orange streamers and confetti rained down all over the stage.

Second by second, reality began to seep back in.

Brodie and I weren't alone.

I was still his manager. And he was still a rock god.

Reluctantly, I stepped away from the spotlight as Holloway, Ronin, and Faisel all offered up their congratulations. They gave me hugs while Holloway yelled, "Why the fuck didn't we know you were a songwriter?"

"What did I tell you?" Brodie spoke into his mic once the crowd had calmed to a gentle roar. "Please give another round of applause to my partner, Ivan Cross."

My body jolted when I heard Brodie murmur the word "partner." I liked it—a lot.

I waved at the crowd and then made my way over to the wings as the band set up for their next song.

Looking over my shoulder at the last minute, I saw Brodie staring at me intently.

It was electric.

All my nervous energy was gone and replaced by a desire that was rising high and fast, crashing over my worries and leaving me with a dangerous kind of recklessness.

Anxieties were for another version of me and another day.

I wanted to soak up this wild feeling and live in it a little while longer. Before reality intruded.

People walked around me, and I'm pretty sure someone asked me a question, but I was too overloaded to pay attention. My body vibrated like a tuning fork.

Until I received a whack on the shoulder and turned to find Ace smiling at me.

"You done good, Van. Didn't know you had it in you."

"Thanks, but it was all Brodie. I just hummed along."

Ace shook his head, his long, blond hair falling over his shoulders. "You did your fair share up there. Gotta say, it sounds like a hit to me. I think you should record it with him."

I placed the guitar aside and ran my hand through my sweat-soaked hair. "No way. He needs a professional singer to partner with."

Ace gave me a knowing smirk and held up his phone, tapping the screen. "I don't know about that. You can't fake chemistry like yours."

My face heated as I stood beside him and watched the video of the performance.

It was all there for anyone to see. Admittedly, I was okay, not great, but the two of us together? Yeah, Ace was right. And fuck, watching me and Brodie singing to each other was the sexiest thing in the world.

I was going to be replaying this—a lot.

Notifications popped up on his phone with people commenting.

"Did you post this?"

Ace shook his head. "Nope, but lots of fans did. It was a pretty intense song. I mean, Brodie was in tears, Van. I know it's not my place, but, are you and him—"

"We don't know what it is yet," I replied quickly and immediately regretted how that sounded.

I wasn't ashamed of my feelings, but I also wasn't ready to answer questions from other people. Fuck's sake, Brodie and I hadn't even kissed yet.

What if he changed his mind?

Ace smiled at me. "I'm not surprised. It's been building for a while now. I see the way you two look at each other."

"I've never crossed that line with someone I worked with. For."

Ace shrugged and patted me on the shoulder. "It happens a lot in this business. We're on the road with each other more than we're home, and when you bond over somethin' like music, well, it don't get much better than that."

I turned to reply to him, but he'd already stepped away.

Instead of watching the rest of the show, I headed to the VIP room to decompress and deal with the influx of calls and texts on my phone.

And to deal with the group of journalists who were readying for the band's post-concert interviews.

Most of the reporters were on their phones when I arrived.

I perused social media and saw various versions of the video being shared and commented on. Almost all of it was high praise, people raving about Brodie's performance and wondering who I was. Not just who I was but who I was to Brodie.

There were also three missed calls from Greg. Shit.

Instead of ignoring them, I stepped back into the hallway for privacy and called him back.

A cold sweat broke out all over my body as I waited for him to answer.

"Van, what the hell is going on?" Greg's voice boomed in my ear.

"We just performed a new hit single; that's what's going on."

"Why were you on stage with Brodie?"

"It was his idea. He found out that I'm Corley Hewitt, and he wanted to test out 'Sideline.'"

"Yeah, but why did he need to perform it with you?"

"He asked; I agreed. It's not complicated, Greg. And it was an honor for me to sing with him. If you've seen the videos on social media, you'll know that the response was overwhelmingly positive."

"I've been watching the videos and photos and reading the comments. And there's a fuckton of chatter about you. They're saying there's something between you and Brodie."

That statement hit me right in the guts.

In the nuts, too.

Yeah, I more than liked the idea of Brodie being mine.

"What do you want me to say, Greg? I can't control what people think. He and I have worked closely together for four years. We have trust and friendship and—"

"I get that; I'm not stupid. But if you're fucking around with my best-selling artist and in direct violation of your contract, then we have a problem."

I paused, unsure of what, if anything, I should say.

I didn't want to lie, but also, it was none of his goddamn business at this point. I was protective of Brodie and me, and this new relationship growing between us. It was the best thing to happen to me, and for once, I didn't care about the implications for my job.

Brodie was a grown man, and so was I, and this was our choice. Neither one of us was heading into this with our eyes closed.

Or maybe I should just up and quit before anything happened. Would that be best?

Then I imagined Brodie's reaction to that news. He'd probably burn the fucking world down.

"I have to get back to work. I've got media here for post-concert interviews."

"Don't think I didn't notice that you didn't answer my question."

"If there's an issue, I will come to you," I bit out and tapped end.

Yeah, I did. I hung up on my boss.

I wanted to tell Greg to take my contract and shove it up his ass, but the timing was all wrong.

My phone buzzed again.

Greg: We are not done with this. What about Brodie's date? How the fuck does that play out in all this?

The date still holds.

Greg: No one's going to buy it now.

Of course they will. He's a rock star. It's not like they assume he's only interested in one person.

Greg: That's a shit answer, Van. You better have more to say when I call you first thing tomorrow.

My boss was going to be sorely disappointed. More than he already was.

CHAPTER 20
VAN

Another hour passed, and the concert was wrapping up.

Stepping back into the VIP room, I shoved my personal feelings aside and got back to work.

By the time the band took their final bows, hydrated, and got their makeup touched up, they were ready for interviews.

The band walked into the room and waved at everyone, then took their seats on the periphery.

Brodie's eyes caught mine, but I quickly turned away, not wanting to draw attention.

I recognized one reporter from rehearsal day. Beau… something. From Channel 10. He and his cameraman were talking. When he noticed me, he walked over and offered his hand.

"Van, good to see you again."

"You too, Beau. You're up first."

"I loved your performance. You really wrote those lyrics?"

I nodded, flustered. This is exactly why I preferred to work backstage. "But this isn't about me."

I motioned for Beau to follow, and we headed over to the band.

"Guys, this is Beau from Channel 10 Entertainment News."

I stood guard as the reporter greeted each member and set up their shot.

Beau looked at the camera and nodded. "I'm reporting live from the Orpheus Theater where America's hottest band, Wayward Lane, finished up their year with a Halloween concert, and all to raise funds for a New Orleans charity. Guys, tell us about your experience tonight."

Beau turned to the band members, and each, in their turn, told him what they loved about the city and the show tonight.

"You also performed a new song with your manager, Ivan Cross, and it's exploding on social media. Can you tell me more about your relationship with him?"

Brodie's face darkened, and I braced myself.

"The response to the song was just what we hoped for," Brodie replied calmly. "Next question."

Beau glanced at me, and I hardened my stare. Thankfully, Beau didn't push any further and pivoted to other questions.

I was enormously relieved. Normally, Brodie wouldn't hesitate to snap at a question he didn't like, but he was restraining himself.

Once Beau was done, I waved in the next journalist.

Beau turned to me with a wide grin. "I'll be working the afterparty. Buy you a drink there later?"

I was caught off guard for a second but quickly found my footing again. "Thanks, but I'll be working."

"Or maybe after?"

I didn't miss the flirty tone or the once-over he gave me. A year ago, that would've gone right over my head.

"I appreciate the offer, but I can't."

He glanced at Brodie and then back at me, a smirk on his lips. "No worries. Have a good night."

I nodded, then turned my attention back to my phone. I perused the band's socials, and Brodie's in particular.

The speculation about who I was to him was running wild through social media, and there was nothing I could do about it. The best thing was to say nothing. Like any news, it would soon be eclipsed by another story. We just had to wait it out.

And really? This was the kind of press that musicians dreamed about. The song was already viral, and it hadn't even been officially recorded yet.

After an hour of interviews, the band was done, and the press filed out of the venue.

"We're ready to take you to the afterparty," Regan called out.

"I need to speak to you in private first," I said to Brodie as I motioned to the door. "Where's Colm?"

"He was talking to Ace in the hallway."

"Let's go to your dressing room."

We headed out of the room and spotted Ace and Colm standing side by side, deep in conversation.

"Brodie and I need to have a quick chat. We'll be back in ten minutes," I called out.

Colm nodded and resumed his conversation with Ace.

Brodie and I made our way down the dark hallway to the basement and the drafty dressing room. I closed the door behind me.

Finally, we had a moment alone.

Brodie sat down at the table, took off his rings, and began to clean off his makeup.

"Wait, what are you doing? You have to leave for the party shortly."

Brodie shook his head. "I messed it up earlier. And it's starting to itch."

I stood behind him and gently placed my hands on his shoulders.

"Have you looked at the socials yet?" I asked quietly.

He nodded. "I have."

"Greg called me. He wants to know what's going on. He

asked if you and I were together. I didn't answer his question."

Brodie grabbed a tissue and wiped the final remnants of makeup off his face. "It's none of his goddamn business what we are."

"It is, Brodie. I signed a contract. I made a promise."

He shrugged off my hands and stood up. Then he turned and faced me, his eyes glittering in the darkness.

"I don't fucking care."

"Are you sure you want this?"

Hell was going to rain down over both of us once Greg found out.

My first instinct was to protect Brodie even if it was from myself.

"Are you really asking me that question? After everything that's happened? After what we shared out there? Couldn't you feel it?"

"Of course I feel it. That song is all about my feelings for you. But I'm trying to be the voice of reason here."

"Well, knock it off! I don't need to rationalize my emotions. That's not who I am."

He turned and made to move around me. No way was I letting him walk away now. We needed to have this out.

"Where are you going?" I demanded.

He stalked over to the door, paused, and leaned against it, facing me.

"If this is all on me, I need to know. I can't keep doing this," he pleaded, his eyes full of sadness.

Before I knew what I was doing, I was right there in front of him, my hands on the door, caging him in.

I took in every detail of his face now that I could see it clearly without the veil of makeup—those stunning eyes framed by inky lashes, the smattering of freckles over his nose, his perfect pink lips.

How many times had I stared at his face? Thousands of times.

Never in my wildest dreams did I imagine we'd end up here.

"It's not all you. I just don't want to fuck this up," I confessed.

His sharp inhale was so satisfying.

"Oh no, honey. I won't let you," he replied and cupped my face.

Brodie touching me and calling me "honey" made my heart clench.

"You feel this?" he asked as he took one of my hands and placed it over his chest. The rapid tempo of his heartbeat mirrored mine. "This is what you do to me. Now I've waited long enough. Kiss me."

My control snapped at his demand.

There was no second guessing. There was no turning back.

I leaned in and took Brodie's mouth—hard, deep, and claiming.

Brodie kissed me back the same way. He became the aggressor, and I'd never been owned like that before.

Every part of me lit up like I had on stage.

Head, heart, body, soul, all of it was perfectly aligned.

And nothing tasted sweeter than him.

We were eager tongues and lips and frantic touches.

I fucking devoured him, and he did the same to me. His wicked tongue teased mine, sparking a pleasure that was decadent and downright filthy. My body shook hard, over-whelmed by every new sensation.

He let out a husky moan, hiking one leg over my hip.

I gripped his leg and rutted against him, thrusting my hips, and the friction, fuck, the feel of his hard cock rubbing against mine, even through the layers of our clothing, was such a fucking turn-on.

I slid one hand under his kilt, my fingertips exploring his smooth thigh.

Higher, higher, until I reached his hip and felt silk and lace under my fingertips.

"You're wearing sexy lingerie?"

"I am."

My dick twitched, and my balls tightened. I paused, trying to get myself under control.

"You like that?" Brodie asked, his hot breath teasing my skin.

"I want to see," I demanded. "Show me."

Brodie pushed my chest, and I reluctantly stepped back from him.

I shivered at the loss of his touch, but he shook his head, turned around, and bent over, lifting up his kilt.

He was wearing a black lace thong, his perfect, round ass cheeks on full display.

I smoothed one hand over his right cheek and rubbed my thumb along his crease, feeling him tremble beneath my touch.

Every part of him was beautiful and deserved to be worshiped.

"It's not the lingerie that's sexy. It's all you."

"Van," Brodie groaned out my name, and it had never sounded better. He pushed his ass against my hand. "You're killing me."

I leaned into him, my denim-covered cock brushing against the heat of his ass cheeks. I kissed his slender shoulder, his neck, and worked my way up to his jaw.

He turned, and I took his mouth as deep as I could at this angle.

I was starved for his taste, addicted after just one kiss, and I didn't think I'd ever get enough.

My cock was painfully hard, and with every brush against him, it throbbed and jerked in my jeans.

My hand slid around Brodie's hip, over more smooth skin and quivering muscles.

Through my lusty haze, I remembered that I'd never touched a man like this before. I knew what I liked and what felt good, so I slid my hand under his sexy thong and took him in hand.

A deep groan erupted from his chest as I began to stroke him, the filthy sound ratcheting my desire even higher.

He was leaking pre-cum, his dick heavy, hard, and pulsing in my hand.

I was the one he wanted, and I wanted to make it good for him—the best.

It was already the most incredible experience for me. Every kiss, every touch burning into my brain and wrapping around my heart.

As if sensing my thoughts, Brodie placed his hand over mine and guided me.

And then we were moving together, in sync, like we were on that stage.

Making music of a different kind.

"Van, I can't hold… I'm gonna—"

His head fell back on my shoulder, and I watched his profile as he shuddered in my arms and came undone. His dick jerked in my grasp, and then my hand was covered in hot cum.

I got so turned on from knowing I was the reason he'd lost control, I came without touching myself.

My balls tightened, my dick twitched, and it was game over. I moaned Brodie's name as the sharp wave of pleasure snapped through my body and I released my load. I held on tightly to him, one aftershock after another rolling through me .

And we'd only just started…

"What did I tell you?" Brodie panted.

I took in his smug expression, flushed cheeks, and swollen lips.

"Shut up and kiss me," I demanded.

"Finally."

I chuckled at Brodie's reply, and the incredible lightness after such an intense orgasm was amazing.

Then he kissed me, and yeah, amazing was an understatement.

I was flying high, the combination of our pleasure and laughter so potent that I wondered how I was ever going to be professional around him again.

I probably wasn't.

And I was okay with that.

CHAPTER 21

BRODIE

Best. Handjob. Ever.

I'd fantasized about being with Van—a lot.

But the reality was so much better than even I could have imagined.

I used to scoff at people who claimed sex with someone you love was different. More intense.

I will admit—and only this time—that I was wrong. So fucking wrong.

Van's kiss alone could sustain me.

I was shaking; he was shaking.

I glanced over my shoulder.

He slipped his hand out from under my kilt and raised it to his mouth, giving it an experimental lick. Then another. It was followed by the dirtiest groan I'd ever heard.

I was not prepared for that.

All the while, his denim blues were watching me, searing me with an intensity I'd never felt from anyone I'd been intimate with. Like he could see right inside me.

And fuck, just watching him taste my cum had more leaking from my half-hard dick.

I turned in his arms to face him, needing to see all of him.

"You taste delicious," he murmured in a husky groan.

And I wasn't prepared for that either.

He unzipped his jeans, delved his hand inside his black briefs, and moaned like a needy porn star. "I'm still hard even though I came in my jeans like a fucking twenty-year-old."

Without hesitation, I dropped to my knees and reached for his briefs.

"Is this okay?" I asked as I looked up at him.

I was so fucked out after that orgasm that I forgot this was new to him. I needed to take things slow.

Instead of answering, he pushed his briefs and his jeans down to his thighs.

Okay, so maybe he was more than all right with moving on to another experience.

And, of course, Van had a gorgeous cock.

Thick, long, and with a perfect head covered in his slick cum.

Mine too.

He was rubbing his dick with our combined cum, and fuck, that was hot. He was still hard. I was getting hard again.

I wanted his load inside me. I wanted him to fill up my ass, but for now, I'd be satisfied with him filling my mouth.

Leaning forward, I gave his cockhead a teasing lick, and fuck, he tasted good. Salty, musky, absolutely intoxicating.

His answering groan had me reaching up to push his hand aside.

I gripped the base of his heavy dick and swallowed him down in one long, smooth glide.

Giving head was always a power rush. Even though I was on my knees, I fucking owned him in that moment.

"Jesus Christ, Brodie, that's... you... so fucking good, I can't..." Van gasped, and I hummed with pleasure.

I wanted Van to lose his fucking mind, and it seemed I was off to a pretty good start.

Van placed his hands on the door above me, leaning in, shoving his dick further down my throat.

I took it all.

I sucked his dick like my life depended on it.

Up and down, over and over, between my hand and my mouth, I didn't let up. I got lost in a primal rhythm that was all about Van. I didn't even care to touch myself. I had no thoughts of my own pleasure.

Only his. Only Van's.

My muse.

My obsession.

And now, my lover.

"Always knew you had a talented mouth," he panted.

I glanced up at him. Beads of sweat rolled down his face as he bit his lip. I sucked harder and watched the bliss wash over his face.

"If you don't want my load, you better pull off right now."

I kept working his cock, licking, sucking, tugging, until I felt him jerk, and suddenly, my aching throat was filled with his hot cum. His deep groan echoed in the room.

I swallowed as much as I could, but some of it spilled out of the sides of my mouth and dripped down my chin.

Then his softened cock slipped out of my mouth.

Van dropped his head back, his chest moving in and out with rapid breaths. I was the same, taking big gulps of air now that I could. I reached under my kilt and touched myself, replaying the sight and sound of Van coming down my throat.

"Stand up," he demanded. "Show me."

I fucking loved when he talked to me like that. Confident, bossy Van was my favorite.

Standing up on shaky legs, I leaned against the door, shoved my kilt and my underwear down my legs, and did as he ordered. I wiped my face and used his cum as lube, tugging my throbbing dick with urgent strokes.

It wouldn't take much. Fuck, my control was non-existent.

"Look at you," he moaned as he gazed into my eyes, never breaking contact. "Do you have any idea what you do to me?"

I nodded, my hand moving faster.

"Same thing you do to me, baby. You wreck me in the best way," I panted as my balls drew up tight, and pleasure snaked like lightning up my spine.

One more tug, and I was done for. I unleashed another load all over Van's dick and balls.

Both of us were a mess, covered in cum, half-naked, our clothes ruined.

I wanted so badly to lean up and kiss him, but I hesitated. Maybe he wouldn't want to do that after coming in my mouth.

This is new to him; slow the fuck down.

That voice of reason had been silent until now.

Then I didn't have to reach up. Or hesitate.

Van bent down and took my mouth, tangling his tongue around mine.

But he didn't just kiss me.

He full-on fucked my mouth. It was deep and dirty and delicious.

My brain melted, my heart ached, and my oversensitive dick twitched.

I whimpered. I fucking keened as he pulled me into his bigger body and nearly crushed me in a passionate embrace.

Next thing I knew, my eyes welled up, and tears threatened. Fucking hell, he'd wrecked me all right.

Permanently.

I finally eased back and smiled at him, blinking away the tears as quickly as they came.

Too late. Van noticed, and his expression fell.

"Brodie, are you—"

Then his phone rang, shattering our intimacy.

The real world was calling. We couldn't stay down in this dressing room forever. Even though that sounded amazing.

Van yanked up his jeans and pulled his phone out of his back pocket. I pulled my kilt back up.

"Shit, it's Colm." He tapped the screen. "Hey, Colm, we're still in the dressing room. We'll be up in ten minutes, okay?"

Van didn't wait for a reply. He tapped the screen again, and shoved his phone back in his pocket.

I motioned to the washroom with a shaky hand. "Let's get cleaned up. I should have a pair of jeans down here you can borrow. Or you can wear one of my kilts," I teased Van.

"I don't think I can pull it off. My legs aren't anywhere near as sexy as yours."

"Are you… okay with everything that happened?"

It wasn't like me to sound unsure.

Van leaned in and gave me a soft kiss. "Very okay."

I smiled against his lips.

"I don't want to go out. Can't we tell Colm I'm sick and go back to the hotel?"

Van shook his head. "We've got obligations."

"Fine," I replied with a sigh. "But after?"

Van nodded. "After."

I took his hand and led him to the bathroom. We washed up as well as we could. A shower would've been better, but we made do.

Van stood behind me, and I glanced at our reflections in the mirror.

It was obvious that we both looked fucked out. I had beard burn, and my lips were red and swollen. Van's hair was mussed, his mouth was puffy like mine, and his permanent grin was a dead giveaway.

He slipped his arms around my waist and pulled me into his big, warm body.

"I don't want to stop touching you," he confessed against

the skin of my neck. "The next few hours are going to be torture."

I gripped his arms and squeezed them tight. "I promise to make it worth your while."

"You've already done that."

After more kisses, we finally pulled ourselves apart.

I found a pair of bootcut jeans that were loose on me and passed them over to Van.

He was able to get them on, but they were skintight on him, showing off his powerful thighs and the outline of his hefty cock. Then he turned and fuck me; his round ass was just as luscious as the rest of him, framed perfectly in my denim.

Next time, I wanted us to ditch all the clothing.

"You look too fucking hot in my jeans," I remarked as I grabbed a sequin kilt and slipped it on. Commando this time.

Van smiled at me. "No underwear for either of us tonight. We're living dangerously."

"I'm willing to walk that edge if you are."

I held out my hand, and he took it, interlocking our fingers.

With his other hand, he yanked on the dressing room door, but it wouldn't budge.

He pulled on the door handle again.

"Oh no. No, no, no," Van muttered as he jiggled the handle again.

A cold draft drifted over me, and I swear something touched my back. I shivered and turned around, but there was nothing there.

Just my ridiculous imagination working overtime.

Fucking Holls and that goddamn ghost story.

Bang.

All the lights went out, and the room was plunged into darkness.

Okay, now I was starting to freak out.

"This better not be one of the guys playing a Halloween prank because it's not funny."

"The door's stuck, that's all," Van assured me. "I'll call Regan and she can open it from the other side."

Van tapped his phone. "Crap. I've got no cell service."

"Let me try mine."

I glanced at my phone, but it was the same. No signal.

"What do we do now?"

"Ace and Regan know we're down here. I'm sure they'll be along any minute now," Van reassured me. "I'll send them a text anyway. Hopefully, it will go through at some point. We'll have to wait for now and save our phone batteries."

He tapped away on his phone and then shoved it back into his pocket.

I could barely make out his form in the darkness, but I reached for him, and he pulled me into his arms.

"This is not how I expected to spend this evening," I confessed as I rested my head on his shoulder. "Not that I'm complaining. I'd rather be locked in a cold, dark room with you than anywhere else."

His husky laugh warmed me. "You took the words right out of my mouth."

CHAPTER 22

VAN

was panicking.

It had nothing to do with the fact that I'd had been intimate with a man for the first time.

No, my anxiety was all about being locked in a room with no power and no means of communication. I was always in touch with someone on the crew. Hell, my phone was like another extension of my body at this point.

Without it, I felt naked.

And speaking of naked… I replayed my first kiss with Brodie. And everything that came after.

No question, it was the best sex of my entire life. And I wanted more with him. So much more.

But right now his safety was top of mind. It was the only thing keeping me grounded.

No matter what, Brodie's well-being was my priority.

We managed to stumble around in the dark and find a couple of chairs to sit on. And I located the mini fridge in the corner. At least we had bottles of water and a few snacks.

I was confident that Regan would come looking for us in the next while.

I hoped.

Then again, I didn't know if the power was off in the entire building or what the hell was going on.

"This reminds me of a time when I was a student and traveled back home to visit my folks," I whispered in the dark. "Did I ever tell you about the infamous ice storm in Montreal?"

"No."

I couldn't see Brodie in the darkness, but I felt him all right.

Every delectable inch of him.

Instead of sitting in his own chair, he moved to my lap, and I wrapped him up in my arms.

"I'd come back home for Christmas break. 1998."

"The dark ages, how appropriate," Brodie teased.

I reached down and pinched his ass.

"Do you want to hear this or not?"

"Of course," he replied as he wiggled in my lap.

My dick should be exhausted after two orgasms, but apparently not around Brodie.

"I could listen to the sound of your voice all day and night, Van. Never stop talking to me."

The things he said.

This sweet side of Brodie was so damn adorable. I kissed his neck and worked my way up to his ear, gently biting the lobe.

"Don't stop that either," Brodie moaned.

I totally lost my train of thought.

"*Câlisse*, I forgot what I was saying."

"Montreal. You were nineteen," Brodie hummed. "I bet you were hot then too."

I chuckled as his compliment. "I don't know about that. But I can dig out some old photos, and you can see for yourself."

"I'd love that." He squeezed my arms. "Now tell your story."

"I was due to fly out of the city on January 4th, but the airport shut down due to a massive ice storm that blanketed most of the province and parts of the northeast. And it was just beginning. We had non-stop freezing rain for six days in a row. We couldn't go anywhere. The power was out for an entire week all across the city. Right in the middle of winter."

"That's really fucking scary."

I nodded. "It was. But we were better off than most. Thank fuck my parents had a wood-burning stove and a full freezer. Others weren't so lucky. But people came together to help each other out. My parents invited our neighbors over since they ran out of firewood after two days. The community came together. It was an experience I'll never forget."

"We only have enough food and water for a couple of hours."

"We're not going to be stuck here for days. I promise."

I heard a loud creak, and then a tendril of icy air brushed the back of my head.

"Did you hear that?" I asked.

"It's this building. It's old, noisy, and drafty."

"Yeah. But I could have sworn something touched the back of my head just now."

"Don't you start too," Brodie muttered.

"What are you talking about?"

"Holls went on about this building being haunted by a ghost, some musician who died onstage back in the 70s."

"Good thing I don't believe in the supernatural."

"Me neither. I think." Brodie paused. "I felt the same cold draft earlier. There must be a vent in the room for the air conditioning."

"There's no air conditioning here in the basement," I replied.

"Oh."

Brodie and I were both silent.

"You know, on the other hand, weird things happened today," Brodie declared.

"I hope you're not talking about us."

"As if." Brodie playfully smacked my arm. "I mean, things were missing on stage after Ace double-checked them. And the power going out. You don't think that maybe the ghost is trying to communicate with us?"

"Come on, Brodie. I know it's New Orleans, but you don't really believe in that stuff, do you?"

He paused. "Well, I don't know. If the crew didn't mess with our equipment, then who did? And what's with the power outages and that strange feeling, like someone's touching you with cold fingers?"

"It's drafty, and the power is hit and miss. And I'm pretty sure someone in the crew was playing a joke. Probably Holloway since he likes to prank everyone. He just told you that story to fuck with your head."

"We prank each other but never on concert day. Shit like that can cause major disruption to the set and schedule."

"Well, if it is a ghost, let's just pray it's a nice one," I quipped. "Hey ghost, we mean you no harm. Please turn the lights back on and open the door for us, and we'll leave you here in peace; thanks so much."

Boom. The lights flickered on again.

Brodie looked at me with wide eyes.

"That's just a coincidence," I reassured him as we both sat up and reached for our phones. "And thank God, we now have cell service again."

I tapped my phone and re-sent the message to Regan.

Then I walked over and tried the door handle again. It was still jammed.

"Well, I'm officially a believer." Brodie looked around the room. "Thank you, spirit, for letting us perform here tonight. We might be back, but only for a short time. This place is all yours."

"What are you doing?" I chuckled.

Brodie's glare had me stifling more laughter.

"What does it sound like? I'm making peace with the entity that lives here."

"The entity? Sounds like you need a rest, sweetheart."

Brodie replied with a middle finger.

We were lovers now, but some things never changed.

I grabbed his hand and kissed his finger.

A knock at the door had us both startling.

"You guys, okay?"

Regan.

"We're fine," I replied. "But we can't get the door open."

"Let me try," Regan replied.

The doorknob jiggled, but it didn't budge. It took a few minutes, but finally, and with a loud creak, the door opened.

"Tell her what happened," Brodie demanded.

"How about on the way to the party? We're already late."

"Agreed," Regan replied and held the door open.

"Don't think I'm gonna forget you making fun of me," he huffed.

Despite looking annoyed, he placed his hand on my lower back as we stepped out into the hallway. Regan glanced at us again, but she made no comment.

Did it look like Brodie and I had been making out? Yes, yes, it did. I had no regrets.

"I was teasing. And you gotta admit, the ghost thing is a bit far-fetched."

I turned and reached for the dressing room door to close it behind us, but it slammed in my face.

That was weird.

A chill teased my neck, and I shivered, looking around. "Did you feel that?"

Regan stared at me like I'd lost my mind.

I turned to Brodie, but he just smirked.

"Don't say a word," I warned.

"I can't promise that."

We made our way toward the ancient stairwell and back up to the main floor.

Ace and Colm were still waiting in the hallway, chatting away.

"Sorry for the delay, folks."

Colm looked at Brodie. "What happened to your face?"

Brodie flushed. Pretty sure I blushed, too, but I pulled out my phone as a distraction.

"I mean, what happened to your makeup?" Colm continued.

"Oh, it started melting under the heat of the stage lights," Brodie replied. "I would've re-applied it, but then the power went off."

Colm stared at him and then glanced at me. I shifted from one foot to another.

"Are we ready to go?" I asked.

"For sure. Are you coming with us?" Colm turned to Ace.

"Nah, I don't go to those things anymore. But thanks."

"Come on, you have to," Colm insisted.

I watched Colm smile at our engineer. And the way Ace was looking back at him… I never would have guessed that.

"Yeah, Ace, come on. You deserve to have some fun after all your hard work," Brodie encouraged.

"All right. But don't expect me to dance," he grumbled.

"You can join Van on the sidelines," Brodie quipped.

"Brodie—"

"Let's move, people! We're already a half hour late," Regan interrupted and waved us on.

All four of us walked the line, Colm sliding in beside Brodie with me and Ace following.

"The whole show was amazing, but that song you guys performed together? That was the highlight for me. It's going to be a huge hit," Colm gushed.

"See?" Brodie looked at me over his shoulder. "I told you the fans would love it."

"And I told Van he should record it with you," Ace replied and nudged me with his elbow.

"That's a great idea!"

I shook my head. "No way; that's ludicrous."

"I agree with Ace," Colm nodded. "You two have something special."

Brodie turned around and winked at me. "We certainly do."

CHAPTER 23
BRODIE

Normally, I relished a party, especially after a performance.

And this one had great music, strong drinks, and plenty of smoking hot eye candy.

None of that interested me.

Still, all my adrenaline needed somewhere to go. Partying and fucking were the usual outlets. But now there was only one person I wanted to party with, and fuck, if only I could get him alone.

I'd sated some of my appetite, but not nearly all of it.

And it wasn't easy trying to keep my distance from Van. Not with the way he was looking at me.

I played along with the date routine with Colm for the first hour until the press shots were done. He was great about it, about the whole evening, really. He was charming, funny, and, yeah, hot as hell. A year ago, I would've flirted and fucked no problem.

But not now.

And funny enough, I don't think he was interested in me that way either.

Not when he was busy eye-fucking our sound engineer

the entire party. I guess I wasn't the only one who appreciated an older man.

Ace was the same, tracking the model with hungry eyes. Maybe I could help those two out and, in turn, buy myself more time with Van.

"The press are gone. Why don't you ask Ace to dance?" I said to Colm.

He let out a nervous laugh.

"I don't think he wants to dance. Not with me, anyway."

"Why not? He hasn't taken his eyes off you all night."

Colm's eyes widened. "Really?"

"Fuck, yes. I can't take the flirty tension anymore," I teased. "Go on."

Colm nodded, finished his drink, and stood up. "Thanks, Brodie."

"For what?"

He shrugged his shoulders. "Being a nice guy. I've met my fair share of assholes in the entertainment industry. I thought you might turn out to be an entitled prick. You know, the usual bad boy of rock. Or at least, that's what the tabloids like to say. But you're not."

"Don't tell anyone. You don't want to ruin my image."

Colm laughed out loud. "I signed the NDA, so we're good."

Then he walked across the room and headed to the bar, where Ace and Van were standing and chatting away.

Colm leaned into Ace and said something. Then Ace nodded, and the two of them headed for the crowded dance floor.

I glanced over to watch my man again, but he was gone.

"Looking for your boyfriend?" Holls shouted as he sat down beside me.

"Shut up, Iain."

He raised his glass and yelled out over the din of the rock

music. "Come on, Dee. Clearly, you got some action earlier. You should be relaxed."

I looked around, but in the packed room with the noise level, no one was paying us any particular attention.

"Can you please lower your voice? He and I are brand fucking new, and not to mention, there's the issue of Greg finding out."

Holls leaned in close to me and whisper-shouted. "Tell me everything."

"Not here. Except to say holy fucking shit." I held up my still trembling hands as proof.

"He's a good kisser, right? Van's got nice lips. And he's so thorough about everything he does. I bet—"

I shoved his arm. "Don't goad me. I'm not above kicking your ass."

"Kicking or kissing it? 'Cause I have to say, I'd prefer the first."

"Where's Ronin and Faise?" I asked, changing the topic.

After we'd done our photographs as a band and individually, we'd all celebrated with several rounds of drinks. But then our bassist and our drummer disappeared. And I hadn't seen them since.

Holls motioned to the left with his glass. "Over there, one of the corner booths. They're in some deep discussion. I think it's about Rae."

I shook my head. "I feel so bad about his brother. I wonder if there's anything else we can do to help."

"Give Faise the time he needs after this. We don't have to be in the studio until the new year."

I nodded. "Yeah. I was thinking a month off, but you're right. Two months will do us good. I'll work on songs with Van."

"On a serious note, how will this play out with him?"

I turned to face Holls. "What do you mean?"

"If you're in a relationship with him, how's that gonna go?

Are you going to tell Greg? What if Greg fires him? Or if Van stays on, and you guys end up breaking up, what then? Do we get another manager? Because that's not optimal. I really like Van, we all do, and he's rare in this business. Someone who's smart as fuck but also completely trustworthy. I don't want to jeopardize that."

"What the fuck, Iain?"

"I'm being a realist, Dee. Come on. When was the last time you had a relationship with someone you fucked?"

I crossed my arms, my party mood taking a serious nosedive.

"Exactly. Never. I hate to burst your love bubble, but you need to think about this shit."

"I don't want to think about it," I bit back. "There's nothing to think about. I told you I'm ready for this. He's what I want."

"I know that. But there are realities here you need to consider. What happens if Van gets another job or Greg reassigns him? You're on the road most of the year. Are you going to do long distance?"

I hadn't thought about that. I didn't want to.

It never occurred to me that there would come a day when Van wasn't working with us. He'd always been there. My anchor, my rock.

I leaned forward, placing my head in my hands.

Was Iain right?

Was this what Van was trying to tell me earlier? He said he didn't want to fuck things up.

I didn't either.

Not for him, or his career. I wanted him to be happy.

"Can I join you guys?"

Van's deep voice had me looking up. Once I met those blues, I was helpless.

"I'm going to grab another drink," Holls stated, patting my shoulder.

I sat back as Van took Holls's place on the lounger.

"Did I interrupt something important?" Van asked me.

I turned to face him. "Iain was just reminding me that I need to think about you and me and the impact our relationship might have on our work, our dynamic, the band, everything."

"He's not wrong."

"I know that," I bit out, my frustration mounting.

"But you're an intuitive person. You make decisions based on feel, not logic."

"Which isn't always a good thing. I'm twenty-nine years old, for fuck's sake. I've never had anything beyond a one-night stand. Iain has a point."

"About what?"

"If Greg re-assigns you, and I'm on the road most of the year, what happens to us?"

My legs bounced, and I gripped my hands tightly together.

Van slid his arm around my shoulders.

"What are you doing?" I asked as I looked around.

"The press is long gone, and this is a private party with NDAs all around," he replied. "And I have to touch you. You're upset."

He was right. I rested my head on his shoulder. All those flutters in my stomach kicked up again.

"Iain's concerns are valid, and so are yours. We'll take things one step at a time," Van reassured me.

I wanted to lean over and kiss him. It felt wrong for me to hold back.

"First off, we have to see how this works out," Van added. "Like, what are your needs and expectations. And not just in the bedroom, but out of it too."

"I'd rather talk about the bedroom part first." I turned to him. "I want you to fuck me. That is, if that's something you want."

Van pulled back and swallowed hard. "I got the impression, from things I've heard, that you usually, you know, that you prefer to top."

"Listening to tour rumors again?"

Van shrugged his shoulders. "It's not a rumor when I see you drag some fan into your hotel room."

"That still doesn't explain your assumption."

Van cocked his head. "I accidentally overheard a guy leaving your trailer. This was, maybe, two years ago? He was very insistent about meeting up again and repeating your... experience."

I nodded, remembering the guy. Only because he wouldn't fucking leave when I asked him to go.

"Yeah, it's true. With hookups, I top. For me, bottoming requires a partner I trust. Implicitly."

Van gave me a knowing grin. "Me."

"You. I want you to own me. I want you to fill my ass with your cum."

"I—" Van licked his lips, a dark stain on his cheeks. "Yeah, I want that. Fuck, I really want that. But, no condoms, are you sure?"

I smiled. "I want to be exclusive. I got tested recently. And I know you haven't been with anyone in, well, *forever*."

"Now who's making assumptions? Maybe I was being discreet?"

"Nah. You're wound tighter than my guitar strings," I joked.

Van reached down and pinched my ass.

"Hey!"

"Brat."

"But I'm *your* brat," I quipped.

Van made a contented growl that told me everything I needed to know.

"Yes, you are mine. And yes, I want to fuck you."

I moaned out loud. I couldn't help it. I wanted him with a need so bad my entire body trembled.

Possessive Van was sexy as fuck.

Lucky, lucky me.

"You, me, and that king-size bed in my hotel room."

"Time to go," he said, jumping to his feet and holding out his hand.

"Are what about you?" I asked as I placed my hand in his. "What about your expectations? Your needs?"

Thank fuck for the low lighting and dark corners because no one could mistake who we were to each other.

"It's not complicated. All I need is you."

CHAPTER 24

VAN

don't remember a damn thing from the car ride back to the hotel. How long it took, who was driving, nothing.

Not when I was consumed with Brodie sitting beside me.

Things I'd tried to push aside before—the intent way he looked at me, his edible scent, his innate sexiness—now overwhelmed me.

Luminous eyes, gorgeous profile. Beautiful, stunning, surreal.

My heart pounded louder than any drumbeat and my dick was so hard I was unable to sit still or find a comfortable position.

Thinking back, I couldn't ever remember being this turned on by anyone.

No, turned on wasn't the right phrase.

I was infatuated, distracted, possessed—words I'd never used to describe myself before.

I was never one to let my dick or my emotions rule my decisions.

Until now.

I just knew that if I didn't get Brodie naked and under me as soon as possible, I would go out of my fucking mind.

Once I'd decided I was in, I was all in.

And I don't think Brodie knew what he was in for.

I don't think I did either.

I was running on adrenaline and instinct. Now that I'd had a taste of him, I wanted all of him.

The SUV pulled to a sudden stop, and Dawson got out and opened the back door.

I practically vaulted out of the vehicle and ran into the hotel, pulling Brodie along with me. It was closing on two a.m., and no one was around, save for the lone cleaning staff.

Dawson accompanied us in the elevator as usual, standing guard in front. I did my best to stare at the ceiling, trying to calm myself down.

Until Brodie, the flirty brat, cupped my ass and gave my left cheek a firm squeeze.

I bit my lip to prevent myself from groaning out loud.

Then Brodie's hand slid lower, down my crease, rubbing in between my legs, over my taint, and fuck me, even with the denim between us, that felt better than good.

I shuffled my feet and spread my legs wider, wanting, no, needing, him to keep touching me like that. Every touch left me wanting more.

Hands down, Brodie was the best kiss I've ever had. Every other sexual experience paled in comparison. Hell, I couldn't even remember anything as satisfying as his kisses.

What other kinds of pleasure would we discover together?

My mind was suddenly spinning with one sexy scenario after another.

A small part of me was nervous about being enough for him, but the bigger part was so consumed with desire that it overrode my anxiety.

Brodie trusted me, yes, but I felt the same way about him.

We were new lovers, but we already had respect and

friendship between us. And knowing that, my heart raced not with fear but with anticipation.

Everything in our working relationship had led us here.

With my hands gripped tightly in front of my body like a shield, I tried taking deep breaths, but it was useless.

Brodie leaned over and gave my neck a teasing kiss.

One whisper-soft touch and I was trembling. I forced myself not to react when all I really wanted to do was manhandle him against the elevator wall and have him ride my thigh.

I didn't have a kink for sex in public places, but it seemed I'd been missing out.

God knows Brodie had been caught by his security fucking around where others could find him—on tour buses, backstage, hotel bars, dressing rooms, airplanes.

Suddenly, I was insanely jealous of every man he'd been with.

And then all I could picture was me and him.

In my fantasy, we were the ones fucking. Others could watch, but only I was allowed to touch him.

No one else.

The possibility of that filthy dream had my balls drawing up tight.

And fuck me, I was about to come in my jeans for the second time in twenty-four hours.

Ping.

We finally reached the penthouse floor.

Dawson left the elevator first and then Brodie, then me.

I was following Brodie down that hallway and into his room, and I didn't give a shit about what Dawson might think.

The bodyguard opened the door to the suite, checked inside, and left just as quickly. "Have a good night, guys."

"Thanks, Dawson," Brodie replied.

At least one of us had enough brain cells left to speak.

I grabbed Brodie by the waist and hauled him inside, slamming the door behind us.

Brodie chuckled as he slipped his hands down my back to cup my ass. "I was going to ask if you're nervous, but I guess not."

I shrugged my shoulders. "I don't know. I mean, I should be. To start with, I have a forty-four-year-old body and you, well, don't."

"Are you kidding me? You're the sexiest fucker I've ever met," Brodie growled.

"Fucker?" I laughed out loud. "You sweet talker, you."

My teasing got me a heated scowl in return. Then, I recognized the real concern in his eyes.

"Please tell me you're not hung up on the age thing, Van."

I shook my head. "I should be. But no. And I'm not nervous. Because I figure, no matter what happens in here, we're gonna be okay. It's you and me."

Brodie gazed up at me, and the smile that revealed itself was so enticing I had to lean down to taste it.

"The first thing we need," Brodie whispered against my lips. "Is a long, hot shower."

So I let him lead me to the bathroom.

My heart was knocking hard against my ribs. Pretty sure it was about to burst free of my chest at any moment.

He opened the glass door and turned on the shower. I toed my shoes off, threw my shirt aside, and undid my jeans... his jeans... unzipping them slowly and pushing them down my hips.

Brodie undid his corset vest, one tiny button at a time. Then he pushed his kilt down and stepped out of it.

I looked my fill of his long, lean body, covered in those stunning tattoos. Unlike me, he was smooth all over.

Slim hips, perfect pink nipples, and a cock that was heavy and hard.

For me.

I kicked the jeans away and stepped into the shower, then reached for him. He stepped in with me until we were finally skin-to-skin, head to toe.

I wanted to feast on him, live inside him, take everything he could give me, and give him everything in return.

"I want the same thing, Van. I want it all with you."

I was so far gone I hadn't realized I'd spoken that thought out loud.

And I'd never forget the way he said my name. Like a longing, a prayer, a plea.

I leaned against the black tile and pulled him in even closer, shifting, slipping my thigh between his legs, encouraging him to ride me.

My hands found purchase in his thick hair, and I tugged, angling his face so I could take his mouth the way I wanted, the way I needed—hard and deep. Brodie moaned just before our lips met.

Finally, I claimed the kiss I wanted more than my next breath.

We were just as voracious as we had been in that dressing room.

Brodie sucked on my tongue, and I teased him right back, reveling in relentless kisses.

My throbbing cock slapped against my belly, my balls aching, so heavy and full. I smoothed one hand over his taut asscheeks and squeezed, pulling him closer.

Brodie gave me one last kiss and leaned back.

"Turn around," he demanded.

I reluctantly let him go and did as he asked, placing my hands on the wet tile. Looking over my shoulder, I watched Brodie watching me—giving me a thorough once-over. Then he leaned in, and I felt his hot breath tease my neck. Despite the heat of the water, goosebumps popped up all along my skin.

"Do you trust me?" he asked, then kissed and sucked on the skin where my neck met my shoulder.

I full-on shivered, never realizing just how sensitive that spot was.

I met his gaze and nodded. "I'm here, aren't I?"

Then he dropped to his knees, and my entire body tightened. Smoothing his hands over my ass, he slipped his thumbs down my crease, and Christ, that felt amazing.

"Yes," I encouraged and licked my lips, tasting him. "Do that again."

Brodie's hand slipped lower, between my legs, teasing me like he had in the elevator.

Warm, wet fingers rubbed my taint, and I let out a groan that echoed inside the steamy enclosure.

"The sounds you make are better than any music I've ever heard," Brodie moaned as he slowly moved his fingers higher, higher, until he slid over my hole.

God, that felt so fucking good; I was ready to come again.

"I want to bury my face in your ass and lick your hole. If that's not something you want, you need to tell me now."

Instead of replying, I pushed my ass out.

I was more than ready for anything he wanted to give me —especially his tongue in my ass.

I'd had plenty of blowjobs, but a rim job? Never.

For a moment, I wondered if he'd want to. I wasn't model smooth like he was.

Brodie pulled my cheeks apart, and the stream of water poured over my overheated skin.

Then his hot tongue slid around my puckered hole and fucking hell...

"Oh God, oh fuck," I moaned as he pushed his face in, his stubble rubbing against my sensitive skin.

Nerve endings I never knew existed were firing, igniting sparks of pleasure so intense my breath hitched.

Brodie's tongue slid lower, over my taint, and back up

again. Teasing, licking, sucking. I was overwhelmed by every new sensation.

With one hand on the tile to brace myself, I reached down with my other and gripped my aching cock, tugging in a frantic motion. The slap of the water against my skin and the echo of our mutual groans filled the air.

I stroked myself over and over, rolling my palm over the sensitive head of my dick.

Until the tip of Brodie's tongue slid into my hole, and then my ability to focus on my dick all but vanished.

God, he was fucking me with that talented tongue of his…

I slapped my hand on the wall, unable to do anything but grunt and moan and revel in the exquisite pleasure. My balls pulled up tight as my climax raced to the finish line.

Then Brodie pulled back, and I nearly screamed in frustration.

"What the—" I turned around.

"You're not coming in here. You're coming in me."

Brodie held out his hand, and I took it, pulling him up until we were face to face again.

He turned suddenly, tilting his head, letting the rain shower wash over his face.

"Kiss me," I demanded.

He shook his head, slicking his hair back. "I just had my tongue in your ass."

"That only makes it hotter," I growled, leaving him no room to pause.

I gripped his chin tightly and devoured his sexy pout.

The mouth that drove his fans crazy. The one that drove me insane.

In more ways than one.

He chuckled. "Didn't take you for the down-and-dirty type."

"Only with you."

CHAPTER 25
BRODIE

stepped away from temptation and stepped out of the shower, grabbing towels and throwing one at Van.

It wasn't smooth or seductive.

I was too far gone.

My hands were trembling along with the rest of me and I knew, I just knew, that if I didn't get Van's cock up my ass in the next few minutes, I was gonna lose it.

As it was, watching his intense reaction to being rimmed had my cock throbbing and nearly spilling my release all over that shower floor.

Maybe someday, but not today.

I was hungering hard for his cum in my ass.

I'd never fucked without a condom, but I wanted Van to own me. I needed to feel him deep inside me as I came apart. I wanted to watch every expression on his face, and I wanted him to see mine. To know how incredible our coming together really was.

"Faster," he demanded as he reached for my towel.

"That's my line," I teased.

He tugged the towel from my hands and rubbed me down with quick, sure strokes.

Then he did the same for himself, drying off at record speed, throwing the towels aside, and steering me into the bedroom.

He let go of me and wandered over to the window, closing the blinds and the curtains, shrouding us in darkness.

I sat on the edge of the bed and glanced at the nightstand.

After turning on the bedside lamp with a shaky hand, I reached into the drawer for the bottle of lube I'd stashed there. I tossed the lube on the bed just as Van moved to stand in between my legs.

His cock was leaking pre-cum, the head red and swollen. I couldn't keep my eyes off his beautiful dick, so hard and heavy, curled up toward his stomach.

My mouth watered at the sight.

Van was perfect in my eyes—broad shoulders, firm pecs covered in dark hair, and a belly that wasn't flat.

He was so fucking gorgeous. And all mine.

Instead of moving forward and taking his cock in my mouth, I leaned back on the bed, opened my legs, and waited for him.

I wanted his weight on me—no barrier between us.

Van kneeled on the bed and crawled up over me, covering my body with his larger one.

"Yes."

His hairy chest met my smooth one, goosebumps popping up all over my skin, my sensitive nipples hardening.

I loved being surrounded by him.

Our gazes locked, and the intensity in his eyes had my trembling turn into shaking.

Van was finally going to be mine. This wasn't a dream. It was so fucking real.

"Sweetheart," Van murmured before he reached for me, mauling my mouth with a desperation that matched my own.

But he didn't just fuck my mouth.

He made love to it, our kisses languid and so deep I didn't know where he began and I ended.

I was too far gone to care. As long as I ended up with him, I was happy.

Sliding my thighs around his waist, I rocked my hips, and the friction of his cock against mine had us both moaning so loud I'm pretty sure everyone on this floor, and the one below, could hear us.

We could come like this, from frotting alone, but it wasn't enough.

He slid his hands slowly up my thighs and over my hips, my chest, and finally, my neck.

"You feel—" He shook his head. "I don't know if I have the words to describe how good this is. What have you done to me?" Van asked as he moved his hands up to cup my face, his callused thumbs sliding over my cheekbones.

God, I could probably come from his words alone.

His deep-set eyes were so dark and full of… everything.

Desire, longing, hell, yes, but more than that. A connection I'd never felt with anyone.

This was Van. I knew him, and he knew me. Just like on stage, we were in tune. Moving to a rhythm we created together.

Leaning down, he sucked on the tender skin of my neck, trailing heated kisses over my collarbone and lower.

When his tongue flicked over one of my sensitive nipples, I let out another moan. My cock jerked, and I knew that I couldn't wait any longer.

I needed him.

"Hold on."

I frantically reached for the lube, flicking open the cap and pouring a generous amount on my fingers.

Van leaned back, sitting on his heels. He swallowed hard and watched as I spread my legs wider. Slowly, I slid one slick finger deep into the heat of my ass.

"That is so fucking sexy," Van groaned and took the lube. "I want to touch you."

The sting of the initial penetration turned to pleasure as I drilled my finger deeper, aiming for my prostate.

All the while, Van was searing me with his gaze, staring at me like a man starved.

I took his trembling hand in mine and guided him.

Gently, he pushed one of his lubed fingers in beside mine.

"Yes," he groaned as he pushed farther, and my eyes rolled back in my head.

I withdrew my finger and let him take over.

"Add more lube and use another finger."

"I don't want to hurt you."

"You won't," I assured him. "And have you ever known me to be shy about telling you what I do and do not like?"

Van's deep chuckle was the only thing I needed to hear.

Then his face turned serious again.

"I want to make you feel good, *mon coeur*."

"I'm already there."

He slid two thick fingers into my ass, drilling slow but deep, and I grabbed onto my knees, holding them up to my chest, opening myself up further.

"God, I'm inside you. Brodie." Van licked his lips, his face and chest flushed, his breathing choppy.

"Wait until your dick is snug in my ass. It's gonna feel so good, nothing but you and me. No condom, just us," I panted as he pushed his fingers deeper, touching my prostate. My body jolted from the mind-blowing pleasure. "Right there, oh fuck, right there."

Van added more lube and began to finger fuck me.

In and out, over and over, until I was a writhing mess, my cock throbbing and leaking, my belly covered in pre-cum.

"Enough," I cautioned. "I need you. Fuck me now."

Van withdrew his fingers, and I bit my lip to keep from

protesting out loud about the loss. I was so empty that nothing but his cock would do.

He kneeled between my legs, pouring lube over his dick and rubbing it back and forth.

My asshole clenched hard. Soon, Van would be inside me, a part of me.

"Ready?" he asked as he notched the head of his dick to my hole.

His chest was moving in and out with rapid breaths, his hands shaking, a sheen of sweat covering his body.

"More than ready," I replied, and our gazes locked. I wanted to drown in those denim blues. "Are you?"

He licked his lips and nodded.

"No going back after this. Now you're mine."

I full-on shuddered—at his words, at his intent expression, at the sheer enormity of my want for this man.

"I've always been yours," I insisted.

His hips pumped, and he pushed inside me. The tight ring of muscle gave way, the biting pain turning to an exquisite pleasure.

It had been so long since I bottomed that I forgot just how primal being claimed like this could be.

And with no condom? God, the intense heat of his bare dick in my ass had another wave of pleasure racing through my veins.

I let out a deep moan of satisfaction.

"Fucking Christ, that feels amazing," Van groaned out as he pushed again, almost all the way inside me. My asshole clenched tightly around his dick, and my thighs quaked. "Shit, are you okay?"

I replied by reaching down to grab his ass cheeks, pulling him deep into my body.

"More than okay. Never want you to leave. I've never had sex without a condom before, and already it's the best thing ever. I guess tonight is full of firsts for both of us."

Van slowly slid all the way in until his heavy balls hit my ass.

I moved my hands up, tracing the curve of his back, higher, up over his broad shoulders and his neck, until I cupped his face.

Van's body went rigid, his expression pained.

"Are you all right?" I asked, worried that I'd said or done something wrong.

"I need a minute," he panted. "I don't want to come yet. And just being inside you has me way too excited."

I pulled his face down, taking his lips in a sultry kiss. Van groaned and shifted as I sucked on his tongue.

Then he pumped his hips, rocking into me.

"Your wicked tongue isn't helping matters," he growled.

I couldn't help but laugh at his put-out tone. And I realized I'd never felt anything like this. Joking and teasing with my hookups was not my jam.

Hot and dirty, for sure.

But fuck me, laughter could be sexy too.

Another first…

He playfully retaliated, biting my neck, sucking on the skin and marking me.

"I know what I want. Now hurry up and fuck me. Take what belongs to you," I demanded.

Van's hips snapped forward.

The buildup between us was finally unleashed.

CHAPTER 26

VAN

should be freaking out by now. I should be freaking out a lot.

But I wasn't.

Being with Brodie, touching him like this, it was as natural to me as breathing.

And every touch between us was hotter than the one that came before. Hotter than anything I'd ever experienced. How the fuck had I been missing this?

All my previous experience with sex was good but not great. Like there was always something missing, and I never had a problem walking away.

But I could never walk away from *him*.

Brodie demanded that I take him, and yes, I wanted him to be mine in every way. I was going to try my hardest, pun definitely intended.

I wanted to get closer, to bury myself so deep inside him that he'd always know I was there.

And the way he was looking at me?

No one had ever looked at me like that before. Like I was the answer to a prayer or a secret he'd just discovered.

Like I was something special.

I was trying to hold on to my control, but it was slipping away.

I shifted to my knees and pulled his gorgeous legs over my arms, then thrust again, going deeper at this angle.

"More, Van. Harder," Brodie grunted. "I said I belong to you. Fucking take me like you mean it."

Holy hell, when he talked to me like that, it lit a fire inside me that burned out of control.

I let out a strangled moan and pumped my hips, pushing in and out of his ass at a punishing pace. I was not holding back.

He met me thrust for thrust, and we moved together in an urgent rhythm as the bed creaked and groaned underneath us.

"Touch yourself," I growled, and Brodie took himself in hand.

All my focus was on the fucking. I wanted to make it good for him. Then I wondered how I'd compare to his previous lovers.

Just the thought of him with anyone else made my inner caveman erupt.

I thrust again, harder this time, and Brodie's body jolted.

"Yes! Faster. And don't you dare stop," he panted.

I moved my hips like a man possessed, my entire being narrowed down to him.

We were one movement, one breath.

Muscles burning, skin glistening, reaching higher and higher for the ultimate point of pleasure.

I gripped his thighs and pulled him in tight with every thrust. All I could hear was the sound of my balls slapping his ass as I rutted in and out of him at a desperate pace.

"Brodie," I groaned, so overcome with pleasure that I could barely voice his name. "I need you."

"Need you more," he replied, his voice hoarse. "I'm almost there."

I snapped my hips and fucked him harder, ignoring the warning tightness in my balls.

I needed Brodie to come first, and I wanted to watch every expression that crossed his stunning face as he found his bliss.

"Van!" he cried as his hole clenched hard around my throbbing dick.

Then he jerked, his cum spilling all over his hand, his cock, his belly.

He was so beautiful when he reached his climax that I couldn't hold on anymore.

Desire sparked in my balls and spread through my body. I punched my hips again, harder, faster, until everything in my body tightened and released in a wave of uncontrollable pleasure.

I screamed Brodie's name and let go as I unloaded deep inside him.

I was shaking so hard, I was barely able to catch my breath. And then I looked down and watched my cum dripping from his hole, around my cock.

Watching Brodie fall apart in my arms was incredible, but the physical proof that I was now a part of him was even more satisfying.

Another wave of pleasure rolled through me, gentler this time but just as heady, and tethered by the affinity that I shared only with him. My emotions were right there on the surface, and there was no doubt about how I felt.

I'd never been closer to anyone in my life.

I glanced up, and his eyes were wet, more green than gold.

"Are you okay? Did I hurt you?" I asked, letting go of his legs and leaning over to cup his face.

The last thing I ever wanted to do was hurt him.

"I'm good, I'm more than that… I'm a bit overwhelmed," he mumbled and sniffed.

Tears welled up and spilled over, slipping down his face.

I gently wiped away the tears with my thumbs, then kissed him.

"And don't you dare tell anyone you saw me crying. I'll deny it," he growled against my lips, and I bit back a laugh.

"Don't worry, *mon coeur*, your secret is safe with me."

My vision blurred, and I quickly blinked away the wetness. Not before Brodie noticed.

I captured the moment in my memory. The way he looked at me was something special. Part of me still could hardly believe it, but the proof was right there in front of me.

My softened cock slipped out of his hole. Looking down the length of his body, I watched my cum continue to drip out of his ass.

He raised himself up, resting on his elbows.

"Seeing your cum on my skin is the hottest thing ever," he confessed as my hand found his hole.

I rubbed his skin in gentle, soothing circles, hoping it felt good. When he threw his head back and moaned deep and low, in that husky way like he did when he was on stage, I knew I was on the right track.

He met my eyes again. "Don't ever stop touching me, Van."

Now that we both knew how good we were together, the wanting would only get stronger.

I had a feeling we'd unlocked a craving that could never be sated.

"So," he paused and licked his lips. "How… I mean, was it good for you?"

He was so hesitant, so unlike the confident, cocky Brodie, I knew I couldn't help but fall a little harder.

"Hands down the most sensual experience of my life. And do you know why?"

He shook his head and wouldn't look me in the eye.

"It has everything to do with how you make me feel."

I captured his mouth and kissed him long and hard, showing him exactly what I meant.

"That good, huh?" His usual smirk was back.

"Don't gloat."

"But I'm so good at it."

"That's not the only thing you're good at."

"Are you flirting with me?"

"Do you see anyone else here?"

That comment got me a hard pinch on the ass.

"I better not. You're mine." Brodie looked up at me as he bit down on his lower lip. "Why the fuck haven't we been doing this for four years?"

I sighed and gave him another kiss.

"It wasn't our time. You were busy building your career and enjoying your fame. And me? I didn't think about my personal life at all. Well, not until I realized that all my focus was always on you, and not just in a professional way."

"Watch me from the sideline," Brodie sang out.

This time, it was my turn to pinch his ass.

Then he pushed me to my back. I willingly fell against the mattress as he slid on top of me. My hands smoothed down his back and over his supple ass.

We made out, slow and easy, kissing and smiling and staring into each other's eyes.

It could have been five minutes or an hour; I had no idea. Time was suspended in our world.

He wasn't a superstar, and I wasn't his manager. We were just Brodie and Van.

"I hate to ruin the moment, but we need another shower," he declared in between languid kisses.

"How about a bath instead? Then we'll order room service."

"Perfect."

Brodie rolled over and sat up on the side of the bed, and I got a fulsome view of the back of his body.

I'd seen his tattoos many times.

Twisted vines and music references were painted down his back and arms in a colorful waterfall.

But I'd never seen them like this, and certainly not the ones that edged along the curve of his ass.

The tattoos were merely a highlight.

Brodie was the real work of art.

Then he turned his head and looked at me over his shoulder.

"Are you going to lie there and stare at me all night, or are we going to have that bath?"

"Now that I see all of you, I can't look anywhere else."

He closed his eyes and licked his lips.

"Fucking hell, you say all the right things."

"I don't know about that. I'm just speaking my truth. It's like my songwriting; I don't hold anything back. Not from you."

I slid out of bed and walked around to stand in front of him.

When I offered my hand, he took it, slowly getting to his feet. I noticed the wince on his face.

"Are you sure I wasn't too rough?" I asked.

"It was everything I wanted," he replied and kissed me.

I pulled back and smiled at him.

Then I bent down, swooped him up in my arms, bridal style, and carried him into the bathroom.

I thought for sure he'd protest. Instead, he surprised me, placed his arms around my neck, and held on tight.

Sharp, sarcastic Brodie had a tender side. One that needed protection, and caring, and, yes, love.

And I was the lucky SOB who was gonna do just that.

CHAPTER 27
BRODIE

After a long soak in the whirlpool tub, we headed back to bed and passed out cold.

Between the concert, the afterparty, and then that spectacular round of sex, our bodies finally succumbed to sleep.

I woke up early.

I thought maybe I was still dreaming, but then I shifted, and the throbbing ache in my ass was all too real.

After a quick trip to the bathroom, I snuck back into bed before Van woke up.

I drifted off again and opened my eyes an hour later with Van wrapped tight around me.

I turned over and woke him up with soft kisses.

We made out for ages and enjoyed mutual morning orgasms.

Trust me, frotting, not coffee, was the best way to start your day.

Van ordered room service—gorgeous eggs benny with crab and spicy béarnaise and a basket of beignets—and we ate our breakfast in bed while watching a movie.

It wasn't that different from how it was when we were on

the road. We often shared meals together, including early morning meetings in hotel rooms.

Except, now we were naked.

I was going to insist on a clothing-prohibited rule from here on out.

And, of course, all during breakfast, our phones kept buzzing.

We ignored them. For a while.

Once we were done eating and the phone calls started to come in, Van finally relented and checked his phone.

"Surprise, surprise. Missed calls from Greg, our PR rep back home, and numbers I don't recognize. Most likely, the media," he muttered, tapping on his phone.

I finished up my last cup of coffee and glanced at my phone. It was mostly text messages from the guys asking how the rest of the night went.

I replied "great" and left it at that for now. I was still reeling from the fact that Van and I were lovers. I truly had no words.

"Did they leave any messages?" I asked.

I hoped to fuck that Greg was going to mind his goddamn business. What Van and I were to each other was private and I wanted it to stay that way. For now.

Van tapped his phone. "No. But I got an email from a reporter looking for a comment about the concert."

"What do you mean? We gave our interviews last night."

"Listen to this article I was tagged on," Van scooted closer and read aloud. "Who is Ivan Cross? The Wayward Lane concert last night was a surprise for fans in New Orleans in more ways than one. The impromptu event included a new song performed by lead singer Brodie James and a songwriter named Ivan Cross. The heartfelt duet had the entire audience, including yours truly, swooning. The video of that perfor-mance has gone viral on social media, with fans clamoring for more. James introduced Cross as a songwriting partner, but he is, in fact, the band's manager. Given their chemistry on stage, there's speculation about what type of partnership they really have. However, James was later pictured with his date for the night, model and actor Colm McDade."

I rested my head on Van's shoulder. "I guess the date was a good idea after all. That'll keep the tabloids guessing for a while."

"I hope so." Van passed over his phone. "This is the picture of you and Colm from last night. Hopefully, that will quell the firestorm."

I glanced at the picture. It was a good shot but practiced.

No one else would be able to tell, but I could.

My heart wasn't in it. Neither was Colm's.

"I'm not sorry I asked you to perform with me. And I'm really happy about the reaction to the song. The fans loved it. If the reporters want a comment, they can wait until the song is officially recorded and released. You and I are no one's business but our own."

"Maybe you should put some thought into who you'd like to record the song with. Then we can steer the press toward that."

"I liked Ace's idea. I want you to record it with me."

Van nearly dropped his phone into my coffee cup. "You can't be serious."

"I wouldn't have mentioned it if I wasn't."

"Greg isn't going to allow that. I'm not a professional singer."

"Greg can go fuck himself. Our performance is already viral. This is what the fans want, and that's what we're gonna give them."

"Can't you record it with Holls? Or maybe another singer who would complement your voice?"

"No."

"Brodie—"

"You're the manager, Van. Make it happen."

Van ran a hand through his hair and tugged at the ends. "Fuck. You are the reason I now have gray hair amongst the brown."

"Good. I have a thing for sexy silver foxes. Or, one in particular."

Van took my cup and put it aside, along with his phone.

Then he playfully pounced on me.

I pretended to fight him off, but really? Who was I kidding? He could manhandle me and pin me to any surface, any time.

After we tussled and he won (I let him), he looked down at me with serious intent in his blue eyes. With his dark morning scruff and his lips swollen from my kisses, I couldn't help but stare back. Van was so beautiful he made my chest ache.

He was disheveled, happy, relaxed.

Too often, he was tense and stressed, always working on solving problems so me and the guys could be the stars and do our thing. But he couldn't keep up that pace all the time.

The industry required you to give a hundred and fifty percent, and even then, there were never really vacations or time off.

You were always focused on the next album, the next tour, the next promo.

The next, the next, the next.

And musicians weren't the only ones in danger of burning out.

"I'll agree to record the song with you. But you need to give me something in return," he replied.

"Anything."

"We have to tell Greg about us."

I shook my head. "He's going to let you go since you violated the terms of your contract."

"Maybe, maybe not. He's been known to bend the rules himself."

"You mean, he's had relationships with musicians on his roster?"

Van sighed and nodded. "I don't like to deal in rumors, but sometimes these things have truth to them. I only know this because of a claim made by one of his ex-wives."

"No surprise there. Most people in this business hook up with each other. I've probably slept with half the guys on our tour roster. And, of course, there are people you meet at music awards and other events, on the road—"

"Stop," Van growled. "Bad enough, I have a good imagination."

I chuckled and tightened my hold on him. "Is it wrong that I find your jealousy hot as hell?"

"I'm in so much fucking trouble," Van admitted and shook his head. "So, are we telling Greg?"

"Let's wait until the new year. We're not in the studio or on tour for the next two months. Let's give ourselves some time together. Just us. Then, before we head back to work in January, we can tell him and go public and deal with all the media craziness."

"Maybe you'll be sick of me by then," Van teased.

"Maybe you should stick to writing songs and not jokes," I returned.

Sick of him? Please. He didn't know it yet, but I would never let him go.

Then, I silenced any more of his insane thinking by kissing him.

And using a lot of tongue to get my point across.

"What are your plans when you return to Nashville?" he asked when I finally let him take a breath of air.

I was not expecting that question. Then, an idea occurred.

"I was going to stay in town for a few weeks and then go see my family in Rhode Island for Thanksgiving. But I think I'd like to go home earlier. Come with me."

His body jolted. "Really?"

"Yeah. We can stay at my cottage."

He smiled. "I love that place. You can see the ocean from every room, and there's no one around for miles."

"Exactly. It's quiet, peaceful, private. I had a studio built this year at the back of the property beside the pool. It's got these huge skylights. At night, when it's clear, you can see all the stars in the sky. It's amazing. We can work on new songs and go for long walks on the beach and, most importantly, fuck under those stars."

"There's only one star I want to get under," Van teased, and I gave him a playful bite on the neck.

"So, you'll come with me?"

"How can I say no? It sounds almost… romantic."

"It is if you're there with me."

I kissed him gently and smiled. I was a total goner for this man, and I didn't care how sappy I sounded.

"What about the guys?" Van asked.

"What about them?"

"Are we going to tell them or hold off until the new year?"

I didn't know how to answer that one.

I did have concerns. Would my band brothers see my partnership with Van as a good thing? Holls's concerns last night still rattled around in the back of my subconscious.

None of us had ever had any serious romantic partners that the others had to contend with. Not until now. Would they be okay if I wanted more time to myself, with Van, or would it cause a rupture between the four of us? Would it mess with our dynamic?

I guess there was only one way to find out.

I loved music and performing, but it couldn't be the only thing in my life.

"Let's tell them. But if Greg starts to suspect and asks them questions, I don't want them to have to lie and cover for us."

"Agreed."

"So, you'll come home with me?"

"Yes. But—"

"My butt is all yours. My butt, my cock, my mouth, everything," I teased.

He nipped my earlobe, and I shivered. Van held me in a crushing embrace, and my cock hardened.

"But we have to keep a low profile. I'll tell Greg I'll be working with you on new songs for the next album. And we'll have to bring security with us. Maybe Dawson?"

"That works. He can stay in the pool house. There's a full bed and bath in there."

"Well, I guess that's settled."

He gave me a wide grin, and I couldn't help but capture those luscious lips of his.

"If you do get tired of me, I can stay in one of the guest rooms—"

I reached down to grab his ass and punched my hips forward, rubbing my hard cock against his. "Does this feel like I'm getting tired of you?"

"It's only been one night. What about three weeks in?"

I shook my head at Van's ridiculousness.

"Stop that thinking and get back to work. And by work, I mean me."

CHAPTER 28

VAN

I couldn't avoid my boss any longer.

Greg had called three times today and texted, and it was nearing four in the afternoon.

Brodie had showered and headed down to Holloway's room to meet with the rest of the guys for dinner and to tell them, quietly, about us.

I headed back to my room and replied to several emails, including more requests from the press. I passed most of them on to our PR team for follow-up, and a few others I replied to directly.

I also received a thank you email from the local charity. They had received an influx of individual donations in addition to the money the concert brought in.

Good news all around from last night.

After another cup of coffee, I was primed and ready to call Greg.

I tapped his number and waited.

"I've been calling and texting you for hours? What the hell, Van?"

I ignored Greg's booming question and put the focus on where it should be.

"Did you see the pictures of Brodie and Colm? They made all the entertainment headlines."

Always lead with the good news and tell them what they want to hear.

"Of course, I saw the picture. What do you think I do every hour of the day and night? This business is my life! It's not like I sleep," he grumbled. "But first, let's get back to the question I asked you last night—"

"I've got nothing to say about that, Greg. You know better than to listen to rumors or media speculation. A performance is just that. If people misinterpret it, it's not our fault. By tomorrow, no one will remember my name."

I didn't like lying about what was going on with me and Brodie, but there was no point mentioning it until we knew for ourselves that we were solid.

And honestly? I was overwhelmed after everything that had happened. My whole world had shifted, and I didn't even know how to make sense of it myself, never mind talking about it with other people.

I was happy about being with Brodie, but it was a lot to process—not just being with a man for the first time but falling so hard.

Falling for the first time in my life.

So yeah, it was better to wait. On several fronts.

I was also saving the bit about me recording the song with Brodie until the new year. No sense in pissing Greg off more than he already was.

"And you'll be glad to know that the band raised over five hundred grand for the local charity. That's also making the media rounds, and fans are loving it."

"Good, let's keep pushing that angle. What else?"

"I'm heading with Brodie and Dawson to Rhode Island when we're done here in New Orleans. Brodie wants to get started on the songs for the new album, and now that he knows I'm Corley Hewitt, we've agreed to write together."

"What about the rest of the guys?"

"They're taking time off. Keep this between ourselves, but Faise is going to California for a while. His brother just entered rehab out there."

"I know."

"Really?"

"I know everything that goes on when it comes to my top-selling artists. Everything. Remember that."

I didn't miss the sharpness of his tone.

"Is there anything else?" I asked calmly.

"Are you sure this thing with you and Brodie is a good idea? I mean, writing songs together," Greg replied.

Right…

"He's the one who does most of the songwriting and selection anyway. Nothing has changed. Except we'll work on pieces together from scratch. We'll create a list, and when everyone is back in January, we'll review them, and the band can decide as a group. Same as always."

"I'll be very curious to see what you and Brodie can create together. If 'Sideline' is any indication, we'll have another best-selling album on our hands. Just make sure you keep your collaboration under the radar. That song has given fans a taste of what's to come, but we want to keep them guessing, keep them hungry. Are we clear?"

Greg was not talking about the next album. But at least he was giving me leeway.

"Yes."

"Good. Send me weekly updates."

"I wi—"

He hung up before I could finish talking, but I didn't give a shit. I was relieved. The call had gone better than I expected.

The concert was a success, I still had my job, and I was about to embark on a month-long trip with Brodie.

A trifecta win in my book.

BRODIE

I knocked on Holls's door and waited.

I was excited to tell the guys about me and Van, but also kinda terrified.

Holls's comments from last night hadn't changed my mind, but still, I knew there would be questions and concerns.

But it was Ronin who opened the door. "You finally surfaced! Where did you go last night? You were MIA at the party. The fuck?"

"I was there for almost two hours, Ro, chill. And can I come in? I don't want to have this conversation in the hallway."

Ronin stepped aside, and I entered Holls's suite. It was the mirror image of mine, complete with a kitchen and dining area.

The earthy smell of pot wafted over me.

Faise and Holls were sitting at the table, munching on snacks and drinking shots of tequila.

Faise raised a glass to salute me. "He has arrived."

I walked over, sat my (tender) ass carefully on a chair, and grabbed the bottle of liquor, pouring a shot for myself and one for Ronin.

Once all four of us had full glasses, Holls raised his. "Here's to another great fucking year!"

"To the city of New Orleans!" Ronin called out. "Great food, great booze, and lots of hot men!"

"To friends!" Faise chimed in.

"To finally fucking my manager!" I blurted out while they took their shots.

The guys choked and spewed tequila all over the table and each other.

I was a good performer, but my timing and delivery weren't always spot-on.

"You all claim to be gay, and yet, none of you know how to swallow," I quipped before I downed my shot and slammed the glass back on the table.

I poured another round for everyone.

They looked like they were going to need it, and I sure as hell did.

I was still in a state of shock that Van and I were lovers. Just thinking about him in my bed had my blood beating fast and hot.

Then I realized three pairs of eyes were staring at me intently.

"What?" I finally bit out.

"You and Van?" Faise's eyeballs looked like they were going to pop right out of his head. "I thought he was straight."

"Yes, me and Van. And he's not straight. Not anymore," I replied with a wide grin.

"Holy fucking shit!" Ronin blurted out and looked at Holls. "Why don't you look as surprised as Faise and me?"

Holls took another shot. "I knew something was up on this trip. They were arguing on the bus on the way down here, and it looked hot and heavy. And who can miss the way Brodie salivates whenever Van is in the room?"

I grabbed a cracker off the platter in front of me and pitched it at Holls's head.

He caught it and shoved it in his mouth. "Come on. I can't be the only one who knew this was coming. I mean, the way they eye-fuck each other? The bickering? How protective Van is of him? How Brodie practically rips someone's head off if he thinks Van is under attack—"

"I think they get it," I interjected.

I hadn't realized I'd been that obvious with my intentions.

"Not to mention that Brodie hasn't had any kind of action in almost a year," Holls teased.

This time, I threw a piece of cheese at him. It hit Holls on the forehead and landed on the table.

"Whoa, one piece of major news at a time," Faise replied and turned to me. "Was this a one-off thing, or are you two—"

"Boyfriends," Holls interrupted and waggled his eyebrows.

I shook my head. "We haven't defined it, but I wouldn't fuck around with him if it didn't mean something. I mean, given that he works with us, there are potential... complications."

"Like Greg," Ronin stated.

"Like Greg," I repeated. "Like Van's contract. We're keeping silent about our relationship for now. Until the new year. This is brand fucking new, so we don't want to say anything to Greg until we know where we're headed. You guys are the only ones who know."

"The new year? That's two months away. This sounds serious," Ronin interjected.

"I can't believe I'm saying this out loud, but yeah. Never felt like this about anyone before. I mean, you saw me on stage last night, singing to him. Couldn't you tell I have it bad?"

They all nodded.

I downed another shot and poured the next one. The guys held their glasses out for another refill.

Ronin rubbed his dark scruff. "We've all seen the way you two interact, but I wasn't sure if Van was into guys. Not only that, but I never thought he'd put his career at risk by crossing a line with someone he worked with."

"Well, he is, and he did," I responded.

"And what if things don't turn out the way you want?" Faise asked. "What if you break up? Are you going to be able to work with him? And him with you? Or what if Greg finds out between now and the new year and fires him? We all know that Van is your rock at home and on the road. If you lose that, are you going to be okay?"

"I'd have to be," I replied and took another shot.

But the very thought of losing Van, of not being around him every day, made me break out in a cold sweat.

"If Van doesn't get fired, maybe he'd be reassigned. Maybe that's better for you, him, and for us in the long run," Holls added. "Not that I want to lose a great manager."

I didn't know how to reply to that, but Holls had a point.

I leaned forward. "Look, I don't have answers right now. I wish I could tell you that everything's going to be fine and drama-free, but it might not end up that way. But no matter what happens with Van and me, I'm still a musician, and I choose this life. And I know I can be a hothead, but I'm also a professional. If Van and I ever got to a point where we couldn't work together, we'd find another manager. I know it wouldn't be ideal, but there's no guarantee he's sticking with us forever anyway."

I wanted him to stick with *me* forever. For now, I'd have to be satisfied with one day at a time.

"And none of us have had a serious relationship, but that doesn't mean it's not gonna happen. You need to think about that. I love what I do, and I'm still happy touring every year, but I can't go at this pace indefinitely. At some point, we'll need a break to focus on other things in our lives. I'm sure you guys feel the same way. This band was our dream, but it's not the only one."

They nodded, but there was silence around the table.

"Okay, enough serious talk. You still need to answer the most important question," Holls leaned forward. "How was the sex?"

I let out a filthy laugh and grabbed the bottle of tequila again.

"You'll need another round."

CHAPTER 29
VAN

After my call with Greg, I headed back to the theater to make sure the crew had finished packing up our stuff and that nothing was left behind.

Given the mishaps over the past few days, I was hesitant about walking back into the venue. I didn't believe in the supernatural, but even I couldn't deny that the place felt haunted.

I was hoping it would be empty and quiet.

Nope.

There were still pieces of equipment on the stage that our crew was moving out, and downstairs, the dressing rooms had yet to be emptied.

I wound my way back up to the rear exit and found Ace in the alleyway behind the building, supervising the equipment haul into our parked trucks.

"How come everything isn't cleared out yet?"

Ace shook his head. "Two of our guys got sick last night, and the door to the dressing room in the basement wouldn't open. I texted you an update this morning."

I checked my phone, but I didn't see any message from him. "I didn't receive it."

"The Wi-Fi signal in this place is shit," Ace grumbled. "Anyway, I went ahead and called building management and told them we'd need until the end of day to get everything out. We got the dressing room door unlocked a half hour ago, but I'm still shorthanded, so it's going to take another few hours."

"I can help move the clothes and stuff out of the basement."

"That'd be great, thanks."

"No problem. Say, did you have a good time last night?"

Ace's face flushed. "I did."

"Cool. Colm seems like a nice guy."

"He is—a true southern gentleman. Did you know he studied engineering at college before getting a modeling contract? He's a tech nerd like me."

I shook my head. "I had no idea."

"Too busy staring at his pretty face?" Ace teased.

"Not quite. Between you and me, I was hoping Colm wouldn't show up at all."

Shit, I couldn't believe I said that.

But this was Ace, and I'd known him for years. The man was a first-hand witness to rockstar shenanigans, and nothing shocked him.

My feelings for Brodie least of all.

"Oh really?" Ace replied with a knowing grin. "Well, no worries there. In fact, I've already made plans to meet up with Colm in L.A. in a few weeks."

"No shit?"

Ace nodded, and his cheeks darkened.

"You aren't worried that… wait, sorry, I shouldn't—"

"Ask your question, Van."

I bit my lip. "You're not concerned about the age difference between you?"

"He's mature for twenty-five, and I work in this crazy business, so I'm probably immature for thirty-eight," he chuckled, then cleared his throat. "I'm more concerned about how quickly everything happened. Like, am I making a fool of myself by chasing after someone I just met?"

"I don't think it's chasing if he's agreed to meet up."

Ace pushed a lock of his long hair behind his ear. "We'll see what happens. God knows this job ain't easy on our personal lives. Still, I can't imagine myself in a nine-to-five life."

"As Brodie would say, do what feels right to you. Lots of people do long-distance long-term. It's not ideal, but there isn't one way to have a relationship." I paused and shook my head. "Listen to me, like I know anything about that."

"So, you and Brodie?" Ace commented.

I glanced around, but no one was close enough to hear, and his crew was too busy loading up the trucks.

"Yeah, me and Brodie. The band knows, but we're not telling Greg yet. Not until we know for sure that what we have is solid."

"Makes sense. I mean, if we had to tell Greg about every coworker we fucked around with, well, he'd be firing all of us, and the company would have no goddamn employees left," Ace chuckled.

"Like I said to Brodie, I don't want to know."

"Yo, Ace!" someone in the crew shouted from the back of the closest truck. "Is that the last of it?"

"Nope, there's still three boxes of equipment on the stage to bring out and all the shit in the basement!" Ace yelled back.

Then Ace turned to me. "If you can start clearing the basement, I'll be back inside in fifteen to help you."

"Will do."

I meandered back into the building and down into the dark basement, only to find Brodie and Dawson standing outside the dressing room.

Brodie was wearing wide-leg jeans, a plain black t-shirt,

and platform booties. He'd shaved his morning scruff and was wearing lip gloss.

All I could think about was the way he kissed me last night with those gorgeous fucking lips of his.

And this morning.

I wanted to walk over and pull him into my arms, but I was highly aware of Dawson's presence.

Not that he didn't suspect already, given where he left us last night.

Not to mention the dopey grins on mine and Brodie's faces right now. Jesus, so much for keeping this under the radar.

"What are you doing here?" I asked.

"I left something in the dressing room," Brodie replied, his hands in his pockets.

"I could've picked it up for you. What did you leave behind?"

"Um, one of my favorite rings. The gold signet with the lion's head. Maybe you can help me look for it?"

Thankfully, whoever had opened the door this morning left it open and added a doorstop so there would be no more locked-in situations.

"I'll wait out here," Dawson announced and leaned against the wall of the hallway.

I motioned for Brodie to go first.

As soon as we were out of sight of Dawson, I slid my arms around Brodie's waist and pulled him in tight against my chest, his ass cradling my crotch. I slid my nose along his neck, inhaling his spicy scent and placing soft kisses and gentle nips on his skin.

"I haven't touched you in three hours," I growled against his skin. "It feels like three days."

Brodie turned his head, and I captured his mouth, kissing him as deep as I could at this angle.

I'd gone four years without his kisses. Now I couldn't

imagine going without for one fucking minute.

"I've unleashed a beast." He smiled against my lips.

I playfully growled and bit his earlobe.

"I can't remember why we're in here," I muttered and kissed his jaw.

Brodie turned in my arms. "It looks like there are racks of clothing and stage items that need to be sent upstairs, not to mention I need to search for my ring."

"Right. I guess we better get to that."

I gave him one last kiss and then headed for the dressing table. "When was the last time you had your ring on?"

"When I took my makeup off after the show. Pretty sure I placed it right here on the table here."

I glanced over the surface, but there was nothing but a box of makeup wipes. I opened the drawers, but they were empty inside.

"Let's move the table; maybe it fell behind."

Brodie and I each took one end and slowly moved the antique dresser away from the wall. There was nothing but dust and cobwebs behind it.

"Search the bathroom. I'll check the clothing racks. Maybe you placed it in a pocket of something you had on."

Ten minutes later, and despite searching everywhere, there was no sign of Brodie's ring.

I shoved the clothing racks into the hallway, and Dawson kindly offered to start taking them upstairs. I did one final sweep of the room and the bathroom.

"I'm sorry, sweetheart; it looks like your ring is gone. Maybe you dropped it on your way to the stage? We can check upstairs if you'd like."

"Yeah, let's do that," Brodie replied, but he didn't move.

"You all right?"

"Better than." He nodded. "I'm just taking a minute to reflect... it's nothing."

He shook his head and looked away.

"What? You know you can tell me anything."

"This probably sounds really lame, but this place feels special to me now. After last night. Our first kiss. I'm never going to forget what happened here."

Brodie finally looked at me, and the heat in his gaze stoked mine. Brodie's sentimental side made my heart ache as fiercely as my cock. Every part of me was wide awake. I'd never felt so alive.

"It's not lame at all. In fact, that's the sweetest thing I've ever heard you say."

I pulled him in tight.

"And I'm sorry about your ring."

"It's okay. Hopefully, someone will find it eventually. Who knows? Maybe it's a sign that we're meant to come back here again."

"Maybe the ghost took it," I teased.

A brush of cold air slid over my neck, and I jolted.

"Did you just touch my neck?"

Brodie's hands squeezed my ass. "Wrong body part."

"I think we should get out of here and let the ghost have their venue back."

"Good idea," Brodie remarked and kissed me.

This trip turned out to be much more than just a concert. It was a turning point in my life. I walked into this place as one version of myself, and I was walking out as another.

Did I have all the answers as to whether Brodie and I would make it long-term?

No, I didn't.

But wherever he was, that's where I wanted to be.

CHAPTER 30
BRODIE

THREE DAYS LATER, NASHVILLE

was ready for a month off.

Three days ago, Holls and I said goodbye to Faise and Ronin, who flew out of New Orleans and headed directly to California. Then it was just me, Van, and Holls on the bus ride home.

It was quiet without half of our quad, but I didn't mind.

It gave Van and me privacy and plenty of time to sneak in make-out sessions. We held off on anything else, though.

And never when Holls or our driver, Sam, was watching.

Things were brand new with Van and me, and I didn't know what he would or wouldn't be comfortable with.

I knew my boundaries. Not that I had many.

Musicians and roadies were used to fucking around in front of each other—most often on tour buses, trailers, and dressing rooms. I never minded if Holls or any of my band-mates witnessed my hookups in the past. Plenty of times, they'd come upon me with some guy and would stay to watch. Always with the consent of my partner at the time, of course. And it was hot—for me, for the guy I was fucking, and for the one watching.

I'd done the same many, many times. I mean, tour buses aren't big, and privacy is limited.

But I was protective when it came to Van.

I knew I would never fucking share him, ever, and I wanted to be the only one he touched. But I wasn't sure it would bother me if, say, Van and I were busy fucking in my bunk, and Holls was watching from his.

Was voyeurism kinky? Maybe to some people.

To musicians? It's just another day on the road.

On the one hand, I wanted all of Van's attention all the time. On the other, well, different kinds of experiences could heighten pleasure. And I wanted Van to have all the pleasure.

We had plenty of time to explore our relationship and discuss our boundaries. I'd have at least a month, maybe two, alone with him. As crazy as it sounded, the reality of that made me more excited than anything I'd ever done in bed.

But a small part of me still worried about all the what-ifs. Van and I were both new at this relationship thing, and God knows I had an artistic temperament that could try the calmest of people.

The past week had been amazing, but reality was now setting in. Would we grow closer together or would working and living as a couple be more than we could handle? I guess only time would tell.

We'd gotten home after a nine-hour bus ride and reluctantly went our separate ways, me to my house on the outskirts and Van to his condo downtown.

I was already counting down the hours until I saw him again. I hated being apart from him before we were lovers, and now even more so.

It was like a vital part of me was missing.

Still, I crashed hard when I got home.

The adrenaline ride of the past week, plus the tour before

that, finally caught up to me. I slept for the better part of two days and woke up to find my assistant Bibi at my door with coffee and my favorite donuts in hand.

She entered my house in her usual whirlwind—talking at fifty miles per hour, her phone buzzing, her long red ponytail whipping around her head. Bibi was a southern ball of energy. She had enough buzz to light up the city and then some.

"I'm glad to see you, but aren't you still technically on vacation?" I asked her as we sat around my kitchen island.

"Yes, but I'm not leaving for Hawaii until next week. And I wanted to stop by since there are a few things we need to deal with before I take off. I brought a ton of promo merch for you to sign; it's in the car. That should be the last of it for the year. Also, and as per your text, I've arranged to have the cottage in Rhode Island cleaned and stocked with food. The private plane is ready for you tomorrow, and there'll be a car waiting when you arrive at the island airport. I've emailed Van and Dawson all the deets."

"Awesome. Thanks for that. You know I hate interrupting your time off, but I didn't want Van to have to deal with it. He was overworked this past week as it was."

She waved me off. "You know me, I'm never really on vacation. The phone is always on, so if you need me, I'm just a text away."

"How would I function without you?"

"You wouldn't," she replied with a wink. "So, you and Van are going to be together for a whole month? How'd that happen?"

She gave me a knowing smirk.

Like everyone in my inner circle, Bibi knew about my long-term crush on Van.

"We're gonna work on songs for the next album," I replied and took a bite of my chocolate-glazed donut. It was good, but I was already missing the beignets from NOLA.

"Is that all?" she asked. "I only ask because you're much more relaxed and happier than when you left here. The European tour was exhausting for everyone, but you were more stressed out than usual."

"Let's just say me and Van have taken our partnership to the next level," I replied with a filthy grin and licked the chocolate off my fingers.

"Thank the Lord Jesus, and finally! I didn't think I could take any more of that sexual tension. Ahh, I'm so happy for y'all!" Bibi screamed and clapped her hands.

I winced at the decibel level of her voice. "You ever consider being on stage yourself? You can project like no one else."

She playfully whacked my arm.

"And keep that info on the down low for now, please," I added as I sipped on my coffee. "We're not going public with our relationship. Yet."

Bibi squealed again and reached for a donut. "These donuts were all for you, but fuck it. This news calls for a celebratory pastry. So, spill. How was it? Are you exclusive? What do the guys think? Are you going to—"

I held up my hand. "Whoa. And to answer your questions, it was amazing, fuck yes, and the guys are cautiously happy for us. And I have no idea what your fourth question was since I interrupted you."

"The guys aren't happy?" she asked before she bit into her glazed donut.

"They are, but they also have concerns. We don't know how this is gonna play out yet, right? I mean, hello, spoiled rock star," I pointed to myself. "Maybe me being his boyfriend and the guy he manages will be too much for him, yeah? Fucking and falling is one thing, the reality of day-to-day living is another."

Bibi blinked and stared at me. "Who is this mature Brodie, and what have you done with my fuckboy?"

I burst out laughing. "Fuckboy is still here, but now there's only one man I fuck."

Bibi took a sip of her coffee and nodded. "And how is Van dealing with all this? He's never mentioned he was gay. In fact, thinking back, he told me about a woman he was dating shortly before he signed on with Bandit, so I always assumed he was straight. Or bi, since I knew the way he looked at you was not the way a manager looks at his artist. Still, he isn't one to talk about his private life."

"Pretty sure he's bi or pan. Whatever the case, so far, he's all in. I thought he'd be freaking out by now, but it hasn't happened."

Part of me worried that there would be a delayed reaction.

Especially once he came out. If and when he wanted to come out. At some point, I wanted to go public with our relationship. But being gay in private versus public were two very different things.

People weren't shy about commenting, and they could be fucking nasty. Van had never dealt with that before. Sure, he witnessed what the guys and I experienced, but it was different when it was aimed at you personally. I'd dealt with haters since I came out, and unfortunately, I probably always would.

Would Van decide I wasn't worth the hassle? He could date a woman with no backlash, no scrutiny.

With me? It would never end.

Bibi placed a gentle hand over mine and squeezed. "Be patient with him and let him feel all the things he needs to."

"That's what I'm worried about. You know me, I'm all in, and that's my only way. Sometimes, I forget not everyone is the same. And patience is not something I'm known for."

"That's not true. You've had feelings for Van for a long time, and look how that turned out." She smiled at me.

"Yeah, but relationships are hard enough. And with the addition of public scrutiny?" I shook my head, wanting to rid myself of these anxieties and self-doubt. I hated feeling inse-cure. "Anyway, I don't want to worry about that now. I don't want to worry at all. I'm so goddamn happy, and fuck every-thing else."

"There's the Brodie I know! Now, let's get that merch signed, and you can tell me all about your trip to NOLA. I want to hear *everything*."

"Not everything. Guy's gotta have some secrets."

Bibi chuckled. "Now I know you're in love."

"Who said anything about that?"

I knew it; of course I did. But I wasn't ready to say the word until I'd said it to Van.

"I know you, and I know love when I see it. For fuck's sake, Dee, I see everything. I haven't been ordering condoms for you for almost a year. I mean, I started to think maybe you were buying them from some secret supplier. Then I realized no randos were walking out of here in the morning either. You've been pining hard for that man for a long time. What else could it be but love?"

My face flushed, and it didn't escape her notice.

"And right there, you're blushing. You, Mr. Rockstar. What the actual fuck?"

"Okay, all right. Man, what you know about my life is frightening, but yes, I do feel for him that way. But I need to take it slow. I don't want to say too much and freak him out."

"Trust your instincts. You'll know when the time is right."

"Thanks, oh wise one."

Bibi grabbed another donut and stuffed it in my mouth. "You got that right."

CHAPTER 31

VAN

I came back to a clean condo, but I'd never felt less at home.

And even though I'd only been away from Brodie for a few days, it felt so much longer.

Like I was going to crawl out of my skin if I didn't get my fix of him soon.

It was crazy how I went from feeling Brodie's presence in my life one day to needing him like the air I breathed in another.

One more day.

In the meantime, I had to get organized for our trip to Rhode Island.

Thankfully, my apartment was easy to maintain. Not that I really maintained it. I had a house cleaning service and grocery delivery once a week. No pets, no plants. It was more like a hotel than a home. Lock the door and leave.

The condo was situated in the heart of the District in downtown Nashville and it was never quiet, not like Forest Hills, where Brodie lived.

When I first moved here, I preferred the noise. Living alone felt lonely enough. At least when I looked out my window or went for a walk, there were people everywhere—talking, walking, and doing their errands during the day. Drinking, laughing, and partying at night. No matter the time of day, it was an endless loop of activity.

Now, though, the endless noise outside was irritating, and the haunting stillness inside unnerving.

It was the events of the past week finally hitting me.

Did facing my sexuality mean that everything else in my life was fair game?

The writer in me yearned for a space to call my own and something that would inspire my work. Maybe the apartment had in the beginning, back when I wrote angrier, edgier stuff. But not lately. And I wondered why I continued to stay here if the place didn't serve me anymore.

I'd never had people over. Not family, not friends. Well, maybe a few times, but I could count them on one hand. Most of my friends were people I worked with. When we did socialize, it was usually at a bar or a club.

And I was either at the office, in the studio, or at one of the band's homes. I came back to my apartment to sleep and shower, and that was it.

There were no memories attached to it.

Unlike Brodie's house. I'd been there many times. But he'd never been to my place.

That made me wonder, had that been me acting professionally, or did I do it to keep him at a distance?

Instead of sitting around asking questions I didn't have answers to, I got my ass up off the couch.

The apartment was seven hundred square feet, small by most standards, but enough space for one person. My idea of decorating was to install my prized guitars on display throughout the living room. And photos of the bands I'd worked with and places I'd traveled to, pics of my family back in Montreal, and, of course, photos of Wayward Lane.

As I walked through the space, I realized just how many

photos of the band—and Brodie in particular—lined the walls of my living room.

And my hallway.

And my bedroom.

There, on the wall directly across from my bed, sat a massive picture taken from Wayward Lane's first international tour.

The stunning black and white photo was focused on Brodie at center stage, wearing only his kilt, his body drenched in sweat as he kneeled before the audience.

Brodie was kneeling before me.

Had I been jerking off to him all this time?

Holy shit, I was like a teenager with a poster of my celebrity crush. He'd tease me to no end if he were here right now.

How could I have been so dense about my interactions with him for so long?

As if we had a psychic connection, my phone pinged.

Brodie: I miss you already. I can't wait until tomorrow.

Instead of replying to him, I took a photo of his photo and sent it to him with the caption "my place."

Brodie: You've got a life-size picture of me in your condo? OMG that's hot!

It's not the only one.

Then I video-called him.

"If there was an award for being totally oblivious, I would win it," I said when his gorgeous face popped up on screen.

Brodie shook his head. "What do you mean?"

"I'm going to walk you through my condo; just watch."

I proceeded to walk down the hallway and then into the living room, all the while aiming the phone at my walls.

"If I didn't know better, I'd say you were an obsessed fan," Brodie quipped. "And you just noticed this now?"

"Yup. It honestly didn't occur to me. I mean, I have pictures of all the musicians I've worked with."

Brodie chuckled. "Yeah, but there's like four of them and fifteen of me."

"Exactly."

"That first one you showed me, is that in your bedroom?"

I nodded. "Right across from my bed."

"You dirty dog, Van. You've been jerking off to me all this time!"

I laughed out loud. "Apparently so."

I hadn't felt this light in ages.

"That is the hottest thing ever."

"You say that about everything," I teased.

"Only when it comes to you, and I can't help it."

"Well, now that I've entertained you, I have to go. I've got laundry—"

"I bet you do. Those sheets must be filthy."

"Brodie—"

"I'd say think of me tonight when you're in bed, but that's a given. Wait until I tell the guys."

"No, and I'm hanging up now."

"Hold on. Did you hear what I said earlier?"

"I did, but how can I miss you when you're right here in my bedroom? And my living room, and my hallway—"

He pursed his lips and blew a raspberry. "Smart ass."

"I guess you're rubbing off on me."

"I will be tomorrow."

Just the thought had my cock chubbing up. "And yes, I miss you too. I'm about to crawl the walls."

"But only the ones with my picture on it," Brodie chuckled.

A loud crash echoed in the background.

"What was that?" I asked.

"Bibi. She's in my kitchen. She actually made me work today, Van. I had to sign merch for over three hours."

I shook my head at his pouty expression. "Poor baby."

"And now she's making me dinner."

"*Câlisse*, you're spoiled."

"I know," he smirked. "I'll see you tomorrow. Sleep well."

"Doubtful. One, you're not here, and two, all I can do now is stare at your sexy body on the wall."

"Next time, it'll be the real thing."

"Looking forward to it."

After I hung up, I unpacked my suitcases, sorted my clothes, and did my laundry.

Four loads later, I re-packed, ordered a pizza, ate half of it, and zonked out on my couch.

I woke up the next morning at nine a.m. to a barrage of texts from Brodie.

> Brodie: We spent one night together, and now I hate sleeping without you. I keep waking up and wondering where you are.

> Brodie: Dawson is picking you up in an hour

> Brodie: You're still coming, right?

Instead of texting, I called.

"Morning, *mon coeur*," I greeted in my gruff morning voice.

"It is now. Did you just wake up?"

I rubbed my eyes. "I did. Normally, I'm up at six, but I guess I needed the sleep."

"Are you gonna be ready in time? Dawson will be arriving at your place in half an hour."

"Shit, shower, and shave in under twenty," I blurted out.

Brodie's responding chuckle had a shiver running through me.

"Why does everything feel so natural between us?" I asked, my tone suddenly serious.

"It's always been that way. Our being intimate hasn't changed anything. You're surprised?"

"A bit." I paused and scratched my scruff. "When I dated women, I always felt oddly on edge. Like, I wasn't sure what to say or what not to say. And I didn't quite know how to relax around them or what they were thinking. I don't really know how else to explain it. But with you, I can just be me. Is that weird?"

"Not at all. First off, we're friends, and there's a level of comfort there. We've both seen each other at our best and our worst. And however you define what we are, I think gender isn't the biggest part of it. We see each other, and I don't just mean our physical forms. Whether we're face to face or texting or on stage the other night, I always feel our connection."

"I feel it too," I admitted, suddenly overcome with emotion. "And that's very deep for first thing in the morning."

"I've been awake for two hours. And being all alone in my big empty house gives me a lot of time to think. Mostly about you."

"I'm going to get up now. Because the sooner I get ready, the faster I get to you."

"I'll see you soon."

I hung up and all but ran into my bathroom.

CHAPTER 32
BRODIE

I t was good to be home.

Not that I didn't love Nashville, but being back near my folks and my sister and being near the ocean again was just what I needed after another grueling year of touring.

I wasn't into holistic healing or anything like that, but there was something about the sea air that gave me new life. Anytime I was burned out, I came here and replenished the creative juices.

And knowing Van was staying with me for the foreseeable future?

I was overloaded with happiness.

After a two-and-a-half-hour plane ride, we landed in Providence. Then Dawson drove us to my cottage in Jamestown.

It was like time had stood still in this place with the stately homes, lush gardens, and miles of unspoiled beaches.

Van hadn't said much since we landed. I worried that it was this morning's talk.

Then I thought about the pictures of me in his home, and I couldn't help but smile. Even if it took a while for him to catch up, a part of him always knew what he wanted.

I turned to find Van glued to his phone.

"What are you reading?" I asked.

"Articles about the concert. Mostly positive. But there are a few more speculating about your relationship with Colm. And with me. Apparently, we're feuding over you."

"I believe the correct term is 'love triangle,'" I quipped.

Van rolled his eyes. "I thought it would've died down by now. Did you notice a car following us when we were headed to the airport?"

"No."

"I did," Van replied and leaned forward near the driver's seat. "Hey, Daws, did you see a blue sedan following us in Nashville?"

"Yeah, we had a tail. Whoever it was, they parked near the arrivals gate and followed us to the entrance. That's when I saw the camera. I tried to shield you as best I could, but he took a few snaps and then took off. I texted Regan. Given that the guy got their shot in a public space and left without incident, there's nothing we can do."

"Thanks." Van leaned back again. "Have you ever had press follow you around here?"

"Don't you remember when I first bought this place? I had that three-day blowout bash, and it caught the attention of local media, and then the entertainment press swarmed in. There were news choppers flying overhead. It was insane."

"I'm afraid I'm not as exciting as a three-day bender."

I slid my hand around his left thigh and squeezed. "I don't want to start our trip with an argument."

"What argument? It's true."

"No, it's not. Look at me."

"Dee, I was—"

"Van, look at me."

As soon as his dark gaze met mine, bam. I felt the impact in my body. My heart jump-started, my dick throbbed, and my chest ached.

Every fucking time.

I shook my head. "This is already the most exciting trip of my life, and it's all because of you."

"But—"

"Put the phone away."

Van slowly slid his phone into his pocket and placed his hands on his thighs. I took his left hand and placed it over my denim-covered cock.

I was hard and aching, and fuck, his big, warm hand felt amazing, cupping my dick. Van inhaled sharply and gently squeezed. I glanced at his face and noticed the flush on his cheeks and the blown pupils.

"You feel that?" I asked as I leaned over. "I've been like that for three fucking days. All because of you. You're the first thing I think about when I wake up and the last thing I want before I sleep. Don't talk down about yourself or what's building between us. Or compare what we have to my past. Just don't. Or I'm gonna handcuff you to my bed and throw the key in the ocean."

Van threw his head back and laughed. Fuck, seeing him smile like that gave me that fluttery feeling inside. His happiness was mine.

"Kinky," he quipped as he rubbed my dick. "I like it."

"I'm not joking."

"Okay."

"I mean it. Stop reading tabloid trash and get that insane comment that you're not exciting enough out of your head."

Van stared at me and nodded. "All right. I get it."

"Good," I bit out, even though I knew that probably wasn't the end of it.

"Fine," Van growled, and our gazes locked.

One moment, we were in a heated staredown, and the next, I was lying flat on my back, Van all over me.

He fucking devoured me, his tongue sucking on mine.

I kissed him back with the same ferocity, desperate for his

taste. And God, the weight of him had me squirming to get closer.

I'm pretty sure I moaned out loud.

Then I remembered we were in a moving vehicle with Dawson.

Van and I were doing a shit job of keeping this relationship under wraps. But I was too far gone to care.

Nothing that felt this good could be wrong.

So, instead of pushing Van away, I licked a path over his jaw and down his neck. I gently bit and sucked on his tender skin, and his loud groan echoed in the confines of the car.

"Um, guys—" Dawson interrupted.

"*Câlisse,*" Van swore and pulled away. "Shit. Fuck."

"I think you missed one," I teased as Van sat up and pulled me with him.

"You didn't see that," Van warned Dawson.

"I didn't hear it either," Dawson replied with a chuckle. "And I've worked for you guys long enough to willfully ignore the shenanigans. The main reason I wanted to interrupt you is because we're pulling into the property. It looks like your dad's waiting by the gate."

I glanced out the window, and sure enough, there he was.

Standing in jeans, rain boots, and a hunter-green jacket, my dad was fiddling with the security keypad. I'd texted him yesterday, and he'd insisted on being there to welcome us.

I took after Mom with dark hair, hazel eyes, a lean body, and a sharp mouth.

Dad, on the other hand, had a thick head of white hair (thanks in no small part to yours truly), a rare smile, and pale green eyes. He was taller than me and bigger, too. But despite my dad's stature and tendency for gruffness, he was the kindest man you'd ever meet. Entirely devoted to my mom and our family.

Everyone I met, I measured up to him. And so far, only one other man had ever met my expectations.

We came to a stop near the gate, and I rushed out of the car to greet him.

"The rockstar has returned!" my dad yelled out and pulled me into a crushing embrace.

"It's so good to be home." I pulled back and smiled at him. "I brought Van with me. He'll be staying on for a while, including Thanksgiving."

"You finally got your man, eh?"

I'd confided to my dad last year about my feelings for Van. He was the only one in my family who knew.

"Shhh. Early days yet. Let's not scare him off."

"Me? You worry about your mom and sisters. They're the nosy ones."

I laughed and turned my head to find Van walking toward us. In his dark wash jeans and an Irish knit sweater, he fit right in with our surroundings. He reached for my dad's hand.

"Lachlan, nice to see you again."

"You as well, Van. You're looking good," Dad remarked and shook his hand. "Keeping my son busy?"

Van's face flushed. "Ah, yes. We're going to work on songs for the next album. No rest in this business."

"Well, if you have to work, you've come to the right place. Great air, stunning views. You'll be inspired in no time."

"Dawson is also staying on." I pointed to the car. Dawson waved. "Some pap was following us this morning as we headed to the airport."

Dad nodded. "Call on us if you need to. Now let's get the gate open so you can unpack and get settled in."

We unlocked the gate, and Dad said his goodbyes.

The gravel driveway was long and meandering until, finally, the cottage came into view.

With gray siding and white trim, the cape cod-style house sat on the edge of a marsh where the river met the ocean. I had five acres of pristine land.

Fresh, briny air, tall grasses, and bursts of autumn colors greeted us. I shivered and pulled my leather jacket tight as the cool New England air surrounded me.

Dawson helped us unload our luggage. I walked with him to the back of the property, where the poolhouse and the studio were located.

Both were built in a similar style to the main house, complete with kitchens and bathrooms. I had enough space on this property to house twenty guests comfortably. Fifty if you didn't care about sharing a bathroom, a bed, or a couch. Five hundred, as per my infamous housewarming party, where we'd set up tents on the grounds.

Once Dawson was settled in, Van and I entered the main house.

Thankfully, the housekeeper had turned on the heating, there was wood stacked up next to the fireplace, and the fridge and cupboards were filled.

"Bibi thought of everything. We could survive the apocalypse in this place," Van declared as he pulled out a bottle of sparkling water.

"She's the best," I replied, sliding my arms around Van's waist. "What do you say we go for a walk on the beach and then hit the hot tub?"

"I say yes. Just let me grab a jacket."

"Meet you on the patio."

I grabbed a gray scarf from the closet and wrapped it around my neck, then slipped outside to the patio that overlooked the pool.

The wind had picked up, and I could hear the crash of the nearby waves as they hit the beach. It was too cold at this time of year to go swimming or surfing, but in the summer, it was cool and refreshing. Too bad I was usually on tour during that time. Next year, we'd be in North America in the spring and summer, so maybe we could schedule a break and come here for a bit.

"You look deep in thought," Van spoke behind me.

I turned and found him smiling at me.

"Just thinking about our tour next year. I'm glad we'll be in the US in the summer. I'd like to come here for a break if possible. When the water is swimmable."

"I think we can make that happen."

Van held out his hand, and I interlocked our fingers.

We walked along the sandy path and up over the dune's crest to a set of wooden stairs that led down to the beach. All beaches in the state were public, but this one was small and remote, so it remained mainly unknown and used by locals.

We were the only ones here on this crisp November day. The massive waves and whitecaps were impressive. No matter the weather, the peace of this place called to me.

"God, I love the air here. You can breathe deep. Reminds me of childhood trips to Maine. My parents would rent a cottage for two weeks every summer."

"You never mentioned that before."

Van bit his lip. "It's still difficult for me to talk about them. Every time a memory hits, I get choked up. But I like sharing the memories with you."

I heard him sniff, and he shook his head. I squeezed his hand tight, offering what comfort I could.

We stepped down onto the sand, and the salt spray hit my cheeks.

"We'd stay in a town called Kennebunkport, it's about a six-hour drive from Montreal. My dad and I would swim too much and get sunburnt. We'd stuff our faces with seafood every night and enjoy the town's quiet charm. This place has the same feeling. It's timeless."

"I know what you mean. When we come back here twenty years from now, it'll still be the same."

"Twenty years, huh?" Van smiled and pulled me into his arms.

"At least."

CHAPTER 33

VAN

After a late supper of corn chowder and baked fish, Brodie and I fell asleep on the couch in front of the fireplace.

I woke up early the next morning with a stiff neck and an even stiffer dick.

But my rock star was still sound asleep, and I knew how rare that was. Not wanting to disturb him, I quietly got up and went for a walk on the beach to clear my head.

But not before I left Brodie a note and told him to meet me in the studio when he woke.

Despite the need to unplug from work, I'd received several notifications, so of course, I had to check. Nothing urgent, thank God.

Then, I checked out the daily media clippings from our PR team. One was flagged.

Brodie James, lead singer of Wayward Lane, is rumored to be in a romantic relationship with his manager, Ivan Cross. Cross joined James on stage for an intimate performance at Halloween in New Orleans. The singer and his manager were seen at the Nashville Airport a day ago, leaving for parts unknown. James was also recently pictured with model Colm McDade. We reached out to Wayward Lane's PR rep, but they had no comment.

The celebrity gossip mill was churning out full force.

Then I thought back to yesterday morning. That reporter had been lying in wait in Brodie's neighborhood at the exact time we were leaving for the airport, and I knew it wasn't a coincidence. Someone had fed them information. And it had to be someone in our inner circle.

I glanced at my social media. I didn't post much personal stuff, but Bandit did require every team member to have accounts to promote the artists.

There were a ton of comments, mostly from supportive fans who wanted confirmation of my relationship status with Brodie.

Jesus, can we have some time to ourselves to figure it out first?

There was also plenty of hateful bullshit from trolls. The vitriol in some of the comments were something I'd never been subjected to before. How did Brodie deal with this daily? And what would happen when we did finally come out as a couple? How bad was it going to get?

Putting my phone and anxieties aside for the time being, I enjoyed my walk and let nature do its thing.

The white noise of the ocean calmed me, but the gathering clouds in the distance looked like a storm was brewing. The waves were higher today, and they crashed into the rocks at the edge of the beach, the salt spray flying everywhere.

It was peace and chaos all at once.

A half-hour later, I was relaxed and ready to write.

I headed for the studio, and man, what a space.

White-washed walls and two big blue sofas sat under the four skylights in the main space. Brodie was not kidding when he talked about the natural light in here. It was perfect.

There was a booth for recording vocals, an editing panel, a

full drum set, a keyboard, and numerous guitars. He'd replicated our studio in Nashville on a smaller scale.

Over to the left, there was a kitchen and a full bathroom.

I headed for the kitchen, popped a pod into the brewing machine, and enjoyed my first cup of coffee while watching the sun break through the thick November clouds.

With caffeinated veins, I grabbed one of the acoustic guitars off the display shelf. Then, I searched the console under the editing board and found several notebooks and pens.

Yeah, I was old-fashioned, writing everything down by hand. It had always been that way, and I didn't question why. I'm sure I could write a hell of a lot more if I typed on my phone or a tablet, but I had my method, and it worked for me.

I sat on one of the sofas and placed the guitar in my lap.

Every songwriter had their routine, but I always started with the music first. A certain idea, a melody, would reverberate in my brain, and once I began to noodle with that on the guitar, the lyrics would flood the empty spaces.

Time seemed to slow down here, and the melody in my head was the same.

I began to hum as I played out the tune.

But it didn't sound like I imagined it. It was too fast.

I started again, slower this time, until I got the rhythm just right.

I played it again. Then, I stopped and jotted down notes. Anything that came to mind and reflected my thoughts and feelings.

The lonesome wail of a foghorn in the distance.

The calm before the incoming storm.

Wild, reckless passion. Deep, all-consuming love.

A longing that was never satisfied. A love that defied logic.

It was a jumble at this point, but you had to start somewhere.

I strummed the guitar again, and I liked what I heard.

"It sounds great already."

Brodie's voice startled me, and I turned my head.

He looked rested, his eyes glowing, his face flushed. He was dressed in ripped black jeans and my Montreal Canadiens hockey t-shirt.

I found it all kinds of sexy that he was wearing my clothes. He was claiming me, and I fucking loved it.

"I didn't hear the door open."

There were so many things I could've said at that moment, but that's what came out of my mouth.

Smooth, Van.

He smiled and sat down beside me. "I tried to be as quiet as I could so I wouldn't interfere with the muse."

"You can't interfere. You're it." I smiled back at him, then leaned over for a kiss.

His soft, eager lips met mine, and hell, I could feast on him for days.

Brodie tasted like coffee and mint. I shoved the guitar to the side and took control of the kiss, pushing him down on the sofa and relishing in his husky moan.

"Nice shirt," I quipped, moving my lips down to tease his neck.

"I figured you wouldn't mind."

"Everything I have is yours," I said as I cupped his face and looked into his luminous eyes.

"That's a dangerous statement. I might assume that you're talking about more than clothes."

"Guess there's only one way to find out."

Then, there was no time for talk.

Or music.

Except the pounding rhythm of our heartbeats.

We frantically removed every scrap of material that separated us as fast as we could. Shirts, jeans, and underwear went flying, scattering over the furniture and floor like confetti.

Then Brodie was lying naked underneath me, splayed out like the rock god he was. Black hair disheveled, pink lips glistening, a dappled flush running down his face and chest.

He looked at me like I was the only thing he wanted.

"You are."

The feverish intensity shifted. Much like the melody in my head, I wanted to touch and taste and savor, to take my time undoing him. To show him that what was happening between us wasn't just a quick fuck but a long, slow dance.

Brodie licked the palm of one hand provocatively and then slipped it around my dick, around both our dicks, rubbing them together.

God, that felt fucking unreal.

He jacked us off in smooth, practiced strokes as I teased his mouth with soft, languid kisses. Our tongues tangled, exploring, tasting.

I was obsessed with his taste, his kisses, and I wondered how I ever survived without them.

His other hand gripped my ass cheek, then gently slid down the crease. When his finger rubbed over my hole, my entire body jolted.

"Does that feel good?"

I nodded because I was too overcome with my emotions to utter a word.

All I wanted was more. More kisses and touches and, fuck yes, I wanted him to rub my hole like that again.

I'd never played with my ass, even though I was curious about things like rimming. And after having Brodie's tongue in my ass the other night, I knew I wanted his fingers there too. Maybe even his cock.

But one step at a time.

I rolled over to straddle him and slid my larger hand over his as we jerked off together.

"Fuck, just keep touching me, Van. Don't stop," Brodie moaned and bit his lower lip.

I was mesmerized by the sight of our hard cocks rubbing together, pre-cum and Brodie's saliva creating a smooth glide.

The pleasure ignited when he tapped my hole.

I swiveled my hips back and forth, unable to decide which sensation was better—the heated grip on my dick or the tormenting finger teasing the rim of my asshole.

"Table. Lube," Brodie whispered as his hands suddenly stopped touching me. "Lie down."

I sat back and did as he ordered, stretching out on the couch, while Brodie reached over to the coffee table beside us. He yanked on the drawer, pulled out a small tube, flicked open the cap, and poured a generous amount into his hand. He rubbed them together, and I caught the scent of vanilla.

Then he was all over me, gripping our dicks in one slick hand while the other slid underneath to torment my ass.

He kept rubbing and circling my hole, but that was it.

I needed more.

"You're driving me insane; just do it," I growled as I lifted my hips, encouraging him.

"Patience, honey. I want you to enjoy this. I want to make it good for you."

A shiver rolled through me when he called me "honey."

"Every time you touch me, it's good. And I know what I want. Please."

I was not above begging if I had to. But Brodie still didn't do anything but continue to rub my sensitive rim as I panted and writhed.

Tormenting witch.

Two could play this game.

I reached down and cupped his smooth balls and rolled them in my palm, then gave a gentle tug.

This time, he was the one who jolted.

My other hand roamed over his taut stomach until I reached his nipples.

"Jesus, don't. You know how sensitive I am there," Brodie panted.

"Then shove your finger in my ass, or I'm going to tease your nipples until you come all over my hand."

Brodie groaned. "Fuck, Van. You talking to me like that is so goddamn sexy."

His callused finger pushed gently into my ass, and then I had nothing more to say.

I jolted from the sting of initial pain, but it was followed by awesome pleasure. I shuddered from the intense sensation and the knowledge that this was Brodie inside me.

He was a part of me, just like I was a part of him.

There was no uncertainty. I could ask, and Brodie would answer, and vice versa. We were partners in every sense of the word.

He drilled his finger deeper, and crooked his fingers. A pleasure I'd never felt before had every muscle in my body lighting up.

"*Câlisse, mon coeur*, do that again," I demanded.

"Welcome to the magic of your prostate." Brodie chuckled as he began to finger fuck me.

Magic was the least of it.

Every time he hit that spot inside me, I was gripped by a cascade of euphoria that had my dick twitching, my toes curling, and my heart kickstarting.

What the fuck had I been missing out on?

"Maybe next time, it'll be my cock in your ass. If that's something you want."

"You want that?" I panted.

"Do you?" he asked, all the while stroking my cock and fingering my ass.

"I…" I was so caught up in my body's pleasure that I had a hard time thinking, never mind talking. "Yeah, I think so."

"I prefer to bottom, but with you, I want to do it all. I want to possess you and, most of all, be possessed by you. I want you in every fucking way."

The passion in Brodie's husky voice made me shiver.

He kept up the steady pace in my ass and on my dick, and then I forgot to do anything but ride the wave of pleasure. The heated friction on my cock and the incredible fullness in my hole was suddenly too much.

I ran my hand up his chest and pinched his nipples. Brodie moaned and squirmed and lost his rhythm for a moment.

It didn't matter. What we were making together wasn't about perfection. It was raw and honest and real.

I wanted him the same way he wanted me—fully, completely, without question.

He leaned over and we reached for each other, kissing frantically.

I was climbing higher and higher, and I didn't know if I would survive the implosion.

All it took was one more stroke on my dick and Brodie growling my name.

My orgasm was so intense I screamed his name in return.

I heard him cry out and felt the heat of our combined cum on my dick and my balls.

His body trembled. Or was it me? It was both of us.

This, us, was an unquenchable fire.

And I didn't care if I got burned.

CHAPTER 34
BRODIE

After we both came down from that explosive high, Van blanketed my body with his heavier one, and we made out.

We couldn't get close enough or kiss enough.

The orgasms with him were amazing, but that wasn't the best part.

It was this.

Us, in the aftermath. We lay on the couch in a sweaty, tangled mess, sharing kisses and talking and laughing.

I had no urge to let go. Far from that. I wasn't lying when I said that I wanted to possess him—every single part.

It was intimate in a way I'd never experienced. As new to me as my finger in his ass was to him.

Hey, I'm a rock star, not a poet. And a finger in the ass can be poetic. Ask around.

"We better shower, or we'll be glued together forever." I gave his jaw a gentle nip.

"I like that idea."

"Until we go to move and the dried cum gives you a wax job you never anticipated."

Van slowly shifted his chest away from mine. I caught his wince when we finally separated.

"Okay, next time, shower right away and save the cuddling for after," Van said as he stood up.

"Cuddling, huh? Didn't take you for a hugger," I teased as he offered his hand to help me.

I stood up and faced him, leaning in for another kiss.

"Don't tell anyone," Van warned as he smiled at me.

"What'll you give me for my silence?"

"More hugs?"

"Sold."

Once we showered and changed, we made ourselves coffee and got to work.

I grabbed a guitar, and we sat on opposite couches.

"What's your usual routine?" I asked.

"Music first, lyrics later. You heard the riff I was playing earlier, so we can start with that and go from there."

Three hours later, we had a good base for a new song.

Van had a great ear for creating a melodic hook that was simple but memorable. I was focused on the rhythm pattern and how that would complement my vocals.

I always gave my input to the songs Van presented to us. And, of course, there were songs I wrote that I would present to him. But this, starting from scratch, creating a song together, was a whole new experience for both of us. And it worked. We bickered back and forth in our usual way until we developed a sound we could both agree on.

"Did you have a look at the recent press clippings?" Van asked as we took a break and shared a coffee on the patio.

Despite the chill, the sea air was energizing.

"Not yet. Anything I should be aware of?"

"There's a photo of you and me at the airport yesterday. There's all kinds of speculation on social media about our relationship," he replied with a frown.

"Okay, well, we agreed to ignore it for now."

Van was silent, sipping his coffee and staring out at the ocean in the distance. He had that worried expression in his eyes that I knew all too well.

"What's wrong?"

He bit his lip and then turned to me.

"I got a lot of comments on my personal accounts. Some are supportive, but there's also a lot of hate. Homophobic rants. It's just so angry. I've never felt that kind of vitriol directed at me before."

Reality was a rude fucking wake-up call.

"Most of the time, your fans far outnumber the haters, but I never fully understood what it's like for you. I mean, I did, but not to the extent I do now," he continued, then reached out to take my hand. "And I worry about what will happen when we come out as a couple. I've never had anyone care who I was with. If I went on a date with a woman, no one looked twice. And I don't like that I'm already worried about how I'm going to handle it."

I tightened my grip on his hand and brought it up to my mouth, gently kissing his knuckles.

"I won't bullshit you, it's not going to be easy. People are going to stop and stare and make comments. There are going to be places we're not welcome, even with my celebrity status. But I learned a long time ago that we can't let other people dictate our happiness. There's always risk in being a high-profile person and being openly gay to boot. And there's also a reason I have PR people monitoring my accounts. If I read every horrible comment, I'd never leave the fucking house."

Van nodded. "Just be patient with me. I may be older, but as far as this goes, you're the wiser one."

"Said no one, ever." I chuckled, trying to ease the tension.

"Sorry, I didn't mean to spoil the mood."

"You didn't. And we have to talk about this. You're being

honest, and I love that about you. I don't ever want you to hold anything back."

Van leaned over and took my lips in a slow kiss.

"You ready to get back to work?"

"I'm ready to write a hit song."

"Let's do it."

We'd just started brainstorming the lyrics when Dawson appeared at the door.

I waved him in.

"Sorry to interrupt, but I wanted you to know that there's a van parked near the gate, and it's been sitting there for an hour. It's a pap. I spotted a professional camera with a tele-photo lens. I don't know how the fuck they found us. I called Regan. She's sending more team members up here, just in case."

"Jesus Christ, can I go, like, a week without having to deal with the press following me? I get that I signed up for this life, but come on. I just want a month off."

Dawson sat down beside me. "I'm sorry, Brodie. We were careful. No one followed us from the airport, and it was a private flight. I don't know how they found us."

"It's not your fault, Daws, and I'm not blaming you." I sighed. "What about my family? My parents and my sister are nearby. I don't want them being harassed."

"We'll place one team member each with your parents and your sister, respectively, if need be."

Van grabbed his phone. "I'm going to make a phone call. I'll be right back."

———

VAN

I stood on the patio as the sea mist sprayed my face and

thanked God for that. I needed something to cool my temper down.

My good mood from earlier had all but vanished.

What started out as the perfect day—mind-blowing morning sex with Brodie followed by a songwriting session—was now marred by concerns that our privacy was about to be breached.

I tapped my phone and waited.

"What's up, Van?" Greg answered.

"Someone leaked word to the press that Brodie and I are in Rhode Island, and I want to know who. We've got a pap camped just outside his gate. Now Regan has to send more team members up here for us and for Brodie's family."

"That's unfortunate, but these things happen," Greg replied.

"That's all you have to say? Are you serious?" I yelled.

I should've been more careful about how I spoke to my boss, but I was fuming.

"This is the business we're in, remember? It's nothing new, so calm the fuck down," Greg snapped back. "They probably followed you from the airport."

He was completely ignoring my suggestion that our location was leaked, and my gut began to churn.

"There was someone in Nashville taking pictures when we left. We took a private charter. And no one followed us when we arrived here."

"You know as well as I do that it's nearly impossible to disappear nowadays. All you can do is listen to the security team, and if you are confronted by the press, ignore them. Unless, of course, you finally have something you want to say."

I caught the sharp tone of his voice and the real meaning of his words. But Brodie and I had an understanding, and we were sticking to our plan.

I could ignore Greg just as easily as he ignored my concerns about a possible leak.

"The band just finished a grueling year, and Brodie needs rest. Now his peace has been shattered," I murmured.

"He'll just have to lay low. The rumor about you and him being a couple has only intensified since the concert. Our social stats are through the roof, considering we're post-tour. So it's not surprising that the media is smelling blood."

"And?"

"And PR is monitoring the situation. If this keeps circulating, they might take over your personal account."

"I better go. Brodie and I have a song to finish."

"Already?"

"Being here is very inspiring."

"I'll bet," he replied. "I'll check in with Regan to ensure she's made Brodie's additional protection a priority."

"Fine."

I hung up with no more answers than before I made the call.

I was tempted to chuck my phone into the waves, but that wasn't smart. For me or the ocean.

"Everything okay?"

Brodie's voice startled me.

I turned and nodded. "Everything's fine. Well, not fine since we won't be able to leave the property without being photographed, but other than that—"

"If Dawson is right and no one followed us here, how did they find us?" Brodie asked.

"Between you and me, I think there's a leak."

Brodie's face fell.

"Someone at Bandit?"

I nodded. "I have my suspicions."

"And?"

I slid my arm around Brodie's waist and pulled him in tightly.

"Only a handful of people knew we were coming here. And the rumor about us isn't dying down. It's generating a huge amount of social engagement. I also checked our sales stats post- concert. Same thing. More photos of us together would only fuel the fire."

Brodie shook his head, his messy waves hitting his cheekbones.

"I get that our music, our brand, is a commodity, but if what you're suggesting is true, if someone internally leaked that info, I'm going to have a serious problem. If we can't trust the people closest to us and we don't receive some measure of privacy when we ask for it, I'm done. And I know the guys will support me on this."

"I have no evidence at this point. It's just a theory."

"But one that makes sense given the circumstances."

"We can't level an accusation without proof. First, I'm going to have Dawson run the van's plates. See if we can find out who's parked outside. We'll go from there."

Brodie leaned up and gave me a kiss. "Do you want to talk about this anymore?"

"Fuck no."

"Good. Because we have a song to work on. And a bed to wreck."

"Maybe we should reverse that," I teased and took his lips again.

It took us a whole week to finish that song.

CHAPTER 35

VAN

Despite the addition of more security, there were now three to four cars parked outside Brodie's property at any given hour, every day.

We hadn't left the compound, and thankfully, the beach was difficult for anyone but property owners to access.

Still, both of us were getting a bit stir-crazy, so we'd agreed to head over to his parents' place for dinner tonight, paparazzi or not.

Thank fuck for shorter days and SUVs with tinted windows.

Between writing and fucking, Brodie and I had been lost in our own world. Not that I was complaining. He had me wrapped around his talented fingers, and every day that passed had me falling a little deeper.

When he was out of sight, I grew restless.

When he was in my arms, I never wanted to let go.

The man in question sauntered into our bedroom, wearing tight pink briefs and a smile that was only for me.

"Do we have to go tonight?" he asked, sliding his hands around my waist and roaming lower, cupping my ass.

"Your mom is going to come storming in here if you don't show your face. And it's a good opportunity to tell them about us. Get your sexy ass dressed," I demanded. "We're already late."

Then I swatted said ass for good measure.

"Now I really don't want to leave," he teased and gave me a kiss. "Do that again."

"No. I'm withholding all sexual activities until later."

"You're so mean."

"You'll survive. And I'm waiting in the living room," I replied as I stepped away from him.

It wasn't easy. We'd been magnetized to each other for weeks.

"Five minutes, sweetheart, don't fuss with your outfit. You're gorgeous no matter what you wear."

"I really want to be mad at you right now, but then you go and say something like that." Brodie huffed and stomped off to his closet.

I watched his ass cheeks flex with every step.

Chuckling at his put-out attitude, I did the smart thing and left the bedroom.

Far away from temptation.

Dawson and Regan were waiting by the front door.

"He'll be ready in a few."

I slipped on my Chelsea boots and my leather jacket, and checked my phone one last time.

Ten minutes later, my sexy man walked out to join us. In tight, black leather jeans and a cream wool turtleneck, he looked entirely too delicious.

"You ready to go?" he asked as I continued to stare.

I wasn't as sure as I was ten minutes ago.

He smirked, took my hand, and we followed Dawson and Regan out to the car.

The air was thick with fog, darkness already settled in. I opened the door for Brodie, and we slid into the backseat.

I'd met his parents a few times, but I was nervous as hell now. Because I wasn't going to be there as his manager but as his boyfriend.

Yes, we'd finally put a label on us, and I liked it. I loved it.

I loved him.

But I was still waiting for the right time to tell him exactly how I felt. For now, I'd show him. And meeting the parents was the first step.

I mentally braced myself for the onslaught of questions and concerns given our working relationship.

Then, my nerves compounded when I thought about who was waiting on the other side of the gate.

As we headed down the driveway, the headlights illuminated several cars parked on the country road.

Once we exited the property, I saw people get out of their vehicles, cameras aimed.

Flashes popped.

It was dark, and our windows were up, so there was no way they got a shot of us. Still, I guess they were hoping. One valuable snap could be worth thousands of dollars.

"Should I lower the window and give them a choice finger? Or moon them? If they were tipped off by someone at the label, a shot of my naked ass would be a memorable fuck you."

I tried to bite back a laugh, but it came out regardless. "Would you listen to me if I said it's not a good idea?"

Brodie smiled knowingly at me. "A few months ago, I might've done the opposite just to get your attention. But now that I have it, I'll be a good little rockstar and behave."

I shook my head. "Don't behave on my account. We don't always agree, but I always respect your decisions. Even when they involved rude gestures."

Brodie smiled and leaned over to kiss me. "You just get me. And that right there is why I fucking love you."

My breath hitched, and my heart took off running.

The mood went from playful to possessive in the blink of an eye, and the words just tumbled out.

"I love you too," I confessed. "I've been wanting to tell you."

I hadn't planned on saying it for the first time in a moving vehicle with bodyguards listening.

But once Brodie had said the words, there was no way I wouldn't let him know I felt the same.

"Even though I sometimes drive you insane?"

"Especially when you drive me insane."

Then I took his lips in a passionate kiss that everyone in the car was a witness to.

Brodie loved me, and I loved him, and fuck everything else.

"I guess my timing is off," he admitted as he looked around.

"Not at all. You felt it, and you didn't hold back. I love it. And I love you."

Brodie's eyes welled up and spilled over. "Fuck, Van, don't make me cry."

"Sorry, *mon coeur*," I whispered as I wiped the tears from his face. My vision blurred, but there was no time for us to savor the moment.

We pulled to a stop, and Regan and Dawson silently got out of the car.

But this time, they didn't open the door right away, giving us a moment of privacy.

"You've called me that before."

"*Mon coeur*," I repeated and took his hand, placing it over my chest. "My heart."

"I love it." Brodie smiled and gave me another kiss. "Holy shit, you said you love me. I'm still in shock."

"I did, and I do," I said as I held onto him, both our bodies trembling. "And you're not the only one. I hope your parents have a well-stocked liquor cabinet because this deserves a celebration."

Brodie smiled and gave me another heated kiss. "Okay, honey, I'm ready now."

A shudder ran through me when he called me "honey" in that husky tone of his.

"I'm not. I need another moment." I pointed to my crotch.

Yeah, my cock was excited about what had just happened, and Brodie's sexy laughter wasn't helping matters either.

Reluctantly separating from him, I took a few deep breaths and got myself under control.

Then I slid over and opened the door, stepping out into the damp air. I wanted to hold my hand out to Brodie, but I was very aware we'd been followed.

Regan and Dawson stood with their backs to the road, blocking us from view. Brodie's parents had a fenced-in property, and the paps that had followed us were now lined up outside their gate.

Our security team quickly ushered us inside the sprawling ranch house. It was filled with amazing aromas and the chatter of conversation and laughter.

"You're finally here!" Brodie's mom, Nia, came rushing down the hallway.

Brodie was the mirror image of her—the hair, the eyes, the smile. She pulled him in tightly, like she was never letting him go.

Then she stood back and playfully whacked his arm. "Why did it take you so long? You've been here two weeks, and you don't come to see your mother!"

"I'm sorry, Mom. We didn't want the press hounding you. And then Van and I got caught up with... you know... songwriting and... stuff."

Brodie was uncharacteristically tongue-tied, and I bit back a grin.

I stepped forward and offered my hand. "It's all my fault, Nia. Forgive me."

"Well, of course, Van, and it's so nice to see you." Nia shook my hand and then turned back to Brodie. "I'm just thrilled you're finally home!"

She reached for him again and they hugged tightly.

Watching the two of them was bittersweet. Moments like these, I missed my mom and dad something fierce.

It kinda made me wish I could fade into the background.

Until Nia let go of Brodie and turned to me. "And a handshake won't do in this family."

She leaned over and gave me a warm hug.

Lachlan walked down the hallway and did the same. "Come on in, boys. What would you like to drink? Vi brought a couple of bottles of bubbly from a local vineyard if you're interested."

"Oh, yeah," Brodie smiled at me. "We've got a lot to celebrate."

"Such as?" His mom glanced between the two of us.

Her hazel eyes were as expressive as Brodie's. Inquiring but also concerned.

"Let's let them say hello to everyone first, then you can start your inquisition," Lachlan teased.

We stepped into the massive living room where Brodie's sister, Vi, and her husband Petyr, were seated. She, too, had Nia's model profile and dark hair. Brodie was standing close beside me, and I was about to reach out to him, but I could feel everyone's eyes on us.

And then Vi broke the tension like only a relative of Brodie's could.

"You're late, asshat."

Vi got up, pulled Brodie in for a hug, and messed up his hair.

"Like you could have a decent party without me, dork."

"Don't mind them," Lachlan assured me as he steered me toward the bar. "They revert back to being twelve years old when they get together."

"I remember that from the housewarming. I seem to recall a rather raucous fight in the pool."

Lachlan nodded and rolled his eyes. "Let's just say we had hefty house insurance premiums for years. Not a week would go by without one of my four children breaking something."

"I bet," I chuckled. "I'm sure Brodie was the chief instigator."

"You know him well."

I leaned against the mahogany bar and glanced over at my love. He was sitting on the couch in between his mom and his sister, telling a story in that animated way of his. Always the center of attention, and no wonder. He had that way of looking at you that made you feel like you were the only one in the room.

Suddenly, a glass of bubbly was set in front of me.

"Oh, thanks. Sorry, I zoned out there," I replied, my face flushing.

Lachlan looked at me intently, then nodded. "It's understandable. I'm like that with Nia. The woman distracts me to no end. And I wouldn't have it any other way."

He poured four other glasses and added them to a tray.

"Let me help you," I offered.

"No way, Van. You're our guest."

We made our way back to join the others and Lachlan passed around the glasses of champagne.

Brodie stood up and walked around to stand beside me, raising his glass. "I just want to say I'm so happy to be back home. I know it's taken me a long time, but that's life on the road. It's been an amazing year for the band and for me personally. And speaking of personal, I—we—" Brodie looked at me and I nodded. "We want to share some news. Van and I are together. We're a couple."

There were a few shocked faces but mostly smiles.

"I knew it! I knew it!" his sister yelled out and turned to me. "He talks about you constantly."

"Oh really?" I commented.

"Vi—" Brodie warned, his face flushing.

"I could tell he had a major crush on you for ages," she continued.

Brodie rolled his eyes. "Oh yeah? Well, Van has pictures of me all over his condo."

Now, it was my turn to blush. I slid my arm around Brodie's waist and pulled him in tight. "Jesus, Brodie, you're such a troublemaker."

"You love my kind of trouble."

Without hesitation, I smiled and kissed him.

Despite all the offers of congratulations and happy smiles, I finally noticed that Brodie's mom was curiously silent.

She put her glass down and stepped forward.

"I don't mean to spoil your news, but are you sure this is a good idea?"

CHAPTER 36
BRODIE

"We haven't informed the label that we're in a relationship, but we will, and soon," Van replied. "But no matter what, Brodie comes first. If I feel there's any personal conflict, I'll recuse myself."

"Van, you don't need to—"

"Brodie, I'm not finished," Mom interrupted. "It's not just your work. There's your age difference. And the tours, your nomadic lifestyle, won't that be difficult on a relationship?"

Van squeezed my side, so I held back on saying anything.

"And I'm not going to lie and say we have all the answers, Nia. We have differences between us, including fifteen years, but Brodie and I also have a bond that has only grown stronger over time. We both understand each other's careers and what that entails. And I can assure you, my feelings for Brodie are very real. I'm in love with your son," Van declared.

Silence descended among my family, and I tightened my grip on Van's waist in return.

"I believe you, but—" my mom started.

"No," I interrupted. "That's it. We're not gonna justify our relationship to you. I'm in love with Van, and he's in love with me. That's all you need to know. He's the best person I've ever met, and everything about us feels right. Be happy for us."

I understood my mom's protectiveness and that it came from a place of love, but I was a grown-ass man who knew my own feelings.

"You're brave, Van, taking this one on," Dad joked as he pointed to me, breaking the tension.

Van shook his head. "Not brave, but very lucky."

Mom walked over and pulled me into another crushing hug. "I'm sorry, baby. You know I love you and support you. You have such a tender heart under all the snark and glamour, and I just want you to be happy."

"I am. Beyond happy."

She pulled back and nodded, wiping away a few tears on her face, and my own eyes filled up.

Then she turned to Van. "Brodie has always spoken highly of you, and he knows his own heart. Always has. Take good care of it."

This time, Van pulled her into a hug. "I will."

"Okay, okay, enough emo stuff," I announced, lightening the mood. "Let's get out the real booze and the cards and play some poker."

"I'm gonna trounce your butt, asshat!" Vi called out.

And just like that, we were back to normal again.

"Dinner first, gambling later," Mom stated. "Do you play poker, Van?"

"A few times. I'm no expert by any means."

My mom smiled at him. "A word of warning: we're hyper-competitive."

"Should I just hand over my wallet now?" he quipped.

I leaned up and gave him a reassuring kiss. My heart skipped a beat when I stared into his denim blues.

"You okay?" I asked.

"Of course."

"Ready to bolt?"

"No way. They'd have to kick me out," Van replied and kissed me back.

After we'd drunk the champagne and opened another bottle, we sat down to an enormous seafood feast. Dad had cooked outside on the grill since the kitchen was still under renovation. Van looked relaxed as he chatted with my dad. He also seemed to enjoy the antics of my sister and the stories my mom told about me when I was young.

When dinner was done, we got out the cards and the poker chips.

Two hours later, my sister and I were the last ones standing. Van, meanwhile, was deep in conversation with my brother-in-law, Petyr.

Until his phone rang.

"I'm terribly sorry, but I need to take this." Van stood up.

"Use my office," Dad urged. "First door on the right at the end of the hallway."

Van nodded and walked off.

I watched the rolling swagger and the flex of his round ass.

Until I felt a tap on my chest and looked down to find a red poker chip in my lap.

"Stop ogling your man and pay attention," my sister teased.

I threw the chip back at her. "If you really want to win this game, you shouldn't say anything and let me be distracted."

I got another chip lobbed at me in response.

———

VAN

Whenever someone from PR called me, my nerves buzzed.

Whenever the head of PR called me directly, my stomach acid churned full force.

I slipped into Lachlan's office and shut the door behind me.

"Zoe, what's up?" I answered.

"I wanted to give you a heads up that Entertainment Now is running a story about your relationship with Brodie."

"Those rumors have circulated since the concert," I countered.

"Yes, but my source claims they have intimate photos of you and Brodie together, which they'll be posting online shortly. And they've dug into your background. I have to inform Greg, but I wanted you to know first."

My stomach sank. "I'm not sure if we should make any comment at this point."

"We're better off getting in front of it sooner rather than later. Control the narrative, remember?"

"Let me talk to Brodie and Greg first, and I'll get back to you, all right?"

"I'll be waiting."

"Fuck!" I exclaimed after I tapped to end the call.

Before I could do anything, my phone rang again. It was Dawson this time.

"Dawson? Aren't you here on site?"

"Regan sent me back to Brodie's. I did some digging on that van, and I got a hit, so I thought you'd want to know right away. The vehicle belongs to a journalist named Jordan Jakes. Odd thing is, he used to work at Bandit seven years ago. He reported directly to Greg."

Son of a bitch.

"Thanks, Dawson. I appreciate the information."

"No worries."

I hung up and started googling Jakes.

There were various pictures of him from 2016 at Bandit

event parties as well as concerts. And one of him and Greg standing side by side at the annual Music Hall of Fame event.

I tapped my phone and dialed Greg. I didn't care that it was late at night, I was so fucking enraged.

"Van."

"Jordan Jakes," I bit out.

"What about him?"

There was only a slight pause in Greg's reply, but I noticed.

"He was the first van parked outside Brodie's. You tipped him off. And I bet you also had that pap in Nashville follow us to the airport."

"I did."

"What the fuck, Greg?"

"I was ticked off by your lack of disclosure after the concert. I know everything that goes on in my business, and from what I was seeing and hearing, albeit from a distance, it was clear that something was going on between you and Brodie. That clause in your contract is there to protect the label. And you and the people you work for and with. Mostly to protect my business. But after the concert videos surfaced and you took off with Brodie to Rhode Island, I had time to think about what was going on. I realized that you and him probably wasn't a one-off thing. And the fans were gonna eat that shit up."

"And so, what, you figured you would have us tailed and photographed for more publicity?"

"Twenty-plus years in this biz, and you're surprised, Van? Come on. Don't act fucking stupid."

"I just got off the phone with Zoe. This reporter dug into my personal life, and I have no idea what the story is going to read like, not to mention that he apparently has photos of me and Brodie when we assumed we had privacy—"

"You know better than most that the love life of a celebrity, especially one as big as Brodie, is always of interest. If you plan to stay with him, get used to it."

I fucking hated to admit it, but Greg had a point.

I was still pissed because, yeah, sending that asshole here to spy on us was a dick move on his part.

But I would have to get used to being in the public eye. There would be no turning back. My privacy, my life as I knew it, was gone.

"What now?" I asked.

"I'll arrange a conference call with you, Zoe, and Brodie. Let's devise a plan to get the most out of this development. Then we'll talk about your re-assignment."

"Now wait—"

"Unless you prefer to get fired?" Greg snapped.

"I think Brodie should have a say in this. And the rest of the guys."

"This isn't a democracy, Van. It's my fucking company. I decide."

"Be prepared for your number one money maker to push back."

"We'll see about that. I'll set up the call one hour from now."

"Fine."

So much for being in our own bubble for a while. All our plans to come out in the new year washed away with the tide.

"*Tabarnak!*" I swore out loud and shoved my phone back into my pocket.

I headed back out to the living room to find Brodie collecting his poker winnings.

I didn't need to say anything. He saw the look on my face and got up, walking toward me.

"What's wrong?"

"We need to have a call with Greg and PR in an hour. I'm afraid we aren't going to get the luxury of coming out when we want. I'll tell you more when we get home."

I didn't want to tell him anything while he was here. I knew he would lose it when I told him what Greg had done.

Brodie nodded and took my hand. Together, we said our goodbyes to his family and promised to return in a week's time.

We headed back out to the SUV and were home ten minutes later. I didn't care if the paps that followed us got our picture.

They were late. Our story was already in progress.

I headed for the bar and poured two glasses of brandy. I passed one to Brodie and sat down beside him.

"Take a sip. Better yet, two," I encouraged.

"Out with it, what's going on?"

"The pap outside, the first one that arrived, his name is Jordan Jakes. He's a gossip reporter and former Bandit employee. Greg purposely tipped him off to follow us around here, and now the guy is running a story about our relationship. Apparently, he has pictures. And he's done a whole story about my background. So, whether I'm ready to come out or not, I'm out. And in no short order, millions of people will know about us."

Brodie slammed his glass on the table in front of him and leaped off the couch. "That fucking piece of shit! How dare he do that to you?"

"I'm not finished. Given all this and the fact that I didn't disclose our relationship, Greg is re-assigning me."

"No!"

"Sweetheart, it might be for the best—"

"I can't believe you would say that!"

I got up and slid my hand around his waist. "He would be well within his rights to fire me, so I think a compromise is not the worst thing. We'll be okay. No matter what happens with my job, I'm not walking away from you."

"But I want you with me, in the studio and on tour. And

writing more songs. I know you won't be working with me forever, but I thought we still had a few years."

I pulled him in tightly and felt his body trembling.

"We can still write together. That won't change," I reassured him.

"Outside of that, what Greg did is wrong, and I'm not going to stand for it," he growled. "No one should be forced to come out."

Brodie pulled away and picked up his phone.

"Who are you calling?"

"Iain first. Then my lawyer."

"Brodie—"

"Van, I'm not going to stand by and not protect you. You do it all the time for me; why can't I do the same for you?"

His passionate statement made my heart take off running.

"I'm not going to stop you, but let's talk to Greg first."

"He deliberately set that reporter on us! I don't know if I can be civil to him ever again. As it is, I want to ram my fist in his smug fucking face."

"We'll work our aggression out in the studio. We can write a kick-ass rock anthem where you sing about kicking his ass."

Brodie scoffed. "Only if I can name it 'Music Mogul Dickhead.'"

"Deal. And we can work our frustration out in other, more pleasurable ways."

Brodie shook his head, but I caught his grin.

"Don't try to make me smile right now. I'm angry as fuck, and I want to stay that way."

"Text Iain and the guys and tell them we'll give them an update once we talk to Greg and Zoe."

Brodie bit his lip, then began to pace.

"I'm still contacting my lawyer. I refuse to continue working with a man and a label who outs people without their consent."

"He gave me an opportunity to tell him—"

"Privately, yes, we could've told him about you and me. But I'm already out; you're not. So he sics a tabloid reporter on us and forces your hand that way? I don't give a shit what your contract says, that's just wrong."

I knew by the stubborn tilt of his chin that Brodie's mind was made up.

And the more I thought about it, the more I agreed with him.

"You're right. And I know exactly what I need to do."

CHAPTER 37

BRODIE

watched Van as we prepared for the call with Greg. We'd had a lengthy discussion and agreed to a plan.

A lot was about to change in both our lives, hopefully for the better.

He hadn't said much in the past ten minutes, though, and I could see the tension in every line of his body.

Like always, Van kept asking if *I* was okay.

The man never once stopped to think about himself. It just made me love him more than I already did. And it made me even more determined to take care of him the same way he took care of me.

I wasn't lying when I said I'd contact my lawyer. I texted her for an emergency request, outlining the gist of what had happened. I didn't give a shit if it was nearing midnight. That's what hefty retainers were for.

Not long after I sent the text, she replied and requested to join the call.

I'd also group texted the guys about what was going on. I didn't want to burden Faise, given the situation with his brother, but he had to know.

My issue wasn't the publicity around my relationship

with Van or even the fact that Greg had purposely sic'd that reporter on us.

It was Van.

It wasn't right to pressure or force anyone to come out. Ever.

And Holls, Faise, and Ronin understood that.

We'd all come out at different times, but always by our choice and on our terms.

So, I wasn't surprised when they texted back in agreement and were willing to stand beside me on this issue. Even if it meant putting our recording contract renewal in jeopardy.

We had enough popularity and power in our brand, and that gave us leverage. If this business had taught me anything over the years, it was to stand up for myself.

Or risk getting run over.

I was curious to see how Greg would spin his reasoning for such a shitty decision. Thank fuck we weren't in Nashville, or there would be a brawl in his office for sure. And I would have no hesitation in throwing the first punch.

"You ready?" Van asked as he tapped on his tablet.

I nodded and offered my hand, linking it with his, holding on tightly.

Zoe and Greg popped up on screen, and then my lawyer, Lila Stevenson. I saw Greg's frown deepen when he recognized her name.

Van squeezed my hand.

"This isn't the way Brodie and I wanted to announce our relationship, but given recent events, here we are. And for the record, we're in a committed, exclusive relationship. That's all I'm going to say about it."

I leaned forward and willed myself to speak slowly and not yell as loud as I wanted to. "And before you speak, Greg, I want to say that forcing Van to come out by having a tabloid reporter tail us in our private moments is the shittiest thing

I've ever been witness to in the four years I've been with this label. Lila?"

I glanced at the screen. She adjusted her glasses. "While it's clear that Van's personal relationship with Brodie violates the terms of his contract, it's also unethical for an employer to force any employee to disclose their sexuality."

"I didn't force anyone to do anything. I assumed Van was already out," Greg replied. "And you can't prove otherwise."

"Bullshit!" I snapped.

"I've never talked to you about my sexuality, so I'm also calling bullshit on this one," Van bit out.

"Your word against mine," Greg challenged. "Suffice to say, I have nothing more to add to that. Except to say that the story of your relationship is now breaking news."

I glanced at my phone and perused the notifications I'd silenced.

Zoe had sent a link with the article and the pictures of me and Van. They were all taken when we were down on the beach—holding hands, kissing, hugging. Despite my anger, I couldn't help but notice that Van and I looked damn good together.

"Zoe, set up interviews for Brodie and Van with national and international entertainment news sites. I want full press coverage," Greg continued. "Let's spin the work relationship angle."

I shook my head. "I'm not saying shit to anyone unless you formally apologize for what you've done. And since our contract is up for renewal next year, I think it's safe to say that Wayward Lane will be looking to make a new start elsewhere."

Greg was silent for a moment, and then he began to laugh.

"Yeah, right. I'm the biggest label there is, so good luck with that. Still, you do what you feel is best for your business, and I'll do what's best for mine. Anything else?"

"Yeah," Van interrupted. "I quit."

"What?" Greg snapped, his surprise showing.

I took great satisfaction in watching Greg's shock.

Van and I had discussed this. He wanted to work on his songwriting full time, and if he freelanced, he could set his own schedule and tour with me. If he continued as a manager with another band, we'd rarely see each other. Neither of us wanted that.

But I'd be lying if I said I wasn't concerned.

I wanted Van to thrive, and there was a lot of uncertainty ahead. A new relationship, a new job, and he'd be under the media microscope with me.

"You heard me. Consider this my official resignation from the label," Van declared.

"But—"

I tapped end and cut off the call before Greg could finish his thought. I didn't care to see his stupid face anymore. Or hear his corporate bullshit.

I sent Lila a text to call me back.

Then, I turned my notifications back on. My phone and Van's began to chime like we'd won the biggest jackpot in Vegas.

Me making headlines was nothing new. But me and Van?

Suddenly, I was terrified that it would be too much for him, and he'd be ready to call it quits.

"It's late, and it's been a long day. Let's call it a night."

Van stood up and held his hand out. I was nervous like I never was and hesitated.

Until I saw the vulnerability in his eyes that mirrored mine.

Both of us were stepping into an unknown situation. I hoped we would walk through it and come out stronger, together.

I could never lose Van. I don't know that I would survive that kind of loss.

I stood on shaky legs and reached up, cupping his face in my hands.

He gave me that rare smile, and I felt his dimple under my palm.

"It's okay, *mon coeur*. We're gonna be okay," Van assured me, and I nodded in return.

I leaned up and took his lips.

The kiss we shared was unlike any other—soft, sweet, and achingly tender.

Then we moved in unison towards my bedroom.

Our bedroom.

We hadn't discussed things like living together, but I already knew I wanted Van with me.

Always.

As our kisses grew frantic, we stumbled down the hallway, our clothes tossed aside.

"So beautiful," Van moaned as he teased my neck.

Him calling me beautiful made me light up inside. Because I knew Van and he wasn't just talking about my looks.

"Honey," I whispered and watched Van's eyes darken.

Then, there were no more words exchanged.

Just sighs and touches and whispers, our bodies reaching for each other in a way that was totally instinctual.

Van manhandled me, and the next thing I knew, I was face down on our bed, and he was licking a path down my back and over my ass.

His confidence—and dominance—in the bedroom had grown over the past two weeks.

He was growing more vocal about what he wanted and was curious about. I, in turn, was only too happy to be his tutor.

But he wasn't the only one learning new things.

I'd discovered that intimacy with him meant letting my

guard down. Showing him the side of me that others rarely saw.

It gave an added depth to our sex life, to our music making, to everything.

Now I understood the intensity of being with your other half.

Van was mine. No question.

I wanted everything with him: a home, a future, a family.

"What are you thinking about?" he asked as he slid his body over mine, his hands running up my arms until they grasped mine, our fingers interlocking tightly.

My heart was running at a furious pace.

"I want everything with you," I admitted in a shaky voice. "I love you so much."

"I love you more," he countered.

Then, we showed each other exactly what we meant.

CHAPTER 38
VAN

A WEEK LATER

Life with Brodie in private was incredible.

Life with Brodie in public took our relationship to a whole new level of intensity.

We'd been busy all week—me fielding inquiring calls from friends and coworkers about Brodie and my (former) job, and Brodie doing pretty much the same. They were all kind, offering us support in any way they could.

I knew I'd done the right thing by resigning, but I also recognized that the reality of this enormous change in my life hadn't hit yet.

Earlier this week, Brodie and I finally ventured outside the gates of his cottage and drove to Providence. With our security team, of course.

We had interviews set up—or, rather, he had interviews. I was there as his partner, no longer as his rep working for Bandit Music.

Before, I'd only had the occasional fan who recognized me from events. But now?

We stopped at a bookstore after the interviews and were

mobbed by a crowd eager for selfies. I still couldn't quite believe it until Dawson and Regan had to usher us out of there as the number of people around us multiplied exponentially.

I'd never felt so strangely anxious and numb at the same time. Like this was happening to me, but it hadn't fully registered yet. For someone who'd spent most of their life working with entertainers and the press, I found the barrage of attention overwhelming.

People were eager to know how we met, how long we'd been in love, and what our plans were. Most were well-meaning, but some were aggressive.

Then there were the online trolls.

Brodie warned me to stay off socials for a while, and he'd been right.

All this to say that it had only been a week since we'd officially come out as a couple, since I was out myself, and I was admittedly feeling the stress.

So was Brodie, but he'd been living in this fishbowl for a while now.

The weird part was I wasn't a Bandit employee anymore, but I still had to deal with Zoe and their PR team because I was Brodie's partner. So, I was in tune with what was happening at the label but on a distanced level.

The only constant in my life was Brodie. And my songwriting.

Losing the pressures of being a manager and focusing on my craft? And collaborating with him? It opened an abundance of creativity inside me. One that was fulfilling in a way I hadn't experienced in my twenty years on the corporate side of the music business.

Still, I wouldn't trade my time as a manager for anything.

It had all led me here. To him. To us.

We'd spent Thanksgiving with Brodie's family on Thursday, and it was the best holiday I'd had in over a year. The loneliness that usually gripped me was tempered with the abundance that was a James family gettogether. Lots of great food, music, and sibling mayhem. By the end of it, my face hurt from smiling so much.

Then Brodie and I went back to work on creating songs for the next album. Like it or not, Wayward Lane was still contracted for that, and there was no way out. Not without a long legal battle. But Brodie vowed that once the album was done, they were done with Bandit.

Meanwhile, Greg had assigned the band a new manager, a guy named Harlow Hines. He was brought in to the company two years ago. His reputation was pretty solid, and the band he managed, Vadium, was now climbing the ranks.

Brodie, of course, was not happy about having someone new to work with and was ignoring the many calls and texts that Harlow was sending. I finally convinced my boyfriend to call him back and talk to him. After all, none of what had transpired lately was Harlow's fault.

Brodie had a video call with Holls, Ronin, and Faise, and everyone agreed on the next plan of action. Their contract renewed in May, and they'd be looking for a new label. Would it mean less money? Probably. Was their brand strong enough to carry them on to continued success without Bandit? Absolutely.

And soon, me and Brodie weren't the only hot topic in the entertainment biz. Rumors of Wayward Lane's unhappiness with Bandit ran wild and fast. Soon, competing labels were sending the guys emails, calls, and gifts to woo them.

Bandit was the biggest music company, but plenty of other successful labels were eager for a shot at representing Wayward Lane.

And finally, Brodie and I both agreed that "Sideline" would wait for a future album. We didn't want Greg anywhere near it. Not when the song meant so much to both of us.

And speaking of meaningful, we were about to make our first public appearance together tonight.

One of Brodie's friends was hosting an art gallery event in Providence. I was nervous like I rarely was, unsure how I would handle being under the microscope.

I'd changed into my navy suit and was wondering if I should remove my necklace when Brodie slid in behind me, wrapping his arms around my waist.

"Don't take it off; I love it," he confessed as his eyes caught mine in the mirror.

I rubbed the silver coin that rested in the divot of my throat. "I bought this when I first moved to Nashville. Every piece the artist made has a musical reference. The coin is made from a metal tuning peg that's been heated and hammered to a flat disk. Then she used guitar wire to string the beads."

"It's very sexy."

Instead of leaving it on, I reached for the clasp and unhooked it.

"What are you—"

I turned and placed it around Brodie's neck.

"It's not platinum or diamond, but I want you to wear it. I love it when you wear my things."

Whether it was a shirt, a hat, or my favorite necklace, there was something primal in seeing him wearing my stuff. I loved claiming him in that way.

Brodie rubbed the disk, just like I had, and stared at me with heated tenderness in his eyes. I didn't know if I would ever get used to him looking at me like that.

"You're in danger of losing your entire wardrobe because I love wearing what's yours. And I don't need platinum or diamonds, just you," he responded and leaned up to kiss me.

He nipped at my lips, and I playfully bit him back. Until his tongue slid around mine, and then all thoughts about playfulness vanished. I buried my hands in his thick hair and angled his head so I could delve deeper and taste every part of his sinful mouth.

"We have to get going; we're already late," Brodie murmured against my lips.

"Or we could naked again and stay here?" I suggested.

He shook his head. "My friend is dying to meet you."

"I'm really nervous."

"They're going to love you," Brodie reassured me.

"I hope so," I replied and held him tightly. "But it's not just that. It's the media attention. It's more than even I expected."

"I know. But it'll calm in a bit. You know these things come in waves."

I nodded in agreement. But while Brodie was confident, I was less so.

And I became more agitated as the evening wore on.

We arrived late to a huge amount of press outside the gallery. The flashes and shouts were something I was used to, just not aimed at me. They were calling out my name along with Brodie's. We stopped for a few shots and then moved on with our security.

Once we got inside, Brodie was swarmed with guests vying for his attention. More pictures and autographs and questions.

His friend, Jojo Raines, the owner of the gallery, was kind and took me under his wing while I let Brodie deal with his fans.

Jojo was a force of blond energy, talking a mile a minute as he paraded me around the room, introducing me to the who's who of the Providence social scene.

"Brodie's always been special. People are drawn to him," Jojo remarked as he passed me a glass of champagne.

"They are."

I was the prime example.

But that niggle of doubt at the back of my mind had me

questioning what Brodie was doing with me. I never considered myself special or deserving of any kind of accolades. And shouldn't he have a partner that shined just as brightly as him?

"When did you two meet?" I asked, trying to distract myself from my negative thoughts.

"In school. Third grade. I was a new student, having just moved here from Vancouver. I was getting picked on during lunch, and Brodie came to my rescue. We've been friends ever since."

That sounded like my Brodie, feisty and protective as always.

"And you didn't want to join his band? Wait, are you the secret fifth member of Wayward Lane?"

Jojo laughed and rolled his eyes. "Please. I couldn't carry a tune to save myself. No, I stick to the visual arts, thank you. My paintings and my gallery."

"You're an artist as well as the owner?"

"That's right. I met my husband at this place when I was a starving creative. Now we run it together."

"I don't think I've met him yet."

"Oh, Ethan isn't here tonight. He's in Spain, visiting his kids. His ex-wife lives in Seville."

"How long have you been together?"

"Five blissful years," Jojo replied with a smile. "So, you and Brodie?"

My face flushed—damn nerves.

"Yeah. Our working relationship evolved."

"I totally understand. You know, he's mentioned you often over the past few years, so I'm not completely surprised at this turn of events. And Brodie's not a person who's easily impressed. Even though you and I don't know each other yet, I can see that you two have something special together."

I nodded, unsure of what, if anything, I should say.

"We do. He's… he's my heart. The most incredible person

I've ever met. But, sometimes, I wonder what he's doing with me. Look at him."

My boyfriend was still holding court, and I was noticing all the men who kept circling him like hungry predators. I couldn't blame them.

Then he looked back at me and smiled, waving me over. But I wasn't sure that was the best thing right now. My nerves were starting to fray, and I'd be likely to snap at anyone who wanted a piece of the man who was mine.

Another fan held up their phone, and Brodie's attention turned to them as he posed for more selfies.

I finished my champagne and turned to the bar.

"Go on and rescue him," Jojo encouraged as he handed me another glass.

"I don't think he needs rescuing."

"He's been following you with his eyes for the past hour. Haven't you noticed?"

The only thing I noticed was my jealousy.

I turned back to find Brodie being greeted by another fan. But not just any fan.

A man I recognized.

A man I once saw walking out of Brodie's trailer.

CHAPTER 39

BRODIE

f I had to smile one more time and pose for another picture, I was gonna scream.

Thirty minutes in, I was good.

An hour in, my social mask began to falter.

Not to mention, my boyfriend had all but disappeared to the outskirts of the gallery, and his vanishing act made me crankier by the second.

Maybe coming here tonight was a bad idea.

Maybe I was a bad idea.

Would Van really want to put up with this shit for the rest of his life? Me, I was used to the attention.

Mostly.

I thought that Jojo's event would be small and quiet, and a way for Van to ease into the public mayhem. But so far, it had been anything but.

I appreciated the fans, I did, but sometimes I wanted a night off.

Like tonight.

Or at least, I wanted Van beside me. I wanted to talk to him and feel him next to me—my little bit of normal.

Something that belonged only to me.

And then the evening took another nosedive.

A man I once fucked was suddenly standing right in front of me.

This cannot be happening right now…

"Remember me? The concert two years ago? It's Shawn."

The handsome brunet man yelled out to me and held open his arms like we were long-lost lovers reuniting in a rom-com.

Did I remember him? Oh yeah, I did.

Not because he or the sex was memorable but because the guy had full-on begged for a return visit, and loudly. Screaming, in fact. All while I tried to get him out of my trailer, with security finally dragging him away.

It was the guy Van had overheard, the one who'd pleaded for another dicking down.

So now my current boyfriend and one of my former fucks were in the same room. Well, I guess it was bound to happen at some point, given I'd been a randy fuckboy.

I looked over and saw Van scowling at me. He downed his glass of champagne and then turned and got lost in the crowd.

Did Van recognize the guy? It was a long time ago, so I doubted it. And who cared anyway? It was in the past.

Van was my present and my future.

Was he leaving? He wouldn't leave, would he?

Then again, if one of Van's former fuck buddies showed up and I was in the room, I'd be less than thrilled.

Okay, I'd make a fucking scene, no doubt. But that's me.

Van was levelheaded. And he wouldn't just run off. Not over something that had nothing to do with us.

"Hey! I'm talking to you!"

I blinked and stared at Shawn, and shook my head. I palmed my phone and texted Regan: SOS.

I was done being polite for the evening.

"I have to go," I stated and then I walked off while Shawn kept screaming my name.

A hush fell over the room, and everyone turned to stare. Christ.

Then I spotted Dawson and Regan moving toward him.

Suddenly, Jojo appeared in front of me. I grabbed his arm and pulled him aside.

"Can you do me a favor? Help Regan get rid of that guy, the psycho one yelling my name," I motioned over my shoulder.

"Shawn?"

"You know him?"

"I invited him. He's one of my lesser-known artists. Talented but squirrely as fuck."

I shook my head. "Well, he and I fucked years ago. He was annoyingly clingy afterward."

"Go back to my office, around the bar, and to your left. I'll text you when he's gone."

"Thanks, Jo. Sorry about this."

"No worries. I can't tell you how many fights I've had to break up in this place. Artists' lives are as dramatic as their creations."

"Have you seen Van?"

"He went to use the washroom," Jojo gave me a knowing smirk. "He's so far gone over you, Dee."

That thought warmed my belly and made me giddy. "Did he tell you that?"

"He did. And even if he'd said nothing, I would know. He has that same lovesick look on his face that you do."

"I love him, Jo. Like crazy kind of love—"

"Brodie! Come back!" Shawn yelled out behind me. I turned to find Regan and Dawson dragging him to the exit.

"Not that kind of crazy." I rolled my eyes. "I'm outta here."

I slid around Jojo and walked to the back of the room, around the bar, and down the hallway to the left.

A moment to myself was desperately needed.

I opened the door to Jojo's office and slid inside the room, the dark silence welcoming.

But I wasn't alone.

A familiar scent teased my nose.

And then I was pulled into Van's embrace, the door slamming shut, my back hitting it soon after.

Van's kiss was demanding, relentless. His tongue was aggressive, sucking on mine, leaving me breathless and boneless.

He was staking his claim and I fucking loved it.

"Let's get out of here," Van suggested, teasing my neck with playful bites.

"Let me text Regan. We may have to wait a bit; she's busy dealing with a security situation."

"Your obsessed fuck buddy?"

"You recognized him?"

"His begging and screaming for seconds was pretty memorable," Van growled.

I reached for his face, rolling my thumbs over the roughness of his scruff and the softness of his lips.

"It probably won't be the last time. And I'm not going to apologize for my past. None of them meant anything more than release."

"I know that. It's just… I feel so damn possessive when it comes to you. Like, ridiculous kind of possessive. And at the same time, I worry you'll wake up one day and change your mind about me. About us."

"Are you fucking serious?"

"*Mon coeur*, you're young and gorgeous and talented and smart and so fucking amazing. You enter a room, and everyone gravitates toward you. You could have—"

I placed my hand over his mouth. "You're my everything, Van. And I'm going to keep telling you that until you believe it. You're the only one I want. The person I love more than anything. My partner in love, in music, in every way that counts. Honey, you need to see what's right in front of you. Cause I sure as fuck see nothing but you. Even when I'm surrounded by other people, I look for you. I feel strange when you're not by my side. Like a piece of me is missing."

Van pulled me in tight, and I notched my head under his chin.

"I love you too, so much it scares me sometimes," Van confessed. "I guess the media nonsense got in my head. There's already rumours about our breakup."

"The only voices that count belong to you and me."

"I know." He kissed the top of my head. "Let's get back to the party."

"I thought you wanted to leave?"

"We should stay. You need time to catch up with Jojo."

"Are you sure?"

"Absolutely."

I reluctantly stepped back and checked my phone. "Regan got rid of that guy. We're all set."

I took Van's hand, and we headed back to the party, cautiously.

Everything seemed normal.

Jojo was standing by the bar and waved when he saw us. "It's safe now."

"Sorry about all this."

Jojo shook his head. "They got rid of Shawn quickly, and everything's fine."

"I hope this doesn't cause issues for you."

Jojo waved me off. "He's one of many temperamental artists I work with. I'll deal with him another day. You're my friend, so you come first."

I leaned over and hugged him.

The bartender poured glasses of champagne, and I grabbed two, passing one to Van. I took a sip and glanced around the room. Thankfully, people were giving us some space.

"So, when's the wedding?" Jojo asked.

Champagne spewed out of Van's mouth like a geyser, and Jojo leaped back before he got sprayed. I choked and snorted bubbles up my nose.

"What are you talking about?" I asked when I finally managed to clear my throat.

"You mean you aren't getting married?" Jojo asked with wide eyes. "It's the talk of the party. Apparently, there's some article that says you two are engaged."

"Jo, that's tabloid talk." I rolled my eyes. "One day they say we're breaking up and the next, we're getting married. Please tell me you don't believe everything you read."

Van was noticeably silent beside me.

"I'm not that naïve. And I swear, one of my guests said the article was legit."

"Well, it's not true," I responded, even though the thought of calling Van my husband had my blood racing hot and fast.

"Not yet," Van stated.

I nearly dropped my glass.

"Will I get an invite to the real thing?" Jojo asked with a smile.

I couldn't breathe.

"Depends on what Brodie wants. What do you think, *mon coeur*? Personally, I like the idea of eloping and then, maybe a week later, having a big party for family and friends."

Was Van asking me to marry him for real? Or was I high? Was there something in this champagne?

Jojo chuckled. "I think you broke Brodie's ability to speak."

"Not an easy task," Van replied and squeezed my waist. I could only stare at him, still in shock.

"Jo!" someone called out.

It was Bianca, Jojo's assistant. "Sorry to interrupt, but Charles Signer has a question about the Lander piece, and I need your help."

"Of course, I'll be right back." Jojo nodded and headed off into the crowd.

I turned to Van.

"Were you joking just now or—"

"About marrying you? No."

"You… want to marry me?"

"Yes."

"Just like that?"

"Just like that."

"Is it crazy to say I want to marry you too?"

Van shook his head and chuckled. Then he drew me in even closer, and I could smell the fruity champagne on his breath.

"Surreal, but not crazy. Leaving this party right now to fly off to Vegas and get married? That would be crazy."

As soon as the words left his mouth, my heart began to pound furiously.

We stared at each other, locked in place.

The people, the chatter, the noise around us, it all faded away.

There was just me and Van and the unmistakable proof of our love.

Hand in hand, we bolted for the door.

CHAPTER 40

VAN

We said a hasty goodbye to Jojo and pulled Regan aside.

"We need your help," I whispered as quietly as I could.

"Sure thing. What's up?"

"We need to organize a private plane ASAP."

"Where and why?"

"Vegas," Brodie explained. "Pretty sure you can figure out the reason why on your own."

Regan's eyebrows nearly reached her hairline.

"I don't care what it costs. This is on me, not the label," Brodie added. "Tonight. Now. And no one is to know. No one."

Were Brodie and I really going to do this?

Yes.

Was it insane?

Not to us.

I saw the love in his eyes. I felt the passion in his voice when he told me earlier that I was his everything. He'd been telling me for a while, but finally, I'd heard him.

And I recognized myself in his words.

Because he was my everything too.

"I'll get it organized." Regan nodded and motioned for Dawson to join her. "Daws, get these two in the SUV. I'll join you in a minute. Then we've got a change in plans."

We followed Dawson outside and walked quickly to the SUV. Not without more photos being taken of us, of course. I hoped the paps weren't psychic because I think the happiness on our faces would've given us away.

Regan joined us shortly after and drove us to a small airfield a half hour away from the gallery.

An hour and a half after that, Brodie and I boarded a private plane with Regan and Dawson in tow.

Thankfully, it had two sofas and comfortable chairs. A five and a half-hour flight meant we'd have time to sleep.

That is, if we could sleep. Both of us were vibrating like kids after eating too much sugar.

I pulled Brodie onto one couch with me, and we snuggled together under a blanket. The soothing hum of the engines and the quiet and darkness of the cabin had us finally drifting off.

We woke up a few hours later to Regan handing us steaming cups of coffee.

"What about your family?" I turned to Brodie as reality filtered in. "Are they going to be upset?"

Brodie shook his head. "They don't expect me to do anything the traditional way, a wedding least of all. We'll organize a reception for everyone when we get back."

I leaned over and kissed him, morning (in this case, night) breath be damned.

"And the guys?"

"Same thing applies. As soon as we start organizing and news leaks, the press will be after us like bloodhounds. I want one moment for just the two of us."

There was a full bathroom on the plane, so we had time to shower.

At just after midnight, we landed in Vegas, and entered the cool desert night.

Brodie and I were both in the clothes we wore from last night—me in my navy suit and him in his black leather kilt, a silky white blouse, and a leather motorcycle jacket.

And he wore my necklace.

In a short time, he'd be wearing my ring.

Mind fucking blown.

Regan and Dawson procured an SUV rental and drove us to the strip.

"I called a few places while you guys were asleep," Regan remarked. "First stop, a jewelry store. Then you're booked in at the Chapel of Everlasting Love in an hour. That still leaves you with enough time if you want to check into a hotel first."

"I don't think we should chance it. Let's get our rings and get to the venue," I replied.

Brodie nodded. "I agree. If someone spots me, we're done. I want to go incognito for as long as possible."

We drove past the gaudy casinos and opulent hotels, the sidewalks packed with people. The energy of the strip was vibrant at this time of night, and most of the partiers were just getting started.

The jewelry store was located in a strip mall on the outskirts of town. The place looked sketchy as fuck, but Regan assured us it was legit and most important, it was open twenty-four seven. Apparently, she'd taken other celebrity clients here when they got married in Vegas.

Trusting in our security lead, we headed inside.

Both Brodie and I preferred simple, classic gold. Forty minutes later, we left with two perfectly fitted wedding bands. Brodie suggested we get matching tattoos on our ring fingers, for those times when wearing a band wouldn't be possible.

"I like that idea."

Being an only child of two parents of the same, and with my grandparents long since passed, I had no cousins or any other relatives close to me now.

But I wasn't alone.

The James family had welcomed me into theirs, and one day, Brodie and I would be creating one of our own.

Brodie and the rest of the guys were true to their word, and in May of the new year, Wayward Lane signed with a new label. Brodie and I had been prolific in our songwriting collaboration, and we had a strong backlist for their next album. The band's popularity skyrocketed even further, beyond even Brodie's expectations.

Bandit Music, on the other hand, went through a rough period of bad press and lower profits when Wayward left, and several other bands followed suit (including Killmine).

Brodie and I had thought about starting our own label, but we weren't sure we'd have the time to dedicate to such a venture. Maybe someday. For now, I was content writing songs for the band and for other artists.

And our life together?

There were still times when he was on the road, or at an event, or an interview, and I stayed home. But for the most part, I was with him. And nothing made me happier.

I may be middle-aged, but after falling in love with Brodie, my heart was forever young.

And our dreams together were just beginning.

BRODIE

After a grueling rehearsal, I was ready to call it a night and blow off some steam.

I turned and found Van standing in the wings, watching me.

Like always, being the center of his attention had me

lighting up. I placed my guitar aside and all but ran over to him.

The guys had been witness to the displays of affection between my husband and me over the past six months and had teased us mercilessly. When they'd start in, Van and I gave them a choice finger and kept on doing whatever we wanted.

And there was nothing I wanted more than him.

Van was the greatest gift of my life. One I never, ever took for granted.

After signing with a new label, the boys and I tested out some of the songs Van and I had written together. Our sound was evolving, and our fans couldn't get enough.

And tonight, we were back in New Orleans. To perform and enjoy an afterparty to celebrate the upcoming release of a new single—the official launch of "Sideline."

Van would be performing the song with me and initiated as our unofficial fifth band member.

We also had a couple of birthdays to celebrate. Me and Holls turned thirty in April, with Faise and Ronin turning the same but later in the year.

Not that entering a new decade had changed us much. When we played together, we still reverted to the loud and snarky teens we started out as.

But offstage? Well, let's just say my rockstar persona had evolved like our music. I was mature now. Most of the time…

And I was good with it. A new decade wasn't something to be feared but embraced.

Van and I had done a lot of talking about our future and the family we wanted together. It may not happen this year, but it was coming down the line.

I could see it as clearly as I saw him.

"Great set, *mon coeur*." Van pulled me into his arms.

"Thanks, honey."

"I've got something for you."

Van held up a familiar gold ring. It was the one I'd lost the last time we were here.

"You found it? Where?"

"I went downstairs to the dressing room to get changed, and there it was. Sitting on the very same table."

"Just like that?"

"Just like that."

I shook my head. "That's too weird. And I know you think it's crazy, but it's gotta be the ghost."

"Between you and me, I'm starting to believe you. It's kind of romantic if you think about it. Maybe the ghost locked us in that room six months ago for a reason?"

"No better reason than love."

Van kissed me. "Too bad we can't thank them."

The lights flickered, and Van and I stared at each other, then burst out laughing.

"Are you excited for tonight?" I asked, getting lost in his blues.

"'Course I'm excited to perform with you. It's afterward that concerns me. Holls told me I'd need tomorrow off to recuperate from the initiation. So tell me, what kind of crazy antics do you four have planned?"

I ignored his question and leaned up to kiss him. "You'll be fine. You're not allergic to Jell-O, are you?"

"No. Why?"

I let out a deep chuckle. "No reason."

"Brodie—" Van warned.

"Relax, honey. I'm teasing you."

My husband, being the smart man he was, didn't buy my answer for a second.

He knew all about rockstars.

And he loved me anyway.

———

THANK YOU for reading Punk-In! Read Iain and Dawson's story in **B-Mine** and Ronin and Faisel in **4-EVER**. You can read more about Brodie and Van in this bonus short Guitar Strings & Pretty Things.
Check out all my books here

"I could also get 'property of Van' tattooed on my ass," Brodie quipped.

"Good. I was already planning on a 'property of Brodie' on mine."

With our rings in hand, we headed directly to the chapel. Tattoos would have to wait.

Brodie and I quietly walked in, with no press or interested fans in sight, and got married. Regan and Dawson were our witnesses.

The wedding was perfect for us. We'd always connected to each other in a special way, and our wedding was no different.

After Brodie stated his vows, he sang to me. Low and soft, he crooned the words I'd penned about him, and I could hear his love for me in every note.

I tried to hold back my tears, but it was useless. Even Regan and Dawson looked choked up.

I swallowed past the lump in my throat and pronounced my vows in turn.

When the officiant announced us husbands, I took Brodie in my arms, and sealed the deal.

Then we wasted no time in group texting photos of our nuptials to his family, the band, and all our friends.

Our phones didn't stop ringing for an entire day.

And, of course, the press got wind of our wedding within a few hours.

But that was fine. We'd had our moment.

I knew I would always have to share a part of Brodie with the rest of the world. And that was okay.

The most important part, his heart, belonged to me.

BRODIE

Rockstar Brodie James marries former manager Ivan Cross in surprise Vegas wedding!

I read the headline on my phone as I sat on a lounger by the pool, the sun warming my skin.

My husband (holy fucking shit, my husband!) was lying beside me, giving me that decadent smile that made my stomach flutter.

After our wedding, Van and I flew down to the U.S. Virgin Islands for our honeymoon.

The lead singer of a band Van used to manage owned a house on St. Thomas, and he was only too happy to let us use it. It was located high on a hill overlooking stunning Magens Bay. We had our own private pool and no neighbors for miles.

Well, sort of.

We didn't realize when we arrived that another famous musical couple hadn't vacated the house yet. Van was so excited to start our honeymoon that as soon as we entered the home, he manhandled me and fucked me over the kitchen island.

It was the hottest thing ever. I know, I know, I say that about everything when it comes to Van, but it's true.

My husband was so intent on railing me, and I was so far gone getting railed that we didn't notice the two men on the other side of the patio doors.

Well, I noticed, but I was already naked by then and too turned on to do anything but grunt Van's name.

Afterwards, all four of us shared ice-cold beers on the patio. Just shooting the shit.

I told you, musicians are used to that kind of thing…

Van confided to me afterward that being watched was something he didn't expect to enjoy but did. But he was never going to share me.

I felt the exact same way.

I glanced at the article again and the picture of me and Van, newly married, as we strolled hand in hand on the Vegas strip. I still couldn't believe we'd done it.

I recalled every moment of the ceremony as Van and I

ABOUT THE AUTHOR

Ava Olsen writes steamy and dreamy MM romance with heartwarming characters, sexy banter, and ALL the romantic feels.

Sign up for my newsletter for the latest updates, cover reveals, and bonus scenes:

http://avaolsenauthor.com

FOLLOW ME

took each other as husbands and committed our lives to each other.

I sang to him; of course I did. I am a rock star, after all.

I'm sure my voice cracked since I was overwhelmed with emotion. It didn't matter.

Just like our Halloween concert, singing Van's song to him was the most meaningful music of my life.

"We look so fucking hot together," I stated as I passed over my phone.

"You should have *that* tattooed on your ass," Van quipped, the sunshine glinting off his sunglasses.

"Are you saying we don't?" I taunted, rolling to my side and propping my head on my hand.

"You're beautiful, no question." Van removed his glasses, looked at the screen, and then stared at me. The Caribbean water had nothing on Van's deep blues. "But it's what's inside that's even better."

I leaned over and gave him a languid kiss.

"I want this picture in our bedroom."

Van's smile widened. "You'll need to find room. I've got those photos from my condo that I need to set up so I can continue to worship at your shrine."

I pinched Van's arm. "Smart ass."

"You've rubbed off on me."

"Well, it is my husbandly duty."

"Come here, then, husband, and get to work."

We both ended up sunburnt but deliriously happy.

EPILOGUE
VAN

SIX MONTHS LATER

After our impromptu Vegas wedding and our honeymoon in the Virgin Islands, we flew back to Rhode Island and organized a massive celebration for all our family and friends. It was another three day party - minus the helicopters…

After that, and just before Christmas, we visited Montreal.

I'd finally decided to put my parents' house up for sale. It was time.

Brodie helped me look through the house and decide what to keep and what to give away. I'm not going to lie. Aside from their funerals, it was the hardest thing I've ever had to do. There were bouts of crying and lots of memories unearthed as we sifted through family photo albums and boxes of my childhood treasures.

I would've managed on my own, but having my husband beside me gave me a strength I will forever be grateful for. And I knew in my heart that my mom and dad would've loved Brodie as their own.

OTHER TITLES BY AVA OLSEN

Sutton U Crew: MM Sports Romance

Catch

Bar Down: MM College Hockey Romance

Rule Breaker

Play Maker

Heart Taker

Stand Alone (enemies to lovers)

Happily Never After

Wayward Lane MM Rockstar Romance

PUNK-IN

B-MINE

4-EVER

Wayward Lane Backstage

Don't Fall For A Rockstar

Don't Fall For A Bodyguard

Don't Fall For A Dreamer

Voyagers Series

Oh Buoy

Starboard

The Cockpit

Endeavor

Nauti or Nice

Stand Alone (Voyagers spin off)

Co-Star

NY Nights

Novel Affair

Troublemaker

Unforgettable You

NY Nights Bodyguard Edition

Hate to Love You

Love Like Yours

Never Knew Love

Stand Alone (novella)

Long Time Coming